COFFIN RANCH
A WESTERN TRIO

WALT COBURN

SAGEBRUSH
Large Print Westerns

First published in Great Britain by Gunsmoke
First published in the United States by Five Star

First Isis Edition
published 2015
by arrangement with
Golden West Literary Agency

A catalogue record for this book is available
from the British Library.

ISBN 978–1–78541–012–3 (pb)

Published by
F. A. Thorpe (Publishing)
Anstey, Leicestershire

Set by Words & Graphics Ltd.
Anstey, Leicestershire
Printed and bound in Great Britain by
T. J. International Ltd., Padstow, Cornwall

This book is printed on acid-free paper

Table of Contents

Foreword
By Jon Tuska

Walter John Coburn, once called "King of the Pulps" by Fred Gipson and promoted by Fiction House as "The Cowboy Author," was born in White Sulphur Springs, Montana Territory, on October 23, 1889. He was the son of cattleman Robert Coburn, then owner of the Circle C Ranch on Beaver Creek within sight of the Little Rockies, whose life story Walt Coburn would later detail in his singular contribution to cow-country history, PIONEER CATTLEMAN IN MONTANA: THE STORY OF THE CIRCLE C RANCH (University of Oklahoma Press, 1968). His mother was Mary Blessing Coburn. Robert Coburn had four sons and three daughters by his first marriage to Mary Morrow and, following her death and his marriage to Mary Blessing, two sons, the first of which, Harold, was six years Walter's senior. Walter's half-sister, Jessie, gave birth to a son a year before Walter was born, thus providing him with a nephew who was older than he was.

Coburn attended the North Side Whittier Grammar School in Great Falls, and it was in this city that he

1

spent his winters growing up. The summers were spent on the Circle C Ranch. As most whose families lived on the north side of town, Coburn attended Great Falls High School, graduating in 1908. In 1909–1910 he attended Manzanita Hall Preparatory School in Palo Alto, California. His father believed a college education vital if Coburn were to be a successful cattleman. Coburn planned to attend Stanford, but his application was rejected. The reason, as Coburn would later recall, was that he "had lost the battle to John Barleycorn." It was not to be the last time he lost that battle. Coburn persuaded his father that a college education was unnecessary for what he planned to do, and his half-brother, Bob, supported him in this conviction. The Coburns now lived in San Diego while still operating the Circle C. Robert Coburn used to commute between Montana and California by train, and he would take his youngest son with him. When Coburn got drunk one night, he had an argument with his father that led to his leaving the family. In the course of his wanderings he entered Mexico and for a brief period actually became an enlisted man in the so-called "*gringo* battalion" of Pancho Villa's army.

By 1911 he had made up with his father and from that year until 1916, when the Circle C was sold, he remained in Montana, drinking heavily and embittered by the awareness that his father was now financially strapped and that his dream of inheriting his share of the great ranch was never to be. In 1914 he smashed his right ankle, but it did not prove a permanent disability. Barb wire and farmers were bringing an end to the large cattle ranches Coburn had known growing up, and it was an experience that never left him. In 1916, after selling out in Montana, Robert Coburn moved the Coburn Cattle Company to Globe, Arizona, where he bought out the remnants of three large cow outfits, leasing graze on the San Carlos Apache Indian Reservation. From 1917 to 1919 Walt Coburn served in the U. S. Army Air Service, Signal Corps, attaining the rank of sergeant first class. After the Great War, Coburn returned to cowboying in Arizona, but this time he injured a kneecap so badly that it would never heal properly. The attending physician warned him that, despite his youth, his bones were brittle. Coburn left Arizona and went to San Diego where his mother, now widowed, still resided. It was mostly there that he had been stationed during the war. He went to work first for the military as a civilian employee and then drifted from one job to another. He read a Western story in the pulp magazine, *Adventure*. It had been written by Robert J. Horton, a man Coburn had known when Horton had been a newspaper sports reporter in Great Falls. Recognizing in Horton's story the nucleus of a tale Coburn had once told him, Coburn wrote to Horton and asked him how one went about becoming a writer. Horton was very responsive, setting down principles that would remain Coburn's working philosophy all of his years: to read Roget's THESAURUS; to read O. Henry, Jack London, and Joseph Conrad, but not other Western fiction writers; to live a story as it was being written, never plotting it out beforehand; and *never* to rewrite.

Coburn put Horton's suggestions into practice and for a year and a half he wrote and wrote, earning endless rejection slips and becoming so depressed at times that, once, he even considered submitting to a glandular transplant offered by a quack doctor. By this time Coburn was living in Del Mar, California, and one day instead of a returned manuscript he received an envelope from the Munsey Publications. Bob Davis, editor of *Argosy All-Story Magazine*, had accepted his short story, "The Peace Treaty of the Seven Up." Payment was twenty-five dollars, and the story appeared in the July 8, 1922 issue. The plot detailed a feud between Bill Crawford of the Seven Up and sheepman Charlie Henderson. They meet on the road and shoot each other. Crawford finds a prescription on Henderson, who is unconscious but not dead, and he thinks it is for medicine for his youngest boy. It isn't. It is a prescription for touching up his wife's graying hair. Although wounded, Crawford fills the prescription, and the two eventually make up, without Crawford's learning the truth about the prescription. It was another six months before a second Coburn story appeared in print, this time in Street & Smith's *Western Story Magazine*. Frank E. Blackwell, then editor of the magazine, wrote Coburn asking to see more stories (as if, Coburn thought, he had not rejected a dozen or more stories before accepting this one). *Western Story Magazine* became an important market for Coburn in 1923. He was writing and selling enough to quit his job in Del Mar and move to Santa Barbara where he rented a small cottage near the old mission. In Santa Barbara, Coburn initiated what would remain his routine. He would try to write at least two thousand words a day, never rewriting, six days a week, with Sundays off, never working more than four or five hours a day, but also never taking a vacation of longer than two or three days once a story was completed.

Coburn had become something of a fixture at *Western Story Magazine* by early 1924 when Jack Kelly came to California to see him. Jack Kelly and J. W. Glenister owned the Fiction House chain of pulp magazines that Kelly edited. Kelly offered Coburn three cents a word and would feature a story every month by Coburn in one or more of their magazines, providing Coburn with cover billing. "I'll build you up, cowboy," he told Coburn, "until you'll be the highest paid Western writer in the game. Max Brand will never catch up with you. While he's a good writer, he knows nothing about the West." To a degree this was pure salesmanship. During the decade of the 1920s Frederick Faust, who wrote as Max Brand, was paid five cents a word by *Western Story Magazine*, and he was writing as much as a million words a year. Coburn never attained that level. However, during the 1930s and 1940s he would average six hundred thousand words a year for the pulp market.

Late in 1924 Fiction House launched a new magazine that, unlike *Action Stories* which was a mixture of genres, would feature only Western fiction. *Lariat Story Magazine* began with the August issue. The first story in the first issue was "Riders of the

Purple" by Walter J. Coburn, the name he used for his fiction, with an illustration by Will James. It is one of Coburn's best stories with the coming of barb wire to the free ranges of Montana as its central theme. I chose to include it in my anthology, SHADOW OF THE LARIAT (Carroll & Graf, 1995). By 1928 Coburn had achieved an even more preferential status at Fiction House, and, while it lasted, it provided him with financial stability. He was paid one hundred dollars a week by Fiction House, and at the first of every month he was sent a check for the difference between the seven hundred and fifty dollars owing for the twenty-five-thousand-word story he was to submit each month, and what had already been paid to him. Fiction House billed Coburn as "The Cowboy Author," running biographical sketches of him and his authentic background, and showcasing his name on covers.

Coburn's early efforts, at *Western Story Magazine* and at Fiction House, stressed humor and comedy. His favorite locations tended to be northern Mexico and Montana. "Tumbleweeds and Trouble" in *Action Stories* (9/25) is actually a better replay of the same elements featured in Coburn's first story accepted by *Argosy All-Story*. Jack Doyle, wagon boss for the Seven Up ranch in Montana, composes a note to Ole Lindstrum, owner of a sheep outfit on Alkali Creek, just outside Chinook, a favorite Coburn location. The dialogue is wholly natural and true to Montana cattlemen of the period. Jack has been told to arbitrate and says, after composing his note: " 'So I borry's that there dictionary uh the cook's an' finds out the meanin'

6

uh this here 'arbitrate' word.'" Jake's idea of arbitration is for Ole to tear down his drift fence, or the Seven Up will tear it down for him. Unfortunately, Jake's letter gets sent to the wrong person, and Lyin' Bill from the Seven Up delivers to Ole a letter from a cowpoke proposing marriage.

The format of *Lariat Story Magazine* could accommodate longer stories, up to forty thousand words, and starting with "Paths to Glory" in *Action Stories* (4/26) Coburn began producing his series of border tales for Fiction House, running primarily in *Action Stories* and *Lariat* but also reprinted in *Action Novels*. These are exemplary stories, many of them highly inventive with a varied and interesting assortment of characters, not only Anglo-Americans and Mexicans but, occasionally, Japanese and Chinese characters as well, and an intriguing group of female characters from both sides of the border. "South of the Law Line" in *Action Stories* (8/24), "*Señor* Satan" in *Action Stories* (6/30), and the only slightly less fine "Border Wolves" in *Action Stories* (12/30) are definitely among the best stories Coburn ever wrote and will eventually be collected. However, no less interesting, especially from an autobiographical point of view, is "He Rides Alone," included in the present trio.

Because of the way he wrote, Coburn's stories in this period are never predictable, and his characters here, as later, are never black and white. Often characters who are ethically culpable will undergo reclamation, at times ironically, as happens in "The Badlands Buckaroo," also found in these pages. God, usually referred to as

Señor Dios, is a frequent character, and His ways are ever seen to be just. Ruth Webster in "The Badlands Buckaroo" is the prototypical Coburn heroine: "In her riding breeches and boots and flannel blouse, a high-crowned Stetson shading her troubled eyes, she looked like a handsome boy."

During the few years Coburn spent in Santa Barbara, he was engaged to a young married woman who had separated from, but not yet divorced, her husband. She had a fifteen-year-old son from that marriage. When she went East, Coburn went on a drunk, flush with money he had just received from *Adventure* for a story. The bender lasted some days, and at the end of it he found himself married to a woman named Blake Beck. This marriage did not last long. Coburn learned that Beck had only married him to get revenge on the woman he had planned to marry. A broken leg, incurred while he was playing touch football, found him in a hospital where he met Mina Acheson Evans, an Irish-Canadian colleen who was his nurse. She had had a brief, unhappy marriage. Coburn called her "Pat" because it seemed more Irish than Mina. They were married July 7, 1927. Later this was the only marriage he would mention, and it lasted for the remainder of his life. Pat was the inspiration for so many Coburn heroines — among them Ruth Webster in "The Badlands Buckaroo," Kathleen Mavoureen Kavanaugh in LAW RIDES THE RANGE (Appleton Century, 1935), and Kathleen Mavourneen Kilgore in "The Block K Rides Tonight!" in *Star Western* (7/39). I included "The Block K Rides

Tonight!" in my anthology, STAR WESTERN (Gramercy Books, 1995). While Coburn wrote myriad stories without any romance at all, when there was one, the heroine was almost invariably modeled after Pat.

It was Jack Kelly who suggested Coburn sign his stories simply "Walt" and from late 1926 on that was the only name he used. Coburn's Golden Age was during the years 1926–1940. Most of what he wrote during this period is better than anything that preceded it and vastly superior to anything that followed. Between 1927 and 1937 he wrote only five novels and none after 1937 until 1951, by which time he was effectively out of the pulp market. THE RINGTAILED RANNYHANS (Century, 1927) was first and was serialized in *Lariat Story Magazine* (3/27–8/27) and reprinted in one installment in *Lariat Story Magazine* (5/43). It is set on the Circle C ranch prior to 1916. Its protagonists are two old cowhands, Hurricane Smith and Calamity Connor, and unlike most Western novels of the period there is no ranch romance. The story is filled with memorable characters, a squaw man and his Cree wife who smokes a Hudson's Bay pipe, their half-breed son, Gabe, Jack Harper, the dude who owns the Circle C, and Milk River Dutton, a rancher as dishonest as they come, " 'a cross between a lightnin'-rod an' a hydrophoby skunk,' " but he is no villain. In fact, Coburn's fiction from his Golden Age rarely has what may be regarded as traditional villains. As Gabe tells Hurricane at one point: " 'You figgered wrong, didn't yuh? I'm a damn 'breed, mister, and I work for a cow thief named Dutton. I'm an ex-convict

9

that was sent up for killin' another man's beef. I reckon I can't blame yuh for thinkin' I'm a sneak an' a squealer to boot.'"

Coburn's second novel, MAVERICKS (Century, 1929), was also serialized in *Lariat Story Magazine* (4/28–9/28) and reprinted in one installment as "Guns of the Dawn Rider" in *Action Stories* (2/42). It is even better. Set in the Chinook district of Montana, Coburn created in it a complex and captivating community of diverse families and social forces. There is a hot-head who in an argument shoots his father, so that his father loses an arm, but they are later reconciled. Lance Mansfield inherits his British father's ranch. He intends to make the Circle 7 a success, only to be framed as a slow-elker. Tonnie Kirby is the heroine, in love with Lance but estranged from him by siding with her brother, Dick, after he shoots their father. The novel falls into three discrete parts: before and after the Great War in Montana and during the war in No Man's Land. Coburn eloquently described the impact of the war on the Montana cowboys, some of whom "would return, even as these utterly weary, soul-sick men were coming back — with the eager light forever gone out of their eyes and, in its stead, the glaze of horror that is war; young men who had lost something that is an essential part of youth. They would never forget, those men who returned. For God has somehow neglected to bless men with that forgetfulness of war pain. He saves that gift for mothers in childbirth."

BARB WIRE (Century, 1931) was first serialized in Fiction House's *Frontier Stories* (2/31–6/31) and was later reprinted in a single installment under the title "The Moon-Trail Maverick" in *Lariat Story Magazine* (1/42). It has neither the eloquence nor the reach of MAVERICKS, but it does have the considerable advantage of a more compact and unified plot along with characters and events that never require the suspension of disbelief as some of the characters do in MAVERICKS. Probably because of its unity and concentration, Coburn's themes, by now familiar from his shorter fiction as well as his two previous novels, are provided here their most refined, powerful, and well-constructed expression. This reason alone would grant this novel a perennial stature. In the relationship between Colleen Driscoll and Buck Rawlins is replayed Coburn's own love affair with Pat; and in the old Montana cattlemen and the banker, Uncle Hank Mayberry, the aged cowhands, and the train robber known as the Nighthawk who had been a good hand once and is still a good man, Coburn embodied all that he knew and loved of the way of life he had experienced on the Circle C. Sheriff Ike Niland, who would return as a character in later stories such as "Water Rights" in *West* (11/32), has to enforce the law in favor of the invading farmers who are destroying the open range with their fences and a way of life for cattlemen and sheepmen alike. The notion of pulling together, so true of the frontier, still strikes a responsive chord in a later time because these characters are people who grew up with that ethic and wouldn't know any other way to behave. It can still be found in Elmer Kelton's masterpiece, THE TIME IT NEVER RAINED

(Doubleday, 1973), set fifty years after the time-frame of BARB WIRE. Coburn's most fascinating character, though, is Fancy Mary who runs a road house. "For all that her skin was black, that she chewed and smoked a cob pipe or a long cigar, that she wore overalls, tended bar, handled half-broken stage horses, drank her whiskey clear, and could swear like a mule skinner, Mary had the friendship of every cowman and common cowhand in the country. She would ride all day to nurse a sick person. She never turned away a hungry man. She counted no favor too great to do for a friend." It is Fancy Mary with her life's savings who comes to the rescue of Mayberry's bank when it is threatened by foreclosure from land speculators.

Jack Kelly died in 1932, and Fiction House went into a period of re-organization. For a time in 1933 publication ceased for all of the company's monthly magazines. It resumed only slowly. *Action Stories* became bi-monthly, then quarterly. *Lariat* became bi-monthly. *Frontier Stories*, which had the longest hiatus from September, 1934 until Spring, 1937, returned as a quarterly. Accordingly, Coburn had to expand his markets. He wrote even more for *Adventure*, wrote again for *Western Story Magazine*, and became a regular contributor to Popular Publications' pulps such as *Dime Western* and *Star Western*. When Popular Publications introduced *10 Story Western* with the January, 1936 issue, Coburn was not among the authors of the early stories, but he became a regular contributor with the August, 1936 issue. The short novel he titled "Coffin Ranch," included in this trio, was one of his best for this magazine.

In 1935, Coburn and Pat moved to Tucson, Arizona, because she suffered from respiratory problems and there built a ranch-style house with a small adobe out back for Walt. The drinking intensified as the years passed. Coburn did not read what others were writing and so, increasingly, what he wrote was but a replay of the same themes and characters and situations. "Man-Trap Ranch" in *Star Western* (4/45) is but a pale reincarnation of the basic plot of BARB WIRE. His remaining novels prior to 1951 — LAW RIDES THE RANGE, earlier serialized in *Lariat Story Magazine* as "Marked Men" (7/29–12/29), and SKY-PILOT COWBOY (Appleton Century, 1937), serialized in *Ace-High Western* as "The Owlhoot Sky-Pilot" (12/36–5/37) — do not have quite the power and ambiance of his earlier novels.

An editor at the New York office of Popular Publications confided to Western author Frank Bonham that most of what Coburn wrote after the Second World War had been written while drunk. It had to be edited severely, the rambling verbosity cut back to the bone while still paying Walt according to his original word count. He was living mostly on his reputation. After Fiction House re-organized, Coburn stories appeared in nearly every issue of *Action Stories* and *Lariat Story Magazine*, but they were reprints from before 1933 with the titles changed. After 1943 even reprints by Coburn stopped appearing in Fiction House magazines.

Jack Burr, who succeeded Frank E. Blackwell as editor of *Western Story Magazine*, would feature Coburn in about every sixth issue after 1940 while the magazine remained a weekly. When it was cut back to a monthly, Coburn was usually represented but only occasionally were his stories showcased on the cover. Before the hiatus at Fiction House, a special issue titled *Walt Coburn's Action Novels* (1931) appeared, consisting of three reprints and one new short novel, but it was a single-issue publication, and it was not until November, 1949, that Popular Publications inaugurated *Walt Coburn's Western Magazine*. The Coburn stories in this magazine were all reprints. Coburn contributed a regular column titled "Walt's Tally Book." This magazine ceased publication in May, 1951, after sixteen issues.

The pulps, of course, were dying. *Western Story* ceased in 1949, *Lariat* in 1950, but Coburn was not a presence in those that continued after 1951. He had never had an agent during his years in the pulps. Now that he intended to try his hand again at book-length fiction, he got one; but many of his novels were published in the United Kingdom first and appeared only sporadically in American paperback editions. When Condé Nast bought Street & Smith, some of Coburn's stories from *Western Story Magazine* were reprinted in a triple-action format, but with the royalties going to the copyright owner and not Coburn. Perhaps his best work in this period is in the original novels Coburn wrote for Ace's double-action series, but they do not bear comparison with the novels from his early years. In this same period Popular Library's editor, Charles N. Heckelmann, reprinted Coburn's finest novels in paperback editions, THE RINGTAILED RANNYHANS, MAVERICKS, BARB WIRE, and SKY-PILOT COWBOY.

In a last, crazy effort to restore himself and write with his old flair, Coburn abandoned Pat and went to Mexico to live where he shared a hovel with a young Mexican girl. It was an act of desperation, and it did not work out for him. Coburn also began contributing his non-fiction column, "Walt's Tally Book," to magazines owned by former pulp Western writer, Joe Austell Small, including *True West* and *Frontier Times*. In STIRRUP HIGH (Messner, 1957) Coburn recorded his recollections of growing up in Montana, and this was followed a decade later by PIONEER CATTLEMAN OF MONTANA. The latter is not only of enduring interest for its general subject but is also an invaluable touchstone for anyone drawn to Coburn's fiction since here was the raw material from which he spun so many of his Montana stories. At the time of his death he was at work on his autobiography, published posthumously as WALT COBURN, WESTERN WORD WRANGLER (Northland Press, 1973). It was prepared for publication by Ramon F. Adams, the Western historian and bibliographer who himself had begun by writing Western fiction for *Western Story Magazine*. The final chapter, about Coburn's career in the pulps, had appeared previously in slightly different form in *True West* (7–8/67). Among the papers he left behind were rambling notes, two of which were

reproduced at the end of his autobiography. One read
in part:

I can't make a hand any more.
Written my last story.
Forgive me, Pat,
This is the only way out.
I leave and bequeath everything to my wife.
I leave the world with no regrets.
So let there be no tears shed.

The home in Tucson had been sold and, after living
in several rentals and briefly owning a home in Del
Mar, the Coburns came to reside in a newly built log
cabin on the outskirts of Prescott where Walt lived, in
his words, "a self-exiled semi-recluse . . ." Home alone
one day, he took a rope and hanged himself. He died
May 24, 1971, terrified that he was going insane as a
consequence of decades of heavy drinking.

His legacy, though, lives after him. MAVERICKS,
BARB WIRE, the marvelous border stories for Fiction
House, the Montana stories for Fiction House, *Western
Story Magazine, Dime Western,* and *Star Western* —
all surely demand to be collected between hard covers
and will be read and enjoyed years hence. In PIONEER
CATTLEMAN OF MONTANA Coburn told of how,
before leaving Montana after the Circle C had been
sold, he had ridden out, sad at heart, to visit with the
old ones he knew among the Assiniboins and Gros
Ventres who now lived as fenced in as the once free
range. "I had sat and smoked with the old ones, once

brave warriors," Coburn recalled. "Still brave at heart, they set an example of splendid courage. It was up to me to pattern the ways of my life after my pioneer father and after these old ones of the Gros Ventres and Assiniboins, once bitter enemies but now living in peace together. Theirs was a far greater sorrow than mine, because I was at the beginning and they were at the end of the trail." As Charles M. Russell and Eugene Manlove Rhodes, two men Walt Coburn had known and admired in life, he captured the cow country and recreated it when it had already passed from sight.

He Rides Alone

This somewhat autobiographical story first appeared as "He Rides Alone" in Fiction House's *Action Stories* in the issue for October, 1927. It was subsequently reprinted by Fiction House under the title "He Heard The Owl Hoot" in *Lariat Story Magazine* for February, 1936. In 1954, after Fiction House had ceased publishing its pulp magazines, Walt Coburn requested assignments of the copyrights for all of his stories that had formerly appeared in their publications and so was able to renew the copyrights in the individual stories as they became eligible for renewal. "He Rides Alone" eventually appeared in a double-action pulp paperback published by Belmont under the title "Reckless!" coupled with "Men of Blood" by E. B. Mann. Coburn had a penchant to capture the way Westerners spoke, in terms of their region and in vernacular speech flavored by their ethnic origins, and it is an integral element in his stories. He drew his characters from life, and readily they engage our sympathy. He did not regard human existence as simple, but rather as desperately complicated, although at the end — if only after suffering the ordeal of living on the frontier — there is finally light. When Fiction House would reprint stories years after their first publication, the editor would occasionally change the names of characters and abridge or rewrite parts of the text so as to conceal from readers the fact that the story was a reprint. For its appearance here both the title and the text of this remarkable story have been restored.

CHAPTER
ONE

"The Crimson Trail"

Powder smoke tainted the air, its acrid fumes piercing the whiskey fog that clouded young Bruce McTavish's brain. A moment before he had been drunk. Now he was sober, white, strained, a look akin to panic in the gray eyes that looked from under heavy black brows through the film of smoke.

"Turn him over, one of you," he croaked hoarsely. "See if he's dead." A last trickle of smoke spiraled thinly from Bruce's gun as he motioned with it toward the huddled form of a man who lay under a poker table in Dutch's Place.

"He's dead enough, kid," snapped Dutch, coming from behind the bar. "Better drag it fer the home ranch. You there, Swift, let the damn' young fool go. His old man'll see he don't quit the country. Swift, put up that gun er I'll make ya eat it. That goes fer yore men, too." And as Dutch rounded the end of the bar, a sawed-off shotgun appeared in his hands.

Bruce McTavish saw the scene as in a dream. The tense faces of Bob Swift and his men, the still form of Jim Harmon, sheepman, half under the poker table, the heavy-framed, cold-eyed Dutch, assuming command of the tense situation as if it were an everyday occurrence to have men shot down in his saloon.

"Drag it, kid!" Dutch's voice, its whiskey huskiness rasping in the dead quiet of the place, shocked the young cowman into action.

"He crowded me, Dutch."

"Save that talk for the jury. Damn it, clear out. I can't keep these men covered all night. Go on home."

Bob Swift, Harmon's foreman, grinned nastily under the cover of Dutch's shotgun. The three Harmon men with him took their cue from the foreman. After all, they were paid to work, not to kill cattlemen.

So Bruce McTavish stepped out of the lighted saloon into a star-filled night. He still held his gun. He shoved it into the waistband of his overalls and swung into the saddle of his waiting horse. A moment and the night had swallowed him.

Thus the prediction of cowland was fulfilled. Old Man McTavish's young 'un had gone bad. It had come, as the cow country had long prophesied it would come, and the man who went down with Bruce McTavish's bullet in him was Jim Harmon from over on Birch Creek.

Sober enough now, filled with mingled emotions that ran the gamut from sheer panic to self-pity and hatred for the man he'd shot, Bruce McTavish rode homeward. Ahead of him lay the ordeal of meeting his father. Later, the reckoning with John Law. And Bruce was twenty-one years old. Prison? The outlaw trail?

Dread of meeting his father's cold gray eyes pulled Bruce to a halt. There, to the south, were the badlands where a man could hide. He feared old Angus McTavish far more than he feared the law and its punishment, for Angus McTavish was a stern man, stern and hard and uncompromising. A just man, they said of him, and an exacting one, with his Bible and his black brier pipe and his piercing gray eyes.

And the one soft spot in his Highland heart now was a memory that lay buried on the little knoll above the ranch house. For Janet McTavish, when she died, had taken his love with her. And that was fifteen years gone by. Nor had rain or snow or sleet kept Angus McTavish from visiting that grave each day. Alone, head bared, his giant frame shielding the Bible from inclement weather, he would pray there each evening. After fifteen years, he spoke of Janet as if it were yesterday that she had been taken from him.

"The wee laddie'll take my place, Angus," she had said, that last day. "Ye'll be a good father to him."

"Aye, lass. But ye'll not be leavin' me, Janet. Tomorrow ye'll be stronger."

"Don't be too hard on the wee bairn, Angus. For it's both mother and father you must be to him."

In his way, according to his lights, Angus McTavish had done his best to carry out the wish of his dead wife. But even the Scriptures cannot supplant the sympathy and understanding that is mother love.

Besides, Montana was a man's country, governed by a man's code. The strong survived, while the weak paid the penalty of their shortcomings. A country where men rode hard, fought hard, drank hard, and, if fate so dealt the cards, died hard.

23

★　★　★

Angus McTavish watched with some misgiving the progress of young Bruce, a black-headed, gray-eyed boy, big-boned like his father, gifted with native strength and a quick temper. He was seventeen when he whipped the bully of Rimrock with his two fists. That fall he won the roping and riding contests at the county fair. But one stain marked these performances. Bruce McTavish had been half drunk.

"The first McTavish," Old Angus told his foreman, "that could not handle his whiskey. The first . . . save one."

"Hell, Angus," returned the grizzled old trail boss whose name was Jake Raine, "the young 'un'll git his wild oats sowed bimeby. Drink'll never hurt that big frame uh his. Show me the young feller aroun' here that don't get drunk. Be easy on the young colt." For young Bruce was the pride of the old trail boss's heart.

"He'll bring disgrace on me in the end. Do ye ken, Jake Raine, the story I was tellin' ye one night aboot that laird o' the clan that brung doon the curse o' God upon the name? D'ye ken, man?"

"The gent yuh called Black Robert?"

"The same. He was hung, man, like a damn' knave."

"There's bin some damn' good men stretch rope," countered Jake, "while there was blackguards amongst them as strung 'em up. Don't fergit it. Scotland er Africa er Montana, there's bin mistakes like that made. Do yuh think it's gonna help that young 'un any tuh keep tellin' him that it's bad blood in him that makes him raise hell? Slingin' Bible verses at his head instead uh talkin' things out with him reasonable? You pay me good money, McTavish, an' I earn it by workin', not runnin' off at the head. But I'm tellin' yuh now, if yuh fire me the next minute, yuh ain't givin' that boy a square deal."

"'Tis such talk that encourages the lad in his wild ways, Jake Raine. In the eyes o' God, I'm a just man."

Old Jake snorted defiantly. "Yeah. Mebby. I calls it mule-headedness."

Repetition of the same arguments arose from time to time during the passing of the years: the time Bruce was arrested for shooting up a saloon in Butte; when he came home from college, expelled for some wild prank that involved the blackening of a professor's eye; and other such occasions. Jake remained staunch in his loyalty, but secretly he nursed that fear that some day young Bruce McTavish would "turn bad."

As for the boy, he had fallen into the habit, through years of custom, of using Jake as a buffer. Jake Raine it was, more than often, who gently broke the news of the son's escapades to old Angus. In due time Bruce came to accept Jake's long-suffering loyalty as he accepted many other favors life gave him, with selfish indifference.

Now, as Bruce McTavish halted in the night, gripped by dread of his father's wrath, he thought of grizzled old Jake. Jake had with his own peculiar brand of cowhand diplomacy eased many a hard situation. Jake would be asleep at the bunkhouse. Jake would advise him. So, somewhat cheered, he rode on toward home.

And it was not until he was covering the last five miles of the thirty that lay between the McTavish ranch and Rimrock that young Bruce felt any qualms of real regret concerning the fate of Jim Harmon — Harmon, who was married and had two kids. For Bruce McTavish's chief concern was of himself. It was not so much that the boy was cold-blooded, for he was not. It was simply the natural panic following the rash act committed in a split-second of whiskey-heated anger.

Reckless, thoughtless, wild as he was, Bruce McTavish was not tainted with the killer's lust, and so he lacked the cold nerve to carry him along, once he had killed. He felt the terrible need of advice, of Jake Raine's advice. Yet, no man could call the boy a coward and stay within the limits of truth.

Harmon crowded me into it, *he reflected bitterly.* Harmon's ornery when he's drunk. He forced the play. Had his gun out when I shot. Maybe he and Swift had it planned. Two-bit poker game. Swift and Harmon sore over boundary lines and those Birch Creek water rights. Looks like they used the poker game to get me into it. Me drunk. Wish it had been Swift that came at me. Harmon's wife and the kids. Damn the luck! I played hell this time. And so help me, I'll play the game to a finish, somehow.

Thirty miles of bitter reflection sobered Bruce McTavish. It was a stiff-backed, steel-eyed Bruce who swung off his horse at the ranch.

26

The first streaks of dawn were lighting the skyline. A light burned in Angus McTavish's room. The bunkhouse windows were yellow with lamplight within. With a sort of shock Bruce remembered the telephone. Dutch, of course, had phoned the ranch and broken the evil tidings.

Bruce grinned mirthlessly and, instead of seeking out Jake Raine, stepped up on the porch, and with spurs tinkling the news of his arrival entered the house of his father.

He met old Angus, fully clad, in the front room. There, in the shadowy light of a low-turned lamp, their eyes met, and Bruce McTavish, white but without flinching, waited in silence for the storm to break in its fury.

CHAPTER
TWO

"The Verdict of Angus"

"Sit ye doon, Bruce." The old man's voice was barely above a whisper. Angus McTavish looked old and, in spite of his giant's frame, a little feeble. Perhaps it was the light. "Ye have killed, lad?" He towered above the boy who had taken a chair. "Ye killed Jim Harmon?"

"Yes, Dad. I was drunk."

"Drunk, eh? God, when ha' ye bin sober these past years? Ha' ye nothin' but that to say to your father? I killed a mon! I was drunk! Do ye ken that the law holds drunkenness as no excuse? A life for a life, says the law, and 'tis but justice. I ha' sent for the sheriff."

Old Angus pulled himself to his full height. A white-maned, bronzed statue of fatherhood. There was something about that deeply-lined face that, hard as it was, touched some chord in the son's heart. He saw his father as he had never before seen him. Not as a harsh disciplinarian, not as the Bible verse quoter, but as a man who lived according to his lights despite whatever penalties God or the devil might inflict.

There was something else in the eyes of Angus McTavish that Bruce could not fathom. A half-hidden something that the boy had sensed faintly once or twice

28

before. The light of that something flickered in the old cowman's eyes for the space of a full minute, as the gaze of father and son met across the low-turned lamp. Then the elder McTavish turned abruptly and for many minutes paced the floor, his great hands knotted behind his back. And Bruce, straight-lipped and steady-eyed, waited in silence.

The boy's panic had left him back along the trail. He held his head high as he stood up on his feet that he might take his verdict standing. For he knew that his father had not done with speech. Straight, black-headed, handsome, he was the living image of Angus McTavish of thirty years ago. It was as if Angus stood there in the room with the image of his own youth before him. As if he now sat in judgment of his own youth with its folly, its temptations, its weakness. But because Bruce was unaware of this striking resemblance, because his father spoke seldom and sparingly of his younger days, and because he could never understand the heart of the man who had sired him, Bruce McTavish could not now understand what lay in the heart of that white-haired giant who walked to and fro with heavy step, chin sunk on the massive, flannel-shirted chest.

From across the room, his head now lifted, Angus McTavish walked up to the son whose wide shoulders leveled his own heavier ones. The father's hands reached out and gripped his son's shoulders. Angus's gray eyes, peering from under the thick, white brows, searched the same gray eyes that met his own from under straight black brows. Angus McTavish was looking back thirty years and was passing judgment not alone on his son, but upon his own youth.

"'Tis a bitter lesson, bairn," he spoke finally, dropping his hands. "Ha' ye learnt it well?"

"I have." Bruce's voice was calm. "But the harm's been done. The lesson came too late. I understand a lot, Dad, that I didn't know last night. I'm not here to whine. I'll take what they give me."

His father nodded curtly. "So I read in your eyes, bairn. Had ye shown me aught else, by the Gad that made ye, I'd die o' the shame. Who made the quarrel, lad?"

"Jim Harmon. But if I'd been sober, I'd have used my fists."

"There'll be witnesses. Swift and his men. Ye've got but a single witness on your side and him a saloonman whose word on the stand is na too good. Like as not, they'll throw his testimony out. 'Tis been done before. 'Twill be unfair to ye, lad. They'll be gi'en ye a long sentence." He stepped to the door, raising his voice. "Jake!"

"Comin'," came Jake's voice as an echo.

The old foreman must have been just outside the door. Bruce saw that Jake was fully clothed, and around his middle sagged a cartridge belt with the old Colt that was wont to hang above his bunk, gathering dust. Jake's seamed face was twisted into an odd grin that was a mixture of excited joy and bitter disappointment. "All set, Angus," he announced. Then he was gone again, and the door closed.

Once more the father and son stood alone in the room. Dawn was creeping in under the drawn blinds.

"Ye'll be goin' awa', bairn," said Angus McTavish in a low, rumbling bass, "awa' from the house o' your birth, awa' fra the grave o' your bonnie mother and fra the father that's breakin' the law by sendin' ye. But before the Gad above me, I'm a just mon. I'll stand by and see no McTavish hung on such evidence as'd be given. So, bairn, I'm sendin' ye awa'. For a' he's a cross-grained mon, Jake Raine loves ye as his own. There ha' been times when I ha' felt 'twas such a love as that which Janet wished. But I dinna ha' it in me to gi' ye softness, lad. I'm na a soft mon. May the Gad forgi' me if I've failed, for 'twas na my nature to be otherwise.

"So I'll be sendin' Jake Raine wi' ye, Bruce. Wi' a letter to a mon that'll gi' ye work. I ha' made my last will and testament, lad. The ranch and all I own goes to Jake Raine. I'm cuttin' ye off wi'out a farthin'. 'Tis na anger, bairn, that guided my pen. Ye ken?"

"I understand, father." Bruce smiled into his father's face. "And I'd rather it would be like that. I'll stand on my own two legs."

"Aye," nodded McTavish. "Aye, lad. I'm gi'en ye the Book. Read it, lad, wi' your own eyes. If I dinna see ye again i' this life, Bruce, 'twill be Gad's will. Ye ha' your lesson learnt. Be the mon Gad meant ye to be. Good bye, bairn."

Across the worn Bible on the table their hands met. Two pairs of gray eyes, misty with unshed tears, spoke mute parting. Then Bruce, the Bible under his arm, found his way to the door.

His saddle was on a fresh horse. Jake, already mounted, held the lead rope of a pack horse. The sun was rising above the notched skyline.

From the open doorway old Angus McTavish watched them go, erect, grim-lipped, a figure of stern grief. And when the two horsemen had rounded a knoll and were gone from his sight, he went back inside, the door swinging shut behind him as if the hand that closed it had grown feeble.

CHAPTER
THREE

"He's Heard the Owl Hoot"

From the badlands in Montana to the mesquite-spotted sands of Arizona is a long ride on horseback — long enough, even if one kept to the well-traveled highways. Longer yet, when the route is devious and the riding is done after dark, for the better part of the way.

It was apparent from the start that Jake Raine knew the route. But when Bruce questioned him about it, or about the men they met from time to time, he was met by a silence that was half tolerance, half apology. The old cow boss seemed somehow changed. There was a hint of swagger in the tilt of his hat and the sagging cartridge belt.

Bruce had always thought of old Jake as a harmless sort of old duffer, good-natured, fond of a jig or a joke, a beef man who understood the business, but unobtrusive and inclined to sidestep brawls. So he puzzled somewhat over this new Jake Raine, who met the hidden challenge of strange men in strange places with a reckless grin and some careless password that made them welcome among men whose eyes were hard and grim and on whose heads the law had set a price.

Wind River, Brown's Park, the Mogollons. Guarded trails where two men, from hidden points, could stand off a company of soldiers. Hidden cabins among the pines. Corrals in box cañons. Log barns that held some of the best horses Bruce McTavish had ever seen.

Men with beards and a few clean shaven. A bantering, fun-loving, care-free company who talked of everything except themselves. Among them Bruce felt young and ill at ease at first. Not so, Jake Raine. He fell into their company as if it were his natural element. It was borne home to Bruce that Jake, like the others, spoke sparingly of himself. Some of the older men in these hidden camps greeted Jake with a heartiness that was thinly disguised under the carelessness of soft-drawled banter.

"Damned if it ain't Jake Raine! Long time no see yuh, homely."

"Ten years ain't so long, feller. Er is it fifteen? Anyhow, yuh ain't no easier on the eyes than yuh usta be." Jake would turn to Bruce. "Meet up with one uh the old-timers, kid. Jim, this is Black Angus's young 'un. Come out tuh hear the owl hoot fer a spell. Yuh recollect Black Angus, don't yuh?"

"Shore thing, Jake. The Box T outfit south uh Rimrock. I taken a hoss from him onct. Year, before I got a chanct tuh send it back."

But it was noticeable that these iron-gray veterans never introduced Bruce to the others in the camp. There was never the formality of introduction. No man asked his name or business. Taking their cue from Jake, they called him "kid."

34

"Just as well yuh don't go airin' yore trouble tuh nobody, Bruce," Jake told him at the start. "Nobody's gonna poke into yore business. Don't git gabby, savvy? Less said, the better."

Over in the Lost Cabin country, Bruce saw a man die with a slug in his chest. He was a big man, big as Angus McTavish. When he coughed, blood gushed from his mouth, and a tow-headed youth with slit eyes wiped away the blood with a dirty neckscarf.

The dying man reached for the cigarette that hung from the tight lips of the slit-eyed boy. The tarp-covered bed was blood-soaked. The boy put the cigarette between the big man's lips.

"Anyhow," said the big man, "this beats hangin'!" And so he died, the cigarette, a sodden thing of blood, still hanging in the corner of his mouth.

They buried him that night. Bruce, with a timidity that Jake Raine approved of with an inward smile, mentioned the Bible in his saddle pocket.

"That's what I calls style," voiced a gray-haired man whose left jaw was indented by a horrible scar. "I'd like the same done fer me when I ford the big river. Have at it, son."

So Bruce McTavish read a brief sermon above the uncoffined remains of a man whose name he never knew. The kid with the corn-colored hair and slit eyes held a lantern to light the page.

" 'The Lord giveth. The Lord taketh away.' "

The slit-eyed youth sought him out later that night.

"A honest-tuh-God parson couldn't uh done better," he told Bruce huskily as they stood in the darkness under a tall pine tree. "I'm obliged." And he gripped Bruce's hard hand, then slid off into the night.

"That big feller that died," Jake told Bruce the next day as they rode along a dim mountain trail, "was the towheaded kid's daddy. He got shot when they stuck up a bank yesterday mornin'."

They camped alone that night and made no campfire. Jake explained that half a dozen posses were scouring the country for the bank robbers.

Late into the night, Bruce lay on his back, staring up at the stars. Now and then the yapping of a coyote broke the stillness. An aching lonesomeness gnawed at the boy's heart. More than ever he felt the bitterness of his forced isolation.

He wondered about the boy with the corn-colored hair. Would he be killed, or hung, or sent to prison? What twisted, torturing grief lay hidden behind the slit eyes that had thanked him under the pine tree? Outlaws. Men hunted like beasts, killed or wounded to die and lie buried in some unmarked grave.

The boom of an owl, close by, made Bruce start. Jake, lying beside him in the bed, spoke without moving.

"Well, kid, yuh heard the owl hoot."

How aptly that expressed it all! The hoot of an owl, weird, unearthly, embodying all the utter lonesomeness of that life beyond the law. No wolf howl, no yapping coyote, dreary as is their call, can so interpret the stark reality of the outlaw's existence as does the boom of that bird of the night that, like the men who hear its call, hides by day and goes forth at night. So cow land speaks of its fallen men: "He's heard the owl hoot."

Fitting epitaph to be carved into the pine slab above the grave of an outlaw. His history written, his sentence passed, his saga sung in those five words: "*He's heard the oul hoot.*"

CHAPTER
FOUR

"Jake Grows Suspicious"

South, always south, Jake Raine's trail led, and Bruce McTavish followed. Each day fresh lessons learned, by lonely campfires or in the motley company of men who had broken their country's laws. A word, a gesture, a lonely grave hidden in some brush thicket, guarded by chattering bluejays. And each day found Bruce more quiet and thoughtful. For he knew that he did not belong to the life that fate had thrust upon him.

Names of men: Billy, the Kid; Butch Cassidy, Black Jack. False idols. Fallen gods of forbidden places, who in their day had worn halos of powder smoke. Names that had always, to Bruce McTavish, conjured up visions of romance and swift-moving drama. Until now he had not reckoned the price those men had paid.

For they had paid, each and all of those knights of the outlaw trail. And because their penalty was hidden beneath a grin, because their code reads that they must cover their regrets with the cloak of bravado, they "played their string out." To those who followed their trails, they bequeathed the heritage of romance. Death claimed their unspoken heartaches. They had died with their boots on.

Jake Raine became more of an enigma each day. Somewhere, some time, Jake had known these men they met along the trail. But Bruce held back his questions.

In between the pages of the Bible was a sealed letter without name or address — the letter from Angus McTavish to some man who was "to give Bruce a job."

"Where are we headed for, Jake?" he asked one day.

"Jail, if yuh don't quit skylightin' yore carcass along the ridges. Gimme the loan of a smoke."

They made camp with a cow outfit one night in the Mogollons. As they sat about, squat-legged, on the ground, gulping down jerky and brown beans and Dutch-oven bread, Jake made careless inquiry of the boss.

"How far tuh Jim Laughlin's place?"

"Acrost that range uh hills. Mebbso a hundred miles. Mebby more. Never could tell distance. Gonna work fer Laughlin?"

"If he kin put us on."

"Yuh come a long ways tuh git a job," grinned the boss. "You boys'll have tuh swap them center-fire saddles fer double-rigged hulls if yo're aimin' tuh make a hand in the rough country."

"Yeah?" Jake munched thoughtfully on a mouthful of jerky, washed it down with black coffee, and grinned at the man who was apparently a stranger to him.

"Yeah. Ever work in the rough country?"

"Some," admitted Jake dryly. "Meanin', I reckon, that yuh call these hills rough?"

"About the slantin'est range I ever rode," announced the boss, with some pride. "I bin slippin' ponies off these slants fer the past five years."

"Yeah?" Jake's grin widened a little. "See that pinnacle yonder?"

"Ol' Baldy?"

"Ol' Baldy," nodded Jake. "Well, mister, I was born an' brung up on a sore-backed mule at the foot uh that pinnacle." And the munching of Jake's jaws broke the silence that followed.

"I reckon, Bruce," said Jake as they spread their bed that night, "that'll hold that curious jasper till we pull out in the mornin'. I seen him lookin' at the Box T brands on our ponies. Our single-rigged hulls tells him we're from the north. Beats hell how some fellers is nosy thataway. Only that we hadn't et fer a day er so, I'd never stopped. Hope nothin' comes uh it. Nosy damn' fool. Orter be herdin' sheep."

"You were born in these hills, Jake?" asked Bruce.

"Never set eyes on 'em till now," chuckled the old cowpuncher. "I come from the windmill country. Staked Plains, an' a few points south. Never knowed where I was born. Raised up on dry jerky an' gyp' water, far back as I kin recomember. They called me 'Button.' When I got old enough, I picked myse'f a name. That name done me for fifteen years. Then I quit that range, an' when I hits New Mexico, I got a new name. Seems like the old 'uns gittin' wore out. Bimeby I drifts outta New Mexico fer one reason er another. I don't quit travelin' till I'm slap-dab ag'in' the Canadian line.

"Ain't seen a human in ten days by then. The bottom's dropped outta the sky, an' I'm crossin' a 'dobe flat that's gonna be a lake directly. Yon side uh the flat I kin see a roundup camp through the sheets uh water that's comin' outta the sky an' down my neck. Boogy? Man, that gumbo'd bog a jacksnipe. I'm a shore sorry-lookin' mess when I hits that cow camp. I sights a big jasper in a yaller slicker that's split up the back. He's settin' on the cook's bed, so I taken him tuh be the boss. I tackles him fer a job an' gets it.

" 'What name?' says he, takin' out a little tally book.

" 'Jake,' says I, pourin' a few gallons uh soft water outta my boots.

" 'Jake who?' says he.

" 'Raine,' said I, feelin' shore sorry about them boots which is new an' gonna be shore tight.

"So the big gent in the yaller slicker writes down a name in his book. The name is 'Jake Raine.' The big jasper in the slicker turns out tuh be Black Angus McTavish. That's bin twenty years ago. You was a yearlin' then. I recollect you chawin' my thumb with a couple uh teeth yuh had. Well, I stayed on with Angus an' kep' the name."

Jake smoked thoughtfully for some minutes, a whimsical smile softening his rough-hewn features.

"Beats hell what a good, honest woman kin do fer a man, Bruce. Fer all that Angus laid store by his Bible, it was yore mammy that slowed me down an' knocked my horns off. She was as close to an angel as they git. She give me the only motherin' I ever had. Me dang nigh old enough tuh be her daddy. A angel, son. I quit drinkin' when . . ."

The old cowpuncher's voice trailed softly into musing silence. Neither man spoke for some time.

"What did that feller say his name was, kid?" Jake finally spoke.

"Huh? What feller, Jake?"

"Yonder straw-boss uh this two-bit pack spread."

"Bullard. His men call him Chick."

"Bullard, eh? Well, son, mark my word, that gent'll bear watchin'. Sorry we hit this camp, but no use borryin' trouble till it's handed yuh. Only keep clear uh him. I know his breed. Now what made me ask how far tuh Jim Laughlin's place? Bruce, I'm gittin' too danged old fer tuh play this game. Too old. My brain is as stove-up as my laigs. Chick Bullard, eh? I'm wonderin', now, Mister Chick Bullard, if you ain't got a nice shiny deputy sheriff star pinned onto yore undershirt?"

CHAPTER
FIVE

"Jake Calls the Turn"

"So you fellers aim tuh hire out tuh Jim Laughlin, eh?" Chick Bullard grinned at the two travelers as they filled their breakfast plates. Bullard, while slightly under six feet in height, was heavily muscled and quick moving. His grin was almost a sneer, and his eyes glinted with suspicion. Bruce took note that he wore his gun within easy reach of a hairy right hand.

"Mebbyso, mebby not," returned Jake Raine easily, "we ain't noways contracted tuh nobody. Ain't that broke."

"No?" Bullard's grin became a one-sided grimace. "Well, you won't be the first two men that went tuh work fer Jim Laughlin with *poco* plenty dough in yore overalls. Laughlin has a habit uh hirin' boys that's plumb well heeled with green money."

One of Bullard's men, who showed a strain of Mexican blood in his veins, laughed insinuatingly and shifted a holstered gun. Three other Bullard men squatted nearby, and each of these men wore a gun. Jake shot Bruce a meaningful look. That look conveyed a warning, even while the old cowpuncher's eyes held dancing lights of sheer joyous excitement. Bruce, sitting on his heels, took in at one swift glance of appraisal the position of each man there. Apparently engrossed in devouring breakfast, he waited for the coming of trouble. For it was plain that Chick Bullard meant trouble.

"I dunno as I quite foller yore drift, mister," drawled old Jake, sopping a biscuit in his gravy.

"Then I reckon, Mister Center-Fire Saddle," leered Bullard, "that it's up tuh me tuh go into details. Jim Laughlin's a ex-convict. A paint horse don't never change color. A cow thief never fergits how tuh build a hungry loop. There's always a job waitin' fer certain folks at the J Bar L Ranch which is owned by one Jim Laughlin. Git me?"

"I git yuh, Bullard," said Jake, sipping at a huge cup of steaming black coffee. "I git yuh, all right. You think me 'n' my pardner is kinda crooked. You got yore authority pinned onto yore undershirt. Just now you got it figgered that me 'n' the kid is bad 'uns an' that you kin build a rep for yorese'f by crowding us tuh fight, then gut shootin' us fer the glory. Well, Bullard, here's at yuh!"

The pint cup of scalding coffee struck Bullard full in the face. At almost the same instant Bruce sprang from his squatting posture, and his right fist sent the half-breed Mexican in a thudding heap among the Dutch ovens. Jake's gun was out, swinging in a short arc that covered every man. Bullard, moaning in agony, held his hands to his face.

"Saddle our horses, kid," grinned old Jake. "Kill any fool that gits in yore way."

"Can you manage the bunch, Jake?"

"Manage 'em? Son, I've et whole herds like 'em in my day. Manage 'em? I'm jest nacherally rearin' tuh play 'Yankee Doodle' on 'em with this ol' Forty-Some-Odd. Shake yore dew-claws, kid, an' git our hulls on them ponies. Bullard, here, is gonna load our pack hoss, directly he finds out he ain't gone blind. Yuh might wean him of that hog-laig he packs in that fancy scabbard. I need a extra gun. Let them others keep their cannons. Mebbyso they might git a rush uh nerve to their yeller hearts an' open the jackpot fer a dollar. Which'll give me a chanct tuh raise 'em a few."

Old Jake was grinning widely. Hat cocked rakishly across one eye, armed now with two guns, he was again the hard-riding, swashbuckling cowboy of thirty years ago.

"Well, Mister Chick Bullard, you ain't half so damn' tough as yuh let on, are yuh? What does that Chick stand fer? I dunno. From the way I reads 'er, she means chicken-hearted. Yeah. Yuh damn' blubberin', over-growed calf! You, a law officer? We got kids in the primer grades up north that'd run yuh outta the country. You begun this. Me 'n' my pard finishes the play. We ain't cow thieves, neither. We're payin' yuh fer what grub we et. We're goin' along our trail tuh where we aim tuh go. You, ner no ten men like yuh, kin run us one inch, *sabe*? If we like this range, we stays. An' Mister Polecat, if you er yore lousy, sheep-smellin', tough-talkin' men gits in our way, we'll make wolf bait outta yuh. Next time yuh cut our sign, tip yore hat to us.

"When yuh git tuh town again an' want tuh tell 'er scary to the bartenders, tell 'em how yuh won glory this mornin', on yore own range, in yore own camp. Outmatchin' us fer numbers three tuh one. Lettin' a wore-out, broke-down, feeble ol' man cuss yuh out! Yeah, tell it scary, Chicken Bullard. Write out a couple uh warrants fer us, why don't yuh? We'll be over at Jim Laughlin's place fer a spell. Drop over any day an' serve 'em, lawman. Try yore luck. Show yore toughness. Yo're a lawman. Well, me 'n' my pardner jest held up a bank up Idaho way. There's a big bounty on our hides. Come an' git us. If I was half blind, had one arm, an' a wooden laig, if I was half-witted an' broke out with boils, I cud still give yuh cards in spades, an' win."

As Bullard's hands came away from his eyes, Jake tossed him his gun. Moreover, the old fellow shoved his own weapon back in its holster and stood spraddle-legged, thumbs hooked in his sagging belt, taunting them. Like an old fire horse at the sound of the alarm, Jake Raine sniffed the air of battle. He swaggered in every gesture, bullied them with his words, and held them helpless with the cold fire of his slitted eyes.

Bruce, returning with the saddled horses and the pack horse, viewed the old fellow with awed surprise.

"There's ten thousand bucks on us, polecats," Jake was lying. "Why don't yuh make a try fer it, huh? You lousy, two-bit, gotch-eared, long-backed, box-ankled, flea-bit sons uh sheep-stealin', mail-order imitations! You bet a nickel an' pinch four cents afore the draw. Yuh figgered yuh had a pat hand, but yuh didn't have the guts tuh play yore cards. Bullard, take that *cholo* that's sleepin' amongst that mess uh biscuits an' spilled jerky. Take him an' load our bed fer us."

So saying, Jake picked up a pail of water and threw the contents into the scared face of the reviving half-breed whom Bruce had knocked cold.

"Men," said Jake, chuckling, "if I was tuh turn the kid here amongst yuh, you'd think you was livin' in a cyclone country. All right, Bullard, git that pony packed. When me 'n' my pard has gone yonderly, put some wet sody on yore face. The hide may peel off, but yuh can't be no homelier than yuh are. Git!"

As Bullard and the half-breed packed the horse, Jake addressed Bruce in an undertone.

"That was our best play, son. Bullard aimed tuh git us. Up tuh us tuh run a long whizzer an' keep him scairt off us if we stay in the country, er he'll be nosin' aroun', huntin' yuh. We got 'em thinkin' we're shore enough bad folks. Keep up the bluff. I knowed that Bullard was a snake, from the start. Dang the luck. May have tuh drift yonderly into Mexico yet."

Evidently Jake's bluff worked, for no one molested them as they rode away. But there was an air of uneasiness about the old-timer that Bruce read by various indications as the day wore on. For Jake had wrapped himself in a brooding silence and glanced back along the trail many times. Twice during the day he called a halt and, hiding in the brush and boulders at some high point, swept the country behind them with field glasses for the better part of an hour.

"Think we're being followed, Jake?"

"Can't see any sign, Bruce. Nary sign. But I'd bet a year's pay somebody's cold trailin' us."

"Bullard?"

"Hard tuh say. Mebby. Most mebby not. Hope I'm wrong. I've knowed these kind uh hunches tuh be all wrong. Still, dang it, I feel 'er in my bones. We ain't makin' no fire tonight. Ner tomorrow night. Ner mebbyso the next night."

"We should make Laughlin's place before then, shouldn't we?"

"Make 'er tomorrow, straight travelin'. But we're doublin' back, come dark. No use bringin' a posse in on Laughlin."

"Look here, Jake," said Bruce earnestly, "don't you think it's about time you cut loose from me? I got into this. Let me be man enough to get myself out. No use in you taking chances because I got drunk and killed a man. I propose we split here. You go on back. I'll play my string out. It's damn' white of you to do what you're doing, and I've learned plenty on this trip. It's come home to me what a fool I've been. What a silly, four-flushing piker I am compared to men that are really game and tough and all those things I tried to be. I've seen myself through the eyes of men like you, Jake, and my lesson is sure well learned. I'm big enough and have enough horse sense to play out the game as the cards come to me. I want you to quit me here."

"Yeah?" Jake eyed him with cold scorn. "Yeah? Well, yuh young warthog, what yuh want an' what yuh git is two differ'nt things. Dang me for a turkey buzzard if I'm gonna let you plumb ruin the only vacation I've had in twenty years. My horns was knocked off about that long ago, but, son, they're sproutin' onct more. I'm havin' the time uh my life, an' I ain't aimin' tuh let no young rascal like you spile it. Chaw on that a while. Another sech crack outta yuh an' I lands on yuh like a week's washin', all spread out. Hear me?"

"You darned old idiot!" Bruce's voice was a little husky.

"You dang young fool!" chuckled Jake.

"Darned if I don't think you're huntin' trouble, Jake?"

"Well, yuh might make a wronger guess, son."

CHAPTER
SIX

"Mystery in the Night"

Piñon trees stood black against the silvery moonlight. Hidden in the shadows of a deep barranca, Bruce and Jake slept the uneasy slumber of hunted men.

A shot, dimmed by distance, broke the night's silence, echoed in the cañons, died into silence again. Bruce and Jake, sitting erect with their guns gripped in startled readiness, looked at one another. Then Jake struck a match and looked at his big silver watch.

"Half after midnight," he mused aloud. "One shot. Come from back yonder on the trail. One shot, kid. I reads the sign as bein' bad. No man's killin' meat this time uh night. Must've shot at a human. Must've hit him square er the second feller'd be bustin' a few caps hisse'f." He threw back the tarp and blankets and reached for his boots.

"You stay here, kid. One man makes less noise than two. Can't be more than half a mile back yonder. I'll go afoot. You lay low. If there's shootin', come back along the trail hell a-whoopin'. But I don't aim tuh shoot ner be skylighted fer another feller's bullet."

Bruce nodded and began dressing himself. "I'll saddle up the ponies and load the bed, Jake. The night's spoiled for sleep, anyhow."

Jake grunted his approval and buckled on his belt. Winchester in the crook of his arm, he faded into the night. Bruce bent himself to the task of breaking up camp.

As he saddled the horses and loaded the bed, he kept listening for sounds. There was something sinister in the silence that should mean peace. The shadows seemed all the blacker for the moonlight, and were oddly shaped to a man whose nerves were rubbed raw.

The horses saddled, the bed loaded, Bruce waited. Minutes dragged past, interminable in their length. Bruce had no watch, and so there was no way of reckoning the time old Jake had been gone.

Bruce rolled a cigarette but dared not light it. Impatience, born of anxiety for the safety of his partner, held the boy in agonized torture — the misshapen shadows that might hide hidden foes, the trifling sounds that held new significance now that he waited for the dread signal. The night was holding its secret, and, high above, the white moon mocked the lonely man whose folly had brought him and his friend into danger.

He cursed that folly now. What a fool he'd been! What an utter idiot! Drinking too much, fighting when a wiser man would have avoided combat and yet retained the respect of men. A silly fool! He'd broken his father's heart. Now he was endangering the life of a man whose affection and loyalty he had taken too lightly. Good old Jake! Must have been an hour now since Jake went. An hour or . . . ?

Bruce tensed. His .45 swung up, pointing. For up on a ridge, five or six hundred yards distant, the silhouette of a horseman showed with cameo clarity against the silver sky. Too far for a six-shooter. A moment and the rider vanished as mysteriously as he had appeared.

Bruce hesitated no longer, orders or no orders. Something had gone wrong. Jake needed help. This damned inactivity! Old Jake might give him hell, but he was going, anyhow.

His horse leaped boulders and brush, slid down a cut bank, scrambled up another. Brush raked the rider's face, lacerating the skin. But Bruce hardly noticed. Each second strengthened the premonition that sent him, heedless of caution, along the trail.

His horse shied, snorted, and plunged off the trail. A leap and Bruce was on the ground, gun ready, running toward a huddled shape that lay in a patch of moonlight. A man. Dark clots smeared silvery hair. Good God! Jake! Dead!

A dry sob shook Bruce McTavish as he bent over the still form of his old partner. Old Jake's head was a sticky smear of blood that oozed across the old fellow's bloodless face.

For a few moments Bruce lost all self-control. Mad with grief and self-condemnation, he held that blood-smeared head in his lap and cursed horribly, tears coursing down his cheeks. Then he broke off in the midst of this weak display of emotion to shove his hand in under Jake's flannel shirt. Was that Jake's heart, beating so feebly? Or was it just the . . . ?

Bruce's profanity became a prayer when a faint moan came from Jake's lips. The boy's incoherent rage and grief now slipped into cool efficiency. He pillowed the beaten head and, taking Jake's hat, went to the little creek nearby for water.

It was on the return trip with the dripping hat that he all but stumbled over the body of a man who lay face down in the trail. In his anxiety to reach his wounded friend, Bruce hardly bestowed a glance upon that dead man. But as he knelt above old Jake, bathing with gentle touch the horrible cuts and abrasions on the old fellow's head and face, Bruce kept an uneasy eye on the brush.

Plainly someone had caught Jake Raine unaware, from behind perhaps, and with a club or gun barrel had beaten the old cowhand into insensibility. Bruce saw quickly enough that Jake was seriously, if not fatally, hurt. Whoever had struck him had wantonly, cold-bloodedly, kept on beating and kicking at the old cowpuncher's head and face.

Jake was breathing steadily now. His pulse, while weak, was regular. To move him would perhaps be fatal.

When he had done all he could for the wounded man, Bruce rode back for Jake's horse and the pack horse. Upon his return he unloaded the bed and spread it on the ground beside Jake, who had not moved. With swift but gentle hands, Bruce took off Jake's clothes and put him in bed. Then, regardless of personal danger, he kindled a fire and heated water.

Like most riders of the range, Bruce had a rudimentary knowledge of first aid. There was iodine in the pack, also a few rolls of gauze bandage. He bathed Jake's wounds in warm water, applied the iodine, and bandaged the lacerations. Jake's six-shooter had been lying beside him on the ground, as if it had fallen from Jake's hand when that blow felled him.

Now that he had done all in his power to make the wounded man easy, Bruce picked up the gun and shoved it in the waistband of his overalls. Then he made his way along the trail to where the dead man lay.

Bitter grief deadened his sense of caution. Nothing mattered to Bruce now except that he must care for Jake. The campfire blazed, sending flickering shadows beyond its rim of yellow light. He was a plain target as he now bent over the dead man.

"Stick 'em up, you damn' skunk!"

Bruce straightened, facing the shadows whence came that cold, menacing command. Scowling, realizing in that one split second of indecision when his gun hand hovered above his weapon, that he was at a horrible disadvantage, Bruce obeyed. Slowly his hands raised.

But he had his ground plans laid in those short seconds that it took to lift his hands above his head. He would wait until the man came from the brush. Had that man wished to kill him, he would have done so ere this. Whoever that man was — and the hidden voice was plainly not that of Chick Bullard — he had no intention of killing Bruce just yet.

"With your left hand drop your guns on the ground," commanded the cold voice. "Be damn' careful how you

54

do it, too. For two bits I'd kill you. But I'd rather see you hang like you deserve."

"And just who in hell," asked Bruce, his nerves now steady, "may *you* be, mister?"

"I may be 'most anybody. But I ain't. I'm Jeff Frazier, United States Deputy Marshal, and you're my meat. You'll swing for killing old Ed. Damn you, I said drop those guns!"

"So you did. Deputy Marshal, eh? So be it." Puzzled at the discovery of the hidden man's identity, Bruce dropped his gun and Jake's on the ground.

"Now, back away from 'em. Keep backin'. Hands in the air. *Whoa.* Now, Mister Killer, put both arms around that saplin'. *Pronto,* you damn' snake. Bear in mind that I'm just rearin' to gut shoot you. The man that lays there murdered was a friend of mine and my boss. Arms around that tree, you . . ."

"You can't call me that when you haven't got the drop," snapped Bruce, suddenly angry. "And you're taking a hell of a lot for granted. If you're a government law officer, act like one, not like a thick-headed cop. Call me that pet name again and I'll be damned if I don't make you play out your hand. You're jumping the wrong man. I never shot your boss. Look at those two guns and you'll see they ain't been fired. My pardner's dying over by the fire. I'm not in a sweet mood myself." He stood there, arms lowered, fists clenched. "If you're the man that hit old Jake," he finished grimly, "I'll kill you if they hang me the next minute."

"Shut up! Put those arms around that saplin'. You fool, I've got you covered."

Bruce put his arms around the tree. The man stepped from the brush nearby, a gun in one hand, shiny handcuffs in the other. The next minute Bruce's wrists were held manacled. For the time being his plans were postponed. This man stood for law — government law. If ever sheer nerve stamped the features of man, it was written in the pinched, almost wizened features of Jeff Frazier. Small of bone, short below the medium stature, he moved with the swift, smooth grace of a pugilist. He had sand-colored hair, well sprinkled with gray, hawk-like features marred by a white scar that twisted one side of his mouth in a perpetually leering grin. One eye socket, sunken, eyeless, marked the upper end of the scar that ran down across a broken cheekbone. The other eye, a thin black slit, squinted at the prisoner. Jeff Frazier held his Colt in a careless grip that told of years of gun wielding. Not a line of mercy in that scarred face! The lipless mouth was bitter in its grim distortion. Bruce wondered why this man hadn't shot him down.

"I'm rearin' to see you hung." It was as if the deputy marshal had read his prisoner's thoughts. Frazier picked up the two six-shooters. With dexterous hands he examined their loads.

"Told you they hadn't been fired," said Bruce.

"So you did," nodded Frazier. "And I don't see the idea of lying when the evidence lays contrary. You admit this is your gun?" It was Jake's old Colt's that he held now.

For a brief second Bruce hesitated. He knew that Jake's gun had not been fired. Only that evening they

56

had cleaned and oiled their weapons as they sat side by side on the bed. Yet Frazier gave him the lie. Jake's gun!

"That's my gun, mister," Bruce lied grimly.

"Ain't been fired, eh?" The law officer ejected an empty shell from a cylinder and showed it to Bruce. Then he carefully replaced it in the gun. Bruce, dumfounded, met Frazier's one-eyed gaze with a level scowl.

"Framing me, eh? Well, Mister Deputy Marshal, bad luck to you, if that's your breed."

"Of course, you'll lie," sneered Frazier, "but it won't save your neck. This empty shell is your death warrant. So Ed got your partner, eh? I heard just one shot."

"And one shot is all there was fired." A sudden thought struck Bruce. "Let me smell that gun barrel."

"If it'll help make you talk, I will."

"I'll talk enough, don't worry. Let's smell it."

Instead, Frazier himself sniffed at the gun barrel. His scarred mouth widened. Whether it was a grin of satisfaction or one of disappointment, Bruce could not say. Then Frazier shoved the gun under his prisoner's nose. The barrel of Jake's gun was free of any taint of burned powder.

"And if you'll take the trouble to look," said Bruce triumphantly, "you'll find the barrel of the gun clean. It was cleaned last evenin'. That empty shell was shot from another gun, then put in that gun."

"Yeah? Who put it there, then?"

"The man that killed your boss. Who else?"

"Hmm! Yeah? And just when, Mister Road Agent, and for how long, was this gun out of your possession?

Get me an answer to that? Looks to me like you'd cleaned the barrel and for some fool reason, probably nervous panic, neglected to eject the empty shell. Your story doesn't hold water. How about it?"

Bruce scowled thoughtfully. The gun that held the empty shell belonged to Jake. If Bruce admitted the true ownership of the weapon, suspicion would naturally be diverted to Jake. Bound to save Jake at any cost, Bruce now grinned brazenly into the scarred face of his captor.

"We'll let 'er go as she lays for now. I'm being framed, that's all. You called me a road agent just now. By what right do you hang that title on me, mister?"

"Say, you're a sweet one," sneered Frazier. "After admitting your identity to Chick Bullard, too. Think I'm plumb dumb? You make a bold bad play at that cow camp, now you begin crawling backwards. Are you drunk or plain loco? You bragged before half a dozen witnesses that you two were the men that held up that Idaho bank. Lucky Ed and I stopped there for supper. We'd just decided to turn back for the Wind River country. Your goose is cooked to a crisp, feller. When I see poor old Ed Hardin laying there, I feel like burning you at the stake. If I was you, I'd pray."

Pray! The word jogged Bruce into fresh mental activity. In his saddle pocket was his father's Bible and between its pages was the sealed letter meant for Jim Laughlin. What was written in that letter? Another complication further to entangle this snarl that fate had wound about him and old Jake? — Jake, his staunch friend, who lay unconscious behind the screen of brush. The firelight was dimming now, as the blaze died to red embers.

CHAPTER
SEVEN

"Jake Sits In"

Jeff Frazier re-kindled the fire. He bent over the unconscious Jake, studying the rugged old features under the merciless glare of a flashlight. Then he went over to Bruce and under the flashlight studied the prisoner's face. His grin became uglier than ever.

"You ain't the bank robbers," he snapped. "But you might as well be. You'll hang anyhow. Looks like your pardner was about to cash in his chips. Ed sure worked him over. I suppose you slipped up and got Ed when he was taking the old renegade. I don't savvy why you lied to Bullard about that bank job. But I'm betting all I got that both of you blackbirds are wanted somewhere on some charge. I'll take a look-see at your stuff when I get Ed taken care of."

Bruce watched the law officer examine the body of his friend. Frazier, his face set and tense in every line, went over the ground, foot by foot, with the aid of his flashlight, reading what sign the ground revealed — tracks, broken brush, the manner in which the dead man lay. Now and then he disappeared in the brush and was gone for many minutes. Finally he covered the body with a blanket from Jake's bed. Then he came over to Bruce.

"You laid for him there by the creek bank. Got him in the back. You must have laid in wait for quite a spell. Smoked four cigarettes there. The horse sign shows that the animal was tied there for quite a while. I can't quite figure how you let poor old Ed live long enough to beat up your pardner, though. You were two to one. Ed's gun is in the scabbard, too. But then you could have put it there."

"The barrel is bloody?" asked Bruce.

"No," admitted Frazier. "It's clean. If it got bloody from beating your friend over the head, it was later washed off. It took me quite a while to get here. I was across the ridge when I heard the shot. You had time to do a lot."

"Don't it strike you, Mister Detective, that if we'd killed this Ed party, we'd be clearing out instead of making camp here?"

"I suppose you thought he was alone," sneered Frazier, "when he rode into your camp."

"Our camp is half a mile from here," said Bruce. "I can take you there. If you read trail sign so well, you'll see that I'm not lying. Turn me loose from this tree and I'll lead you to where we were camped and sleeping when the shot that killed your Ed woke us up."

"Maybe, later. Just now, keep your shirt on. I'm going to look through your war sack."

"While you're at it," said Bruce carelessly, "look in my left-hand saddle pocket. There's a Bible there. You suggested praying. I'm taking you up on the proposition."

"Bible, eh?" Frazier's tone was frankly incredulous. "It won't help you none to play jokes."

"I'm not joking. Take a look. If it ain't there, shoot me."

Frazier's one eye searched the unshaven face of Bruce McTavish. Secretly, in his manhunter's brain, there were some odd kinks about this situation that were wholly confusing. Jeff Frazier had been a law officer for thirty years. In his mind were catalogued the pictures of a thousand and one men wanted by John Law. Types of men were also classed in his mind, criminal types of all sorts. Now, as he searched the frank, open face of his prisoner, he could not find a line of condemnation in the boy's face. No criminal tendency showed there, quite the contrary.

Now the young fellow was asking for a Bible. And while not of the criminal type, neither was his prisoner of a type that, when adversity comes, falls back on the God whom he neglects in times of prosperity. So it was that, when Jeff Frazier handed Bruce McTavish his Bible, then retired to a boulder and constructed a cigarette, there was no letter between the thumbed leaves of the book.

"It's in my pocket, feller," grinned Frazier, meeting Bruce's questioning look. So saying, he drew forth the unaddressed envelope and carefully, by aid of his flashlight, scrutinized it, turning it over in his hand without breaking the seal. Covertly that one eye watched the prisoner's face, now visible in the firelight. Bruce, holding the Bible in his manacled hands, smiled ruefully.

"You win that jackpot, Frazier. Why don't you read it?"

"In due time," nodded the law officer, "I will." And he fell to examining the envelope again, as if he expected to find on the blank white paper some hidden clue. Finally he replaced the letter, still unopened, in his vest pocket.

"I suppose that's some sort of subtle third degree, eh?" said Bruce.

"Perhaps. You don't talk like a common cowhand, mister. Who are you and where is your range, anyhow?" He laughed shortly. "Not that I expect an answer. I'm just talking to make conversation."

"I thought, by the way you played Sherlock Holmes, you'd have that part of the mystery solved," returned Bruce.

"Well, for that matter, McTavish," said Frazier, his crooked grin widening, "maybe I have."

Bruce was dumfounded for the moment that he should be called by name.

"Once more you win, Frazier. Know any more funny tricks?"

"A few. Your name is Bruce McTavish. Your father is Black Angus McTavish, up in Montana. You and Jake are headed for Jim Laughlin's place. This letter is to Laughlin? From Black Angus McTavish? It'll pay you, Bruce McTavish, to tell the truth."

There was something in Frazier's attitude that told Bruce he was deadly earnest. He sensed again that odd feeling that had so often obsessed him since leaving home: that he was playing a part in some hidden game he did not understand, that he was a more or less useless cog in a machine the working of which he did not know.

"The letter," he said steadily, looking straight into Frazier's one eye, "is to Jim Laughlin from my father. I don't . . ."

A harsh laugh from Frazier broke into Bruce's words. It was a nasty laugh that grated on the listener's senses. The laugh was followed by a sting of cursing, loud, insulting, fighting names that paled the color in Bruce McTavish's face. Then, with a light, swift spring, Frazier crossed to where Bruce was handcuffed to the tree and, with a pair of gloves held in his hand, slapped the prisoner across the face several times.

Bruce, struggling vainly to free himself, stared, white-lipped, into Frazier's face.

"Kill my friend, eh?" snarled Frazier, slapping him with the gloves. "Murder old Ed, eh? Damn your skunk heart!"

A coarse laugh came from beyond the firelight, a laugh that Bruce quickly identified. The next instant Chick Bullard, a drawn gun in his hand, stepped into the firelight, an ugly grin on his face.

"What's the rip, Frazier?"

"I got my men, that's all," panted Frazier, who was breathing heavily as if hot anger had shortened his wind. "They killed the boss."

"The hell!"

"From behind." Frazier's gloves had drawn blood from Bruce's tight lips.

"You dirty coward!" Bruce jerked at the handcuffs till his wrists bled. "You yellow cur! Take these cuffs off, then try to hit me, you ugly little weasel. Turn me loose, and I'll take on the whole lot of you. Give me my two mitts and you'll quit like sheep. Tough as hell, ain't you? You lousy little pack rat!"

Bruce missed by inches a kick that would have ruined Jeff Frazier's face. The deputy marshal laughed and slapped Bruce once more.

"Get a stretcher rigged up, Bullard," ordered Frazier, somewhat curtly, "to carry Ed on. I'm takin' his body to town. Another stretcher for the old gent with the mashed head. I'll leave the black-muzzled young badman with you. You'll be responsible for his safety, savvy? Feed him, treat him decent, ride close herd on him. If he makes his getaway, I'll hold you responsible. Also, Bullard, no necktie party or pot shooting him for making a try to escape. You've used that once. It won't work a second time.

"Now rustle those stretchers. I'll only need them till I get to the Laughlin place and get a wagon there. Pick four gentle mules. Put on pack saddles and I'll rig jockey-sticks to the hackamores and pack saddles so they won't jamb the two men on the stretchers."

"If you hurt old Jake," Bruce said hotly, "I'll live to kill you, Frazier."

Bullard laughed and, taking all but one man, rode off.

"Mebby. Most mebby you won't, though. They hang 'em fast in my country. Don't fret about your Jake. I've

packed more than a few wounded boys on blanket-
rigged stretchers. What jolts he gets won't hurt him. It
won't surprise me if he comes out of it and can get a
horse by the time we're ready to . . . I told you."

He pointed to the bed where old Jake lay. The
grizzled veteran of cowland was slowly sitting up.

For a long moment he looked squarely at Bruce.
Deliberately old Jake's left eye closed, then opened.
Ludicrous, ghastly, that wink! Bruce's lips, opening to
speak, shut tightly. Jake was talking, his voice a little
thick as if he had drunk too much.

"The herd was spooky. I done told that Gila Bend
Kid tuh be keerful about strikin' a light . . . But he
done 'er. Had tuh smoke his cigareet . . . I feels like the
whole damn' beef herd had run over an' tromped me.
Will some jasper stake me to a smoke?"

"Told you he'd come out of it." Jeff Frazier stepped
to the bed and, stooping, shoved his cigarette in Jake's
mouth.

"I'm obliged, Kid. Is it the same one yuh lit on
herd?" Jake grinned through his bandages.

"He's a little nutty," said Frazier, "but he'll be all
right after a while. He's tough. Thinks he's been in a
stampede. Thinks I'm the Gila Bend Kid."

The deputy marshal straightened up. As he did so, a
gun was jammed against his stomach. It was his own
gun, now held by the grinning, blood-smeared Jake
Raine.

"Untie that maverick yuh got fastened to the tree,
Kid!" snapped Jake. "I ain't in no fit humor tuh be
monkeyed with. *Pronto*, or I'll kill yuh! And you over

yonder, you cowboy in the big hat, reach fer heaven er I'll send yuh to hell on a one-way ticket. 'At's it. Move quick, now!"

Frazier moved. His scarred face was an enigmatic mask as he unlocked the handcuffs. Bruce's first act was to pick up his own gun and Jake's from where they lay near the blanket-covered dead marshal.

"Tie him to the tree like he had you tied," chuckled Jake. "Them's shore purty cuffs. Tie up the Gila Bend Kid an' make him swaller the key. Then git yore pony an' drag it . . . I bet the whole damn' herd tromped on my face as they went over. Twelve hundred head uh dogie steers. Hurry up there, black whiskers." Jake laughed crazily.

Bruce, none too gentle in his handling of the deputy marshal, handcuffed that gentleman to the tree.

"Better give me the key instead uh makin' the Kid swaller it," suggested Jake. "Fetch it here, an' gimme a light for this smoke."

Bruce, puzzled and worried by the odd mixture of clarity and maudlin talk of his partner, stepped to the bed.

"Hold me a light fer this cigarette, I tell yuh."

Bruce obeyed. As he held the match, Jake's lips moved in a faint but clear-worded whisper.

"Drag it, Bruce. Fer Laughlin's. I ain't fit tuh go along. Do as I say. Keep yore face shet. When yuh meet Laughlin, yuh'll understand."

"But I won't leave you here with . . ."

"Do like I say, yuh idiot. Run fer it. You can't do no good here. I ain't fit tuh ride. I'm safe with . . . with the

Gila Bend Kid." And Jake winked again. "Drag it, Bruce."

"Don't forget the Bible," sneered Jeff Frazier, as Bruce passed him on his way to his horse.

Bruce picked up the Bible. Beside it, on the ground, lay the unopened letter to Jim Laughlin. It must have fallen from Frazier's vest pocket.

From up the cañon came the clatter of horses' shod hoofs. Bruce swung up into the saddle and, whirling his horse, was gone. He got one last, swift picture of Jake, grinning crazily, covering Frazier and the Bullard man with Frazier's gun.

CHAPTER
EIGHT

"Deeper into Mystery"

As he rode into the graying dawn, Bruce tried to make something of the odd puzzle. Jake was playing some sort of crafty game, that was plain. He had called Jeff Frazier the Gila Bend Kid. Crazy, yet not so crazy, either. The name meant something. Some link to Jake's past? Perhaps. There had been an odd sort of look on Jeff Frazier's face. Did Jake have something on Frazier? Had Frazier let Jake steal his gun and alter the situation? And why had Frazier slapped him with his gloves — when Bullard showed up on the scene? More play-acting?

Bruce swung off the trail and climbed a steep slope. Choosing a roundabout course, he headed for the broken peaks where he judged Jim Laughlin's place to be. He felt like a yellow dog for leaving Jake, yet something in the old 'puncher's attitude, something in Jess Frazier's odd behavior, told him that he was not wanted there. Jake had said that Jim Laughlin would explain things.

So be it. He'd not pull up until he found Laughlin and gotten a solution to this mystery. He stowed the letter in his chaps.

In doing so, his hand touched Jake's gun, and he pulled it out of his chaps pocket to examine the weapon again. For the first time, he saw a tightly-rolled cylinder of white paper peeping from the gun barrel. Puzzled, he drew it forth and unrolled it. In the uncertain light, he scanned the penciled words.

Save this gun as it is and give it to Laughlin unfired.
Do as Jake says. Don't act the fool.

There was no signature, but Bruce knew that none other than Jeff Frazier had penciled those words. So the whole thing had been framed for his getaway. Jake must have regained consciousness before Bullard came. He and Frazier must have planned the thing somehow. Yet, there had been little time. And why had they not let him in on it?

"Hell," Bruce gave it up in disgust, "I quit. It beats me. Step along, pony. We're not out of the woods yet."

Avoiding open spaces, keeping to the brush and away from beaten trails, Bruce followed a circuitous course. Hours passed. The sun mounted higher in a cloudless sky. Noon found him at a little creek that watered innumerable cattle that wore Jim Laughlin's J Bar L brand.

"Must be getting close to the home ranch," mused Bruce, as he watered his horse and removed the saddle to let the animal's back cool. He squatted on his heels and watched his horse roll luxuriously.

Weary, drowsy, he fought off the desire to take a nap. He rolled a cigarette and leaned back against the broad trunk of a hackberry tree. He felt safe from pursuit now. His horse began grazing hungrily. Bruce relaxed his position and stretched out on the ground. A little nap while his horse grazed? Half an hour? His eyes closed wearily.

He woke with a start. Even as his eyes came open, he was on his feet, his gun in his hand. From somewhere behind him came rippling laughter. Whirling, he faced a young person who, at first glance, he took to be a boy, with wide-brimmed hat, flannel shirt, chaps, boots. And then, with a start of embarrassment, he saw that it was a girl. She sat easily in her saddle. Her horse, a chestnut sorrel, was a keen-limbed, slim animal whose fine breeding showed in every line of its splendid body.

"I'd have ridden right past without seeing you," she told him with frankly smiling eyes, "only that you were snoring like a buzz saw. You ought to sleep without snoring. Do you always pull a gun on a lady?"

"Not as a rule," admitted Bruce, reddening as he sheathed his gun. "You should have given me some warning. Lucky you weren't shot."

"It's your habit, I reckon," she mocked him, her voice the lazy, slurring voice of the Southwesterner, "to shoot ladies who overlook the formality of properly announcing themselves. I might add that in my country men remove their hats in the presence of a lady."

"My mistake." Bruce swung off his hat and bowed. "I seem full of 'em today." He was eyeing her appraisingly, now that the first shock of embarrassment was passing.

"Maybe I ought to be wearing spats and a monocle and a morning coat."

"I wouldn't go quite that far," said the girl, looking him over with a frankness that was almost rude, "but I'll tell the world a shave wouldn't hurt you much. And I bet a dollar Mex' that your neck's dirty."

Bruce dug down in his pocket and found a dollar that he tossed. She caught it in a small gloved hand.

"I owe you four bits," she told him. "This cart wheel is worth two 'dobe dollars. If it's any of my business, cowboy, how bad do they want you and how far behind is the sheriff?"

"Hate to be rude, lady," replied Bruce, his eyes hardening a little, "but I'm afraid that concerns just me."

"Perhaps. I wasn't aiming to be nosy. A man's affairs are his own personal property . . . that is, usually. But when you run over into another man's back yard, looking over your shoulder, you're more or less sharing your misfortune with the fellow that owns the back yard, no?"

"This is the J Bar L range, isn't it?"

"It sure is," admitted the girl easily, "and I'm the main rod of the J Bar L. Laugh that off."

"You mean you . . . ?"

"I'm Jim Laughlin's kid. Jim being away just now, I'm the boss. I bet another dollar you were heading for the ranch."

"I owe you another buck," said Bruce. "I wish you'd quit it. I'm broke! You say Jim Laughlin is away?"

"Left the ranch last night. Rode this way to head off a couple of renegades who were about due. We've got

72

guests at the ranch. Bunch of dudes. Jim was afraid there'd be some killing and didn't want any Eastern friends to get a bad impression. Gosh knows why Jim has to hide every renegade that heads south, but he does. We're getting a hard name on account of it."

"Well, Miss Laughlin," said Bruce stiffly, "you needn't feel that I'll cause you any annoyance by showing up. I wouldn't go within cannon range of the place." Turning his back on her, he picked up his saddle and blanket and walked toward his horse.

He saddled in scowling silence. The girl, smiling faintly, watched him. Not until he jerked the latigo tight and unhooked the stirrup from the saddle horn did she break the silence. Her throaty laugh made Bruce's ears redden. Without glancing at her, he swung into the saddle.

"Jim said that you'd probably be black-headed and red-tempered," she said. "A stiff-necked Scotchman. I was just hoorawing you, Bruce McTavish. Now ride over here and shake and quit sulking. Cuss some, if it will help. I'm used to cussing."

"First the marshal calls me by name," groaned Bruce. "Now you hang a label on me. And I thought I was playing the game undercover. I've been treated like a damn' school kid ever since I left the ranch. Ignored, patronized, tolerated. I'm sick of it. Sick of the whole works, damn it!"

"Atta boy!" the girl encouraged him. "Cuss. Get it off your chest. Then roll a smoke and you'll feel better. When did you eat last?"

"What's that got to do with it?" Bruce found his temper cooling in spite of himself. He tried not to return her grin.

"Nothing much, only that most men folks ain't fit to live with if they miss their coffee. If you'll give me your word not to fight your head like a bronc', I'll pilot you to a place where we can eat this lunch I brought. You can cook the coffee. By the way, where's your pardner?"

"The last I saw of Jake," said Bruce, "he was sitting up in bed with his head tied up, holding a gun on a man while I ran off like a coyote."

"He told you to run, didn't he?"

"How'd you guess that?"

"Well, you don't look like a foot racer, I suppose. Now let's go eat and you spill me the news while we're resting. Gosh, you look tough. I think I'll have to take you to the ranch and give the effete East a thrill. There's a cute blonde that'll have a fit over you. Vamp the shirt off your back. She took away every man I ever hooked at school. Coming?"

She whirled her horse, and, as she led the way along a twisting trail, she dodged catclaw limbs with the ease of a veteran brush hand. Bruce, following, was torn between annoyance and admiration.

Truly, this daughter of Jim Laughlin was easy to look at — reddish-brown hair, gray-eyed, with a mocking smile on her lips. A square, little jaw denoted strength of character, and there was a reckless tilt to the close-cropped, curly head that seemed to belong under a creamy white Stetson. She hummed softly as she rode, as if life were one glorious adventure and she loved each moment of it. It was like her to call her father, "Jim."

"I gave Lige the slip back yonder about ten miles," she called over her shoulder. "We jumped a maverick, and I let him outrun me. Then I back tracked on him. He'll be pawing the dirt when he comes up. Lige is my chaperon. His bark is worse than his bite, so don't mind him. I've tagged at Lige's heels since I was knee-high to a rattlesnake . . . Has your mother gray eyes like yours? And does she worry about you and make you put on woolen undies?"

"My mother's dead," said Bruce.

She reined up, half turning her horse. The smile was gone from her lips, and her eyes were no longer mocking.

"I . . . I beg your pardon. I didn't know. I'm always saying the wrong thing. It was rotten of me, and I'm truly sorry."

"You needn't be, Miss Laughlin. You didn't know. Forget it." He grinned reassuringly. He was wondering if she ever cried like other girls.

"I can't even remember my mother," she told him, still grave, "but they say I look like her a lot. I take after Jimmer in temperament. I'm a little roughneck for all the polishing off, the most of it at finishing school. I suppose they shipped you to college? How long before they canned you?"

"I didn't last long."

"Harvard?"

"Stanford."

"No?"

"Sure. Why not?"

"I didn't mean it that way. I was just getting a contact . . . Just a second now till I work the old brain. McTavish. Bruce McTavish. Stanford. I get you now. Stew Bum McTavish. Sweet name. You captained the freshman team. Made quarterback on the varsity next year. Then, when your school needed you most, you broke training, went on a bust, and pulled some poor prof's nose or something. They should have lynched you. Oh, yeah. I suppose you were all tight the night of the prom when you cut a dance with a hero-worshipping little chump with red hair and a green dress? I didn't recognize the great, notorious Stew Bum McTavish in his whiskers and homespun. Got any defense?"

"Nary line of defense. Did I do that?"

"Among your other cute tricks, you sure did. And I'll even that score, if I break both legs trying. Just for that little oversight on your part, I'm dragging you into the ranch as you are. Whiskers, sweat, dirty ears, a true specimen of the great unwashed."

"No! Listen . . ."

"I recall your exact words that night of the prom. You were queening some blonde doll from San Francisco. She looked like a chorine. You asked Cub Milburne who this jane was on your ticket. Cub pointed me out.

"'That?' says the great Stew McTavish. 'That washout? Tell her something, Cub. Tell her I got a wooden leg. Something. Anything. I'm smoking this one in company with the queen of paradise.'"

76

"Cub lied like a gentleman till I cornered him and got your verdict *verbatim*. Only that I'd been polished off and made over into a lady, I'd have spoken to you in the language of the great open spaces. Mad? I was madder yet when you got canned. I had a week's allowance bet on Stanford and couldn't hedge. Oh, what a lot you have coming!"

She had been talking over her shoulder, letting her horse pick its own trail. Now they came to a little clearing where a spring bubbled out from under some granite boulders. Leaning against a boulder was a white-mustached, snowy-haired, old cowpuncher whose sky-blue eyes looked out from under heavy white brows.

"The next time, Jerry Laughlin," he said lazily, "that you come a Injun trick on me, I'll wear out a good ketch rope on yuh. Howdy, McTavish. Where's Jake?"

"This is Lige Taylor," explained the girl. "They got in some kind of tight, Lige. Bruce had to dig out."

"Chick Bullard's spread?" questioned Lige with what seemed mild unconcern.

"Partly. There was a U. S. marshal and his deputy mixed into it."

"What?" Lige was fully awake now. "Say that over."

"Marshal named Ed Hardin. His deputy was Jeff Frazier. Somebody shot Hardin in the back."

"And Jeff Frazier?" It was the girl who spoke. Her face was like chalk and her voice a rasping whisper. "Was he hurt?"

"No. But what . . . ?"

"Easy, Jerry, easy, little 'un," said Lige, on his feet and beside the girl's horse. "Git off an' set a while now, an' young McTavish'll spill the news. Bein's yuh know this much, yuh'd as well hear it all. Give us the story, son. Jerry's shakin' like a leaf. Who killed pore ol' Ed Hardin?"

"I don't know," said Bruce.

The girl, now on the ground, came to him and looked up into his face, her eyes searching his. "You are sure that . . . that Jeff Frazier is not hurt?" she asked. "Tell the truth, please."

"Not a scratch on him."

"Thank God for that!"

Bruce caught himself wondering if this handsome girl could be in love with the one-eyed, disfigured Jeff Frazier. He was older than she, and his face was almost repulsive. Yet, there was a certain fascination about the man. He had magnetism and no doubt a fascinating background as a peace officer.

CHAPTER
NINE

"Lige Makes a Bet"

Simply, in a straightforward manner, Bruce told of his
finding Jake unconscious near the dead body of Ed
Hardin, how Frazier had captured him, and how Jake
had effected his escape. His audience of two listened
with rapt attention.

"There's the whole yarn," he finished. "Make what
you can out of it. Jake says nothing. Frazier's a clam. I
feel like a fool."

"Naturally." Jerry Laughlin's voice was like a slap in
the face. "Running away like that and leaving old Jake
at the mercy of Frazier and Chick Bullard. After the
way Jeff Frazier treated you, too. What will he be doing
to Jake Raine?"

"Easy, Jerry, easy," cautioned Lige, his voice soft and
once more lazy. "Let 'im alone. He's taken his orders."

"Sure he did, when the orders said . . . 'Beat it!'"

Bruce took the insult smiling. Was she getting even
for that silly affair at college? Or did she really think
him a coward? But a short while ago she had told him
he did not look like the running kind. Now she was
deliberately calling him a coward. Bruce's quick temper
surged redly into his face.

From his pocket he took the unaddressed letter from Angus McTavish to Jim Laughlin and tossed it in the fire where Lige was cooking lunch.

"That's that," he smiled thinly, and turned to his horse. "I'm all caught up on this mystery business. I'll get off your range as quick as a leg-weary horse can pack me. I'd advise you, Miss Laughlin, to go back to that finishing school and tell them they left off too quick with their polishing. *Adiós!*"

And without touching the stirrups, Bruce was in the saddle and his horse was in motion.

"Hi, young feller!" called Lige. "Hold on. You dunno what yo're runnin' into."

"Nor I don't give a damn," called Bruce, twisting from sight in the brush as his horse carried him back along the trail.

"Think that over."

Lige turned to the girl, who stood sullenly by the fire, her eyes gazing at the burning letter.

"Ain't you got no sense a-tall?" snapped the old cow-puncher.

"Plenty." She lifted her head and smiled mockingly at him. "Bruce McTavish is a spoiled colt, Lige. He needs busting. Let 'im go. I suppose that's the letter to Jimmer. Well, I'm glad he has enough grit not to be using his father's good name to save his own neck. I'm all fed up on these funny friends of Jim's. Why should we keep open house for every bum between the Pecos and Canada? What have they got on Jimmer, anyhow? And listen, Lige, I want the truth on this. Who killed Ed Hardin? Was it Bullard or Jimmer? Both of 'em had reason enough. Especially Jim. I've heard Jim say before witnesses that Hardin's never quit watching him since they let Jim out of the pen thirty years ago. Hardin was a manhunter, pure and simple. So is Jeff Frazier. Lige, why in the devil can't you say something?" She stamped a booted foot.

"It's bin about ten years, Jerry," said Lige, "since I turned yuh across my knee an' spanked yuh. But I've a mind tuh do it now. You shore played hell, sending young McTavish away. He was tuh go to the ranch."

"But that telegram from Angus McTavish said . . .'"

"Never mind the telegram. Only that the telegraph operator has sheep brains, you'd never uh seen that wire. Now, looky here. You've raised enough plain an' fancy hell fer one day. Coaxin' me tuh let yuh come along. Runnin' off from me. Then bawlin' up the game by sendin' that young idiot to git shot down like a beef. Yeah, that's what I said. Shot. Hear me? Now yuh fork that single-footin' pacer an' hit fer home. Don't pull up till yuh git there, neither. Then stay put amongst yore danged shorthorn friends that's lollygaggin' aroun' the ranch. Young McTavish, drunk er sober, is worth the whole pack of 'em. He's a man, anyhow. That's more'n you kin say uh that yaller-headed dude that butters his hair an' wears knee pants . . . yore *fee-awn-say* pilgrim with his fancy duds. He calls us servants, the young, spineless . . ."

"You can leave Bert out of this. Because he never killed anybody or got drunk and shot up a saloon, you think he's yellow. Well, let me tell you something. He'll lick Bruce McTavish any time and any place. He was heavyweight champ at Yale and captain of his polo team. He doesn't chew tobacco or let his shirt hang out, but he's as much of a man as you or Stew Bum McTavish. Home? You bet I'm going home. I was a darn fool to come out. I only came out to head off that drunken bully. Bad enough to live down the rep of a father who did time in the pen. Now he drags in all the renegades in the country when I'm entertaining a party of decent people."

"Decent?" Lige snorted disgustedly. "Them gals goes swimmin' with them things you call men and wearin' a swimmin' suit that ain't big enough tuh flag a antelope. Gals smokin' cigareets an' drinkin' licker. The men all wearin' white panties an' butter on their hair. Decent? Hell! A sheepherder grades high alongside 'em. That yaller-headed dude whup Bruce McTavish? What'll yuh bet?"

"My horse against yours."

"I calls the bet. Send tuh town fer a case ah arnica an' bandages. That dude'll be needin' 'em. Now you high tail it fer the ranch. I'm gonna fetch McTavish back."

"Be sure you do, Lige dear," she said sweetly. "I want Bert and the gang to see what a real badman looks like. He's a four-flusher, and I'll prove it. *Adiós*, Lige. See you in a better humor. Take good care of papa's boy that was naughty and ran away from home."

Lige swore at length as he took the hobbles off his horse and, tightening the cinch, set out after Bruce.

"Wimmen," he concluded his lengthy burst of profanity, "beat all hell. That kid'd put gray hairs on a

82

billiard ball. The older she gits the harder she is tuh figger. Now why does she hate that young McTavish?"

Lige, could he have seen the girl just then, would have been more puzzled than ever. For as she rode along the trail, she was sobbing bitterly. Nor was she heading for home. Instead, she swung off to the side and climbed a steep trail that would almost parallel the course taken by Bruce McTavish.

CHAPTER
TEN

"The Knockout"

Bruce, the white heat of his anger cooling, kept doggedly on his back trail. He was glad he had burned the letter. He was going to play his own game after his own dictates. He'd rescue Jake Raine if he had to shed blood doing it. From now on, he'd stand on his two feet and fight. He was wanted for killing that sheepman. Now another murder charge hung over him. He'd rescue Jake, then make Jake go back home. And he, Bruce, would take life as it came to him — Mexico, South America . . .

"Darn that girl," he muttered. "Only for her nasty temper, she'd be a knockout. Wonder if she's riding me because of that fool dance." And in spite of himself, he grinned.

He was in a better humor now. He felt free for the first time in weeks, and the feeling of independence made him a new man.

From ahead came the clatter of shod hoofs and the muffled, indistinct sounds of men talking. Bruce swung his tired horse off the trail and waited with drawn gun.

Two men rode down the trail, side by side. One of the men was Jeff Frazier, the other Jake Raine. Frazier led a pack mule that carried a tarp-covered burden that Bruce knew must be the body of Ed Hardin. Jake and the deputy were conversing earnestly. Certainly Jake did not seem to be a prisoner.

"Wish you'd gotten a peep at the man who hit you, Jake," Frazier was saying. "It's a cinch that's our man. Ed had plenty enemies. You didn't kill him. Neither did McTavish. It simmers down to Bullard or Jim Laughlin. Bullard claims an alibi without being asked to do so. That sounds fishy. Maybe a guilty conscience. ¿Quien sabe? But somehow I got a hunch that it wasn't Bullard. Laughlin hated Ed like poison."

"Who didn't?" grunted old Jake. "He was a killer, fer all his badge. He was the only man in this country I wasn't trustin' when I come back. It was like him tuh serve that old warrant, jest tuh prove he had a good memory."

"You're admitting a lot for a prisoner," grinned Frazier. "Even if young McTavish had sense enough to throw away that gun, I can swear I found by examination that one shell had been fired."

"And don't fergit, Frazier," said Jake, "that Bruce'll swear the barrel uh that gun was clean. Whoever shoved that shell in 'er should uh remembered that a fired shell leaves a fouled barrel. You kep' your word about turnin' the kid loose. I'll go to jail peaceful. But it takes more'n that empty shell tuh hang me fer killin' Ed Hardin."

They were almost abreast of Bruce's hiding place now. He had heard enough to guide his actions. His gun was covering Jeff Frazier as he called out: "Pull up,

Frazier, and keep your mitts high and in sight. I'd kill you for a plugged nickel. *High*, I said!"

"Keep yore shirt on, kid," called Jake. "Yuh don't understand what the . . ."

"Never mind what I don't understand," snapped Bruce. "Ride out of line, Jake. Frazier's so skinny the bullet may go plumb through and nick you. I'm taking this jackpot, and I'm not calling for advice. Take his guns, Jake, and make it fast. The day's getting short."

"Quit actin' the fool, Bruce, an' . . ."

"Clean the guns off that one-eyed snake, I tell you. Then I'm going to thrash him within an inch of his life. I'll teach him to slap a man that's handcuffed. I'll make him eat all those sweet names he called me. Skin his artillery off, Jake."

Jake groaned audibly and obeyed. Frazier, his twisted mouth in a grin, fixed his one eye on Bruce with a venomous glare.

"Got anything to say, Frazier, before I wipe up the dust in the trail with your carcass?"

"Only that you're about the biggest fool I ever met," snapped Frazier. "Hold my hat, Jake, while I drag some conceit out of Black Angus's black cub." And with a quick leap, Jeff Frazier was on the ground, his freckled fists clenched, his wiry body moving as if on springs.

"Bruce, fer gosh sake, quit . . . ," Jake said. "Sweet onions!"

For Bruce was also on the ground, and the two men were at it. Youth and weight favored Bruce. But experience in rough-and-tumble fighting, coupled with the swift, punishing power of a tiger, evened the odds.

86

The battle was swift, terrific, merciless. Bruce fought fair, probably because he had been tutored in ring fighting rather than this sort of combat. But Jeff Frazier fought dirty and taunted Bruce for not doing likewise. The deputy bit, kicked, butted, and hit low.

Bruce, his face ashen with agony from a blow in the groin, swung at Frazier's leering face. The blow sent the peace officer staggering back. Another short-arm swing and Frazier went down. But Bruce did not kick the fallen man as he had been kicked a few moments before when he had tripped and gone down. Instead, he stood back, his bruised lips snarling taunts.

"Get up, you dirty-fighting skunk, and get the rest of what you got coming! Stand up and fight, you quitter!"

Frazier was on his hands and knees. Blood was spilling from a smashed nose. He seemed exhausted. But the next second he was catapulting through the air, arms flailing, head lowered. That head hit Bruce under the belt. A moan slipped from Bruce's lips, and he sank to his knees. Frazier's boot smashed into his face as he dropped. Then the deputy, snarling like a beast, was on him, gouging at Bruce's eyes.

Red pain shot through the younger man's eyeballs as those terrible, blood-smeared thumbs gouged deeper.

"One-eyed . . . snake, eh?" sobbed Frazier. "You're . . . damn' well . . . right. How's this, eh?"

Red, blinding pain! Bruce, dizzy with nausea, felt like screaming. Then his arm swung up and over Frazier's neck, jerked, twisted, pulled that ugly face into his own. His hand found that scarred face and ripped at it. With a tremendous effort, he rolled on top of the deputy, wrenched free, and staggered to his feet.

He stood there, his vision now a reddish blur. Blindly he swung with all his strength at that moving red shadow that must be Frazier. The blow spatted on flesh. Bruce's hand and arm went suddenly numb with terrifying pain.

His hand was broken!

But there in the dust, a red, huddled heap, lay Jeff Frazier. The blind blow had caught him on the point of the jaw, lifted him from his feet, dropped him senseless and beaten, unconscious.

Jake bent over the fallen man. "He ain't dead, though the devil only knows why. You sure played hell again, kid. Come on. Somebody's comin'."

Bruce, his breath coming in sobbing gasps, staggered blindly forward. Frazier had, in those swift minutes, given him a terrific punishing. Half blind, sick from the foul blows, he groped for his horse.

Jake, cursing him for an idiot, led him to the saddle. "Come on, kid, come on. Oh, you fool! You damned fool!"

"Quit it," grunted Bruce, mounting. "Lead my horse. Can't see a thing! Wait. Where's my hat?"

"Here's Frazier's hat. Never mind yours. Hurry. Stay on that horse. He leads like a rock. Somebody's . . . sweet snakes!"

A bullet had ripped through the air close to them. Another shot. The two fugitives spurted for shelter, Jake leading Bruce's horse. Above the sound of firing bawled Chick Bullard's loud voice.

"They've found Frazier," growled Jake. "Oh, you fool!"

"Save the bawling out, Jake." Bruce's vision was clearing a little. Reaching forward, he jerked his bridle reins from Jake's hand. "I'm no baby. Either let up on me or cut your sting. I'm sick of it."

He whirled his horse and, jerking his gun, faced about. Still sick, his vision a swimming blur of red shadows and light, he tore back along the trail, his horse on the run.

Brush ripped his face. He cursed a little. Around a blind angle in the trail there was a terrific thud. He and his galloping horse had collided with another horse and rider. There was a moment of mad, desperate scramble, and then the horses kicked free and were again on their feet. In the swirling dust lay Chick Bullard, and Bruce was on top of him. The thud of a six-shooter barrel and Bullard lay quiet.

A cowpuncher came up, slid his horse to a running halt, and whirled the animal as Bruce's bullet ripped a hole in his hat. Bruce's laugh followed the fleeing Bullard man, who spurred away in mad haste.

"Come on, you skunks!" bawled Bruce. "Come and get it!" He emptied his gun at the brush ahead. The clatter of rocks and breaking brush told the flight of Bullard's henchmen. Then Jake, white-lipped, furious, rode up, a smoking gun in his hand. Bruce, then, had not been alone in victory.

"A shore purty mess uh sour beans, I call it," he growled. "Oh, you bonehead!" Then his seamed old face crinkled into a broad grin. "Yuh young warthog.

Black Angus's spittin' image. If only Jim Laughlin had bin here tuh see this show. Is Bullard dead?"

"Just out for a long count, I reckon. I couldn't see very well, and I may have hit him a little high. He's got a skull like a mountain sheep, so I'm afraid he'll live."

"And will yuh tell a man jest what in hell's gone wrong with that haired-over hunk uh neck that yuh call yore head? I told yuh tuh flag it fer Laughlin's place."

"So you did. Man, that Jeff Frazier's a fightin' fool, ain't he? He sure scratched my eyes plenty. I got a hunch Bullard's men will try to make a comeback, Jake. Pick us a good place for a stand-off."

"Come along, then," growled Jake. "We're into 'er now. Hired fer a tough hand an' plays my string out." He looked up at the taller Bruce McTavish from under a rakish hat brim, spat tobacco juice at a rock, and grinned. "I can't swear on no stack uh Bibles that I'm sorry, neither. Done my best tuh foller out Angus's orders. No man kin do more. Luck's turned up the joker, an' the devil declares deuces wild. Ante, gents, ante! She's gonna be the biggest jackpot New Mexico ever seen, barrin' the Lincoln County war. I was askin' yuh what turned yuh back from Laughlin's?"

"How about that nest of boulders up yonder?" grinned Bruce.

"Ain't yuh the close-mouthed thing. All right, yearlin', keep yore secret. I'll keep mine. Directly yuh begin tuh act human, I'll let yuh in on somethin'."

They had ridden up on a knoll and, dismounting, took shelter among a cluster of granite boulders. Bruce's eyes were swelling badly and were becoming green. His lips were split and swollen. His broken left hand must have caused excruciating pain. But he did not complain. He grinned widely as a volley of shots spatted against the rocks.

"The game's open, Jake."

"An' she'll be a shore big jackpot afore long. Us outnumbered about five to one. No water, no grub, an' our horses laig weary. You, with yore mule-headedness, blowed up the works, jest when things is goin' sweet. Frazier'll be after yore hide now, I reckon. He's ornery. Bin ornery since he was a kid down in the Gila Bend country. Run a beef herd over me onct, because he wanted a cigareet an' was too bullheaded tuh ride into a coulée tuh strike a match. Then like tuh killed hisse'f tryin' tuh drag me out when my hoss went down in a 'dog hole. That's where he got that scar on his face. A long-horned Chihuahua steer jest nacherally ripped his face open, but he brung me out. Saved my life, I reckon. I bet he never was licked in his life till today. He may wake up an' go gunnin' fer yuh. On the other hand, he may be the best friend yuh ever had. Depends on how he takes a lickin'. Kid, yuh shore blew up the works, no foolin'."

"How come?"

Jake grinned tauntingly. "Tell me, fust, how come yuh didn't go to Laughlin's place?"

But Bruce laughed shortly and took a snap shot at some moving brush. A yelp of pain came from the brush.

"Score one, Jake. We should keep tally."

CHAPTER
ELEVEN

"Jerry Stands Siege"

From a high pinnacle, Jerry Laughlin watched with field glasses. She had, from that point, witnessed the battle between Bruce and Jeff Frazier. The powerful glasses had focused on the grisly fight so that she saw each ugly detail of the combat. She had seen Bruce and Jake ride away. She had watched Bruce turn back and ride down Chick Bullard. Now, as she watched the two men crouched behind the boulders, a dizziness swept over her. This was war — a man's war, unfit for the eyes of a woman.

Bullard had come to his senses and slipped out of sight in the brush. But she could hear his harsh voice, shouting orders. Other men were coming down the cañon from the Bullard camp, attracted, no doubt, by the sound of rifle fire.

Jeff Frazier was getting slowly to his feet now. Two Bullard men were helping him.

A man was slipping through the brush toward the boulders where Jake and Bruce squatted. She knew that man. It was old Lige.

Jake had detected Lige's approach now. He must have called a challenge, for Lige halted, stood erect for a moment, and waved his hat. Then, as bullets from the Bullard guns rattled about him, Lige dropped on all fours and kept on. A few moments and he had joined Bruce and Jake. The girl saw the two old fellows shake hands. Then Lige took a position among the rocks, Winchester peeping out to seek a target.

Now her glasses swept the hillsides, probed the depths of the cañons. Fear and doubt stamped her flushed face. With a dry little sob, she lowered the glasses.

"Jim!" she sobbed aloud. "Daddy Jim! Please, God, where is he?" A stray shot ricocheted past her like the drone of a hornet. She dodged, her lips quivering.

She wanted to make a dash for those boulders below where Lige was, but she knew the folly of such an attempt. In her masculine garb she would be taken for a man and shot down by one faction or another. Her every path of escape was blocked by men with death-spitting guns. Panic held her for some minutes, and she crouched in the brush and rocks, shaking as if stricken by a chill.

Huddled there, frightened, she sobbed out incoherent little prayers. Friends of the flippant, self-sure Jerry Laughlin would scarcely have recognized this badly frightened and wholly chastened girl who wished with all her heart that she was safe at home.

She thought of the ranch. The cool, white adobe walls, the flowers, the feathery pepper trees, the gay laughter of her Eastern guests who lounged about on the verandah or perhaps danced or played bridge while Chin Lee served cool drinks and sandwiches. A wave of resentment swept over her. Those people — what did they know of bloodshed, of feuds, of raw life? Wealthy idlers, a trifle superior in a well-bred way, somewhat bored by a week or two of ranch life, loafing, dancing, riding behind the hounds, sipping highballs. Did she belong to them, there on the verandah, or was her place here among the bullet-scarred rocks where unshaven men fought without water or food and perhaps died with tight lips spread in a grin? Which were *her* people?

She had promised Bert Atchison that she would accompany the party to New York next week, had given her "Yes" to his question. She had told him, as she told herself, that she belonged back there. After three years in the East, the Southwest seemed crude and terrible. Her friends here seemed boorish and uncouth, coarse and grating. At times she was almost ashamed of her father, who, for all that he was a college man, had fallen into the habits and customs of the cow country.

Then, there was that black stain on Jim Laughlin's life. That prison term. Why did he not try to conceal it? Why did he mention it with that same casual lightness that one might use in speaking of a siege in the hospital?

What would Bert Atchison do if he were here, undergoing this baptism of whining lead? Would he weaken? Or would he sit on his heels, a cigarette in his mouth, as Bruce McTavish now sat, a hot-barreled gun in his hand?

In split seconds, these questions, these comparisons, flickered through the brain of Jerry Laughlin. And no answer came to solve a single one of her perplexities.

Frightened, worried, hiding like some hunted animal, she crouched there. Then another whining bullet sent her into new panic. She heard the clatter of shod hoofs as her frightened horse bolted. Her plight was more serious than ever now.

And to harass the girl further there came the conviction that she had sent Bruce McTavish back to precipitate this bloodshed. Why had she taunted him? Why had she insulted him? Because of that silly school-day affair? Jerry Laughlin questioned herself but found no answer.

"Why did he come here?" she panted audibly. "I hate him!" But her cheeks flushed. Perhaps that flush was the answer to some of her questions. For the hearts of women are beyond all fathoming, and, therefore, they are all the more lovable. In their weakness lies their strength.

"I hate him!" Throwing herself face downward, her cropped curls buried in her arms, she sobbed as if her heart were broken. So poignant was her grief that she did not hear the stealthy approach of a man. Not until a pair of thick arms picked her up in rough embrace did she know that she was not alone. Startled, she squirmed about in that strong embrace to look up into the leering face of Chick Bullard.

"Oh! You . . . you filthy beast!" She tried to jerk free, but he held her and laughed through tobacco-smeared lips.

"I was slippin' acrost the ridge when yore pony like tuh run over me. Last time we met, you was too damn' high-toned tuh speak tuh a common cowhand. I'll drag

95

that nonsense outta you afore I'm through. Too good fer Chick Bullard, eh? Got a dude fer a lover, eh? Well, he's home milkin' the ducks today, an' I'm halter-breakin' yuh. Yore ol' man's a ex-convict an' a cow thief. Who are you tuh be high-tonin' a deputy sheriff an' part owner of a cow outfit as big as Jim Laughlin's spread? I'll learn yuh some decent manners."

He pulled her closer, his hot breath almost choking her. "God!" He let go, cursing, for she had bitten his wrist to the bone.

Her fear was gone now, and she stood for a moment, eyes flashing fire. A heavy, shot-loaded quirt hung from her wrist. Viciously she swung at him, again and again. Bullard, covering his welted face with his arms, stood his ground for some moments, mouthing curses at her as the quirt slashed him. Then he rushed. But she was too swift for him.

Quitting the shelter, she ran headlong down the hillside toward the cluster of boulders where Bruce, Jake, and Lige were returning a scattered hail of bullets from the brush below.

Bruce was the first to see the girl. Heedless of his own safety, he leaped to his feet and ran to meet her. Bullets screamed all around him. Luck seemed with him, for the shooting was wild. They met on a bare stretch of open park, and Bruce grasped her arm none too gently.

"This way! Don't you know enough to keep to cover?" And he half dragged, half carried her to the shelter of brush that flanked the clearing. "Bend low now, and keep right behind me. *Low!* Want to get us both shot? That's better. Now keep close and don't fall. Crawl here. Faster, can't you? Better. All right. Now run for it. Behind me, I said! One more spurt now. In you go!" And he all but threw her bodily into Lige's lap.

"Well, pull out my eyeballs if it ain't a gal!" gasped Jake.

"I might uh knowed she wouldn't go home," groaned Lige. "Are yuh hurt, honey?"

The old fellow was holding her, and Jerry clung to him, weak and almost hysterical. Bruce absently wiped away a stream of blood that came from a bullet-ripped cheek. Chick Bullard had almost made a bull's-eye.

"You keep on like you bin doin', kid," growled Jake to Bruce, his hands shaking a little as he pulled out a plug of tobacco, "an' they'll whittle yuh to pieces so's yuh won't make even a respectable corpse. If you ain't a sweet-lookin' thing! If that bullet had gone a half inch to one side, you'd be shakin' hands right now with the devil. Who's the lady?"

"Ask her," suggested Bruce, tying a handkerchief across his face. "She'll tell yuh how welcome we are on this range."

Jake whistled soundlessly and looked at Lige, who was patting the girl's shoulder as she sobbed, clinging to him tightly. Lige winked broadly, and Jake resumed his former position behind the boulders, a grin on his face that made Bruce flush.

"Don't be a darned fool, Jake," Bruce muttered, shoving shells in the magazine of his carbine. "Wise, ain't yuh?"

"Plumb," agreed old Jake, and punctuated the terse comment with a shot that sent a Bullard man into cover.

Oh, I held her hand in mine an'
looked into her eyes of brown,
An' I told her that I loved her
when the leaves came driftin' down.

Jake, squinting along the blue gun barrel, sang around his tobacco plug in an off-key baritone. Lige chuckled. Jerry Laughlin, more quiet now, ignored the song and the singer.

"Lige," she whispered, "where's Daddy Jimmer?"

"Dunno, baby. Ain't seen hide ner hair uh him. Now go set down over yonder where nothin' kin hurt yuh. We'll be outta this directly. Bet on this, Jim's safe, wherever he is. The fightin' is all goin' on right here, an' he ain't within miles uh this spot. Now go set down till we git ready tuh go home. Keep yore nerve, honey."

"Is . . . is this my fault, Lige?"

"Shucks, no. It's bin cookin' to a boil fer fifteen years. She's boilin' now an' no mistake."

"I don't understand, Lige."

"No, don't reckon yuh do. Don't aim that yuh will. Go over there now an' set, or I'll spank yuh."

She obeyed meekly. Lige went back to his business of taking shots at whatever moved in the brush below. Of Bruce, all Jerry saw was a broad-shouldered back, sweat-streaked, dusty, the tail of his flannel shirt partly out above the waistband of his overalls. His left hand, swollen and discolored, was across his lap, and he was using only one hand and a rock for a gun rest. Now and then, he dipped into the hat beside him and brought out cartridges that he methodically shoved in the gun magazine. He was as coldly calm as his two veteran companions.

Jake made a grisly picture, his head swathed in soiled, blood-stained bandages, jaws munching contentedly on a huge cud of tobacco, humming, talking to himself, squinting along his gun sights. "Ma'am," he called over his shoulder, "this ain't no pink tea, an' we done run out uh cake an' cookies. The music is kinda all one tune, too. I'd be proud tuh escort yuh home when the party's broke up. Too bad yuh didn't bring along yore knittin'. Are yuh anyways scairt?"

"Who wouldn't be?" she smiled as he turned to look her way. "I'm petrified."

"Me, too," said Jake. "My off-laig's gone tuh sleep. Didn't see nothin' of a Barlow knife with one busted blade, did yuh, as yuh come off the hill?"

Jerry smiled faintly. For all his gruesome bandages, there was something ludicrous about old Jake.

"There's one thing we kin be thankful fer up here," he went on, "the flies ner muskeeters ain't bad. Got cut off onct by some fellers. Had me bushed up along a boggy crick. Muskeeters like tuh gnawed me tuh death afore I snuk out. Ner it ain't snowin', nuther. Mind the time, Lige, when the Dodson boys kep' us all night an' most uh the next day in that norther?"

"You froze a ear, didn't yuh?" questioned Lige.

"A ear? Dang yore hide, there wa'n't a square inch uh hide on me that didn't need thawin' out. Ner it ain't rainin', nuther. Hate tuh scrap in the rain. Gits down a man's neck when he sights. Makes a man mean."

"Recollect that time when the Rangers pushed us acrost the Rio," called Lige. "We taken off our clothes. *Rurales* on the other side jumps us, an' we don't git time tuh re-sume them garments? Traveled ten miles through catclaws an' mesquite thorns. Looked like we'd tried tuh whup a herd uh bobcats."

"I suppose," said Jerry Laughlin, really smiling now, "that you two old cow dodgers are trying to get me over the shakes? I'm not as scared as I was. Can I help in some way?"

"You kin tie up Bruce's face," suggested Jake. "He's bleedin' all over the place."

"Send him over, then."

"My face is my own property," grunted Bruce, "and I'm all through being sent anywhere."

"Then I'll come over where you are, Stew," she called. "Call it a day and let me fix you up. You're a mess. Anyhow, you got hurt dragging me down the hill. Swearing at me every jump, too. Now crawl over, and let's fix you up. I won't try to hold hands. Come on, or I'll stand up and . . ."

"Sit down," snapped Bruce when she made as if to rise and invite a shower of bullets. "I'll be there in a minute."

"When yuh git white-headed, kid," chuckled old Jake, "yuh'll learn that when a woman wants her way, she'll git it."

100

"Er git shot tryin'," added Lige dryly. "Rise outta yore seat, Jerry Laughlin, an' I'll rope yuh an' tie yuh down. They bin havin' a dang fool argument, Jake. May have tuh knock 'em both on the head yet tuh git any peace aroun' here. It's shore tough when a man can't even fight in peace."

"Git over there," Jake told Bruce. "Yuh look sick."

Bruce obeyed slowly. Jake made no idle comment when he said Bruce was sick. Loss of blood, pain from his broken hand throbbing into his shoulder, his eyes swollen almost shut, he was a ghastly sight. Jerry stifled a cry of alarm as she saw his face, gray with suffering, unshaven and blood-smeared. He grinned at her, and she shuddered.

"Am I that hard to look at?" he asked.

"You are."

"Sorry."

"Don't be. I feel rotten enough about getting you into this. What'll we use for bandages?"

"In books, the lady uses her petticoat," grinned Bruce. "But you being shy the garment, we'll use my undershirt, I reckon. None too clean, but it'll do. Can you roll a cigarette? My one-handed efforts are *no bueno.*"

"Give me the makings. Then peel off that shirt. I'll try to build you some sort of smoke."

"Party's gettin' rough," grinned Bruce, and peeled off his shirt. Jerry handed him a rather sickly looking cigarette and, taking the undershirt, ripped it into strips. She was calmer now. She was getting accustomed to the spattering bullets that so far had

101

done no harm. Once over her first shudder of nausea at the sight of blood, she smiled gamely.

"You'll do," Bruce grinned his approval. "For all the polishing, you didn't let the tenderfoot schools spoil you. Say, I bet if you had to live back there for keeps, you'd pine away like a caged animal."

"You think so?" Jerry was thinking of Bert Atchison. In less than ten days she was scheduled to go East, there to remain always.

"*Think* so? I know it. Thanks for the bandage . . . and the smoke. Gotta get back on the job now. Don't worry any. We'll be out of this mess directly."

Cheerful liar was her inward comment, but she smiled.

CHAPTER
TWELVE

"Frazier Comes Clean"

Five riders seemed to drop out of the sky and into the cañon where Chick Bullard and his men lay hidden. In reality they came from five different compass points, riding at reckless speed down the steep slopes of the cañon.

"Eat 'em up, boys!" boomed a big voice. "Give 'em hell!"

"Jimmer!" screeched Jerry Laughlin. Bruce caught a swift glimpse of a man on a sweaty black horse as he tore down the slope, a red-faced man with a graying, sand-colored mustache who rode on an easy rein, a gun in his hand.

"Jim Laughlin hisse'f," bawled Lige, and leaped to his feet.

"An' about time he got here," grunted Jake. "I'm dry fer water an' ga'n't fer grub an' my chawin's about tuh give out. Lookit them Bullard snakes drag it fer home."

True enough, the enemy was in flight, Chick Bullard leading the retreat. Presently Jim Laughlin and another man came back up the slope toward the boulders. The man with Laughlin was Jeff Frazier.

Bruce's lips tightened.

"Don't go off half cocked now, kid," warned Jake. "You made one bad play whuppin' him. Don't foller it up with another mistake."

"If he starts it, I'll play what cards I have," defended Bruce.

"Shore thing. But I don't think Jeff Frazier's gonna begin nothin'. Leastways, not now. He's outmatched too bad. Keep yore ears open an' yore face shut."

Their horses blowing from the climb, Jim Laughlin and Jeff Frazier drew rein. Jake, Lige, Bruce and the girl were now all standing up to greet them.

Jim Laughlin had the appearance of being a big man without actually weighing more than a middleweight. Despite his years, his build was that of an athlete, thin-flanked, wide-shouldered, thick-chested. His features were blunt and clean cut — a handsome man, in spite of his rough garb. A good-natured grin spread his wide mouth as he beheld his daughter.

"So you had to get your feet wet, did you, Jerry? How do you like it out West as far as you've been?"

"Nothing to write back East about, Jimmer. We ran out of water. Well, here's your two men. Been keeping them for you. Bruce McTavish got a little mussed up, and somebody wrapped a gun barrel across Jake's skull, but they'll be O K in a week or two. You sure missed one sweet fight."

Her eyes shifted to Jeff Frazier who, bruised and battered, sat his horse in silence. The deputy marshal's face was mask-like, but his one eye was fixed on Bruce McTavish. The glint in that one eye might mean anything. Bruce, carelessly toying with his .45, watched Frazier like a cat watching a mouse.

Jim Laughlin swung to the ground and, stepping over to Jake, gripped the old cowpuncher's hand hard.

"Long time no see you, Jake."

"Quite a spell, ain't it, Jim?"

Casual, yet their glances exchanged a world of hidden greetings, for their kind hate emotional display.

Jeff Frazier got slowly to the ground and came toward Bruce. The deputy marshal's scarred face twitched in some sort of grimace. Then he held out a hand.

"You fought fair, boy," he said, "and whipped me clean. You're the only man alive that can boast of whipping Jeff Frazier. I'd like tuh shake hands."

"You gave me the worst beating I ever took, Frazier," grinned Bruce. "Put 'er there." And their hands gripped and held.

"Oh, ho!" boomed Jim Laughlin, "so that's the way the cow jumps, eh? You didn't say who worked you over, Jeff. The boy's a better man than old Angus, eh? Whipped you, did he? By gad, that's good, eh, Jake? Recall the time Jeff and Black Angus fought? And the terrier whipped the bear, for that was the way Jeff and that big black Scot lined up. Reckon it's time I shook the hand of Black Angus's son and heir."

"Son, but no heir," grinned Bruce, when Laughlin's hand found his.

"No heir, eh? Well, you can tell me about that later, Bruce." He chuckled to himself, and Lige winked at Jerry. Again Bruce felt that some hidden joke was being

105

played. "Well, Angus's misfortune is our gain," said Laughlin, sobering now. "We need a real friend or two. You seem to fit the bill and bulge over. And old Jake's a sight for weak eyes. Now we'd better be drifting for home. This is just a curtain-raiser compared to what's coming."

"What do you mean, Jimmer?" asked Jerry.

"Just what I said. I was hopin' you'd be safe out of the country before it tightened. Married and flitting around among the white lights. But they opened up the game, and, from the looks of things, they're going to go on through with it till they're licked." Laughlin turned to Frazier. "Well, Jeff, appears like we've come to the forks of the trail. You can't take sides while you've got that badge on. If Angus was here, he'd vote with me. Draw out of the game. I'm not holding you to that old oath. I swore I'd kill you on sight, but you came to me under the white flag, back there on the divide. There's still time for you to ride out of the picture and no harm done. You and Ed Hardin came onto my range hunting trouble. Hardin got his just punishment. Because I want no government officer's blood on my hands, I'm giving you your chance. You'd better be drifting, Jeff. Next time, you come a-shootin'."

Jeff Frazier grinned twistedly and deftly made a cigarette. "What if I told you I wasn't leaving, Jim?"

"I hope," said Laughlin coldly, "that whatever you do, you'll run true to form. You have your faults, but you never was a sneak about anything. I suppose you acted according to your lights in the past. Stick to your game, Jeff Frazier. Don't turn traitor."

"Them's hard words fer a man to take, Jim." It was old Jake who spoke. "I reckon it's time I put a white chip into the ante. I kep' my trap shut a long time, a good many long years. Because I give Jeff Frazier my word to do so. But Ed Hardin's dead now, an' I kin talk. It was Hardin, not Jeff Frazier, that done you an' Black Angus dirt. I knowed it all along. Jeff has bin on the level with you an' with Angus."

"Hmm!" Jim Laughlin raised a skeptical eyebrow. "I'll need proof of that."

Jeff Frazier grinned wider and, unpinning his badge, handed it to Jim Laughlin. "I already burned up the warrants for you, Lige, and Jake. Rather, I gave 'em to Jake back yonder where Ed was killed, and Jake burned 'em. The past is closed. When Ed Hardin died, my job as deputy marshal ceased automatically. Now, if you'll have me, Jim Laughlin, I'll pool my bets with you boys. You'll be needing an extra gun when Bullard's partner gets into motion. Bullard may be yellow, but Pat Green ain't. Green will fight to the finish, and he'll kill Bullard, if Bullard weakens. Will you have me, Jim?"

"I'd rather have you with me than against me," admitted Laughlin, "but I don't savvy yet what your idea is throwing in with me. You've always been against me. You stuck by Ed Hardin and Pat Green. Green used his money to have tin stars pinned on his killers. Because I wouldn't stoop to such methods, I was called an outlaw and a cow thief. On perjured evidence I was sent to the pen along with Angus McTavish, a man who never broke a law of God or man in his life. You and Hardin pulled out, but Green stayed. After twenty-five

107

years of preparation, Green plans another coup. You and Hardin come down the trail from Idaho or Wyoming with bench warrants for Bruce McTavish and Jake Raine. You knew they'd head for here when Bruce shot a man named Jim Harmon, up in Montana."

Jeff Frazier nodded, his one eye glinting with a hard, bright light. Jake and Lige shifted uneasily, their spurs tinkling nervously.

"Jim," said Frazier in a somewhat husky voice, "I know things look black for me. From all evidence, I've been a cold-blooded killer. I can't explain things, and you'll have to take my word for it. I did what I was bound to do. Hardin's dead, and I'm free. Will you take the word of Jake Raine or Lige Taylor for it?"

"And my word, Daddy Jim?" put in Jerry Laughlin.

"And just what, young lady, do you know about it?" asked Laughlin.

Bruce, still watching Frazier, saw the deputy marshal go chalk white. Lige was red and pale by turns. Jake looked puzzled and tried to catch Lige's eye, but Lige avoided his glance. Laughlin's face was a study. Bruce was more bewildered than ever.

"Well, Jerry?" questioned Laughlin. "Speak up. What do you know about Jeff Frazier? I wasn't aware that you knew him except by hearsay."

"Now, Jimmer," Jerry resorted to woman's tactics, "don't be so darn stubborn. You're outvoted. Never mind how much I know. Let Jeff Frazier come along. I want to show our tenderfoot guests what a real honest-to-gosh manhunter looks like."

"Hmm! Well, tell 'em, for good measure, that he's the manhunter that helped send Jim Laughlin to the penitentiary. It should give 'em a thrill. Outvoted, eh? Looks that way. Which way do you vote, Bruce McTavish? For or against Jeff Frazier?"

"Me? Well, being as I'm absolutely a blank and know less than yonder horse about the whole works, I reckon I'll stay neutral. I'll say this much. Frazier took his licking like a white man. That's something."

"Then I reckon, Frazier," said Laughlin, "that you come along."

"Will you shake on that?"

Laughlin shoved out a hand, and Frazier gripped it. "Perhaps, some day, Jim, I can explain."

"Hope so, Jeff. At least you never were underhanded. Always fought in the open."

Jerry came close to Bruce and addressed him in a low tone. "We're even, Stew McTavish, for that dance. You spoke up like a white man." And she squeezed his hand, laughing a shaky little laugh.

"By the way, Frazier," said Bruce, "here's that gun that you claimed killed Ed Hardin." He held out Jake's gun, butt first, the weapon still unfired.

Jeff Frazier took it. All eyes were on him as he smiled twistedly, then returned the gun to Bruce. "Thanks, McTavish, but I won't be needing it. Give it back to Jake. I knew all along that it was his gun. Also, I knew that the gun was not the weapon that killed Ed Hardin. I was being watched with field glasses from nearby. Chick Bullard was spying. That's why I slapped you when you were handcuffed to the tree. Wanted to make

109

a play for Bullard's benefit. As a matter of fact, I know who killed Ed Hardin."

"You sure were convincing," said Bruce. "You didn't pull your blows any when you slapped me."

"I had to make the play strong. Bullard was suspicious. I didn't want to tip my hand."

"Say," said Jake suddenly, "I'm wonderin' if you know who hid in the brush an' bent a gun acrost my head when I stopped over Hardin's body?"

"I could make a good guess, Jake."

"It wa'n't you?"

"No. It was Chick Bullard."

"Then it was Chick Bullard that killed Ed Hardin?"

"No," said Frazier, "Chick Bullard didn't kill Hardin."

"Then who did?"

"For certain reasons, boys, I can't tell you just now. When the time comes, I'll tell. We'll have to let it go at that. Jim, we'd better be moving along. Green and Bullard mean business. They'll head for your ranch, come dark."

"Then let's get goin'." Laughlin paused before he mounted. "Jerry, you an' Bruce go on ahead. If you can, load those Eastern folks in the car and send 'em to town. And you go with 'em, understand? What's coming off is no woman's party. Us boys will swing in by Sacatone and gather up what boys we find. Now kiss your dad and light out. Wire me from Chicago or 'Frisco or some safe place."

He held her close for a minute, kissed her, then sent her away with a forced grin.

110

"I'll come back East for the wedding," he called after her, as she and Bruce rode off.

"Just do that, won't you, Jimmer?" she called back. "*Adiós*. Take care of yourself. You boys keep an eye on him. See you in jail, folks."

"That's what I call a darn flippant farewell," frowned Bruce, as he rode beside her.

"Farewell, you say? Not much. If Jim Laughlin or you or Lige or anyone else thinks I'm going to run away, you're loco. We'll ship off the gang, but little Jerry is going to see the big show. Grin, cowboy. Do you have only one expression . . . a scowl?"

And she spurred ahead, leaving Bruce to follow.

CHAPTER
THIRTEEN

"Bullard Makes a Capture"

What Chick Bullard lacked in cold nerve, he made up for in cunning. He ran, but never ran so far as to lose contact with his pursuers. In times gone by, he had traded on that very contempt men felt for him. So it came about that, when Bullard sent his men to a rendezvous where they were to meet another faction of gunmen under Pat Green, he himself lurked behind to spy on the movements of his enemies.

There were men in the Southwest who claimed that the blood in Chick Bullard's veins was a mixture of Negro, Apache, and renegade white, that his mother was a half-breed Apache daughter of an outlaw. While not dark, Bullard had the thick lips and broad nose of the Negro, and there was a peculiar tone to his laugh. Also, in his cunning, he was more Indian than white.

He watched Bruce and Jerry leave the others and ride toward the J Bar L Ranch. His field glasses told him that Bruce's left arm was in a makeshift sling and that his face was bandaged. From this distance it appeared that the injuries were serious.

Bullard felt gingerly of his head, bruised and swollen from the blow of Bruce's gun. Chick Bullard was never a man to forget a blow or a cursing. In his own way, at the proper time, he would again take up this quarrel. Sometimes in the open, more often from ambush, he had collected his black debts. Because his gun was a coward's gun, it was the more to be feared by brave men.

First, he made sure of the direction taken by Bruce and the girl. Then, he remained long enough to ascertain the movements of Jim Laughlin and his three companions. Choosing a short trail that would intercept the one taken by Jerry and Bruce, he rode hard and with a wide, self-satisfied grin on his thick lips.

But even the most cunning of plotters cannot foresee the improbable. An odd chance it was that brought Bert Atchison, tenderfoot, along that trail. He had started out with some vague, romantic idea of somewhere meeting Jerry Laughlin and enjoying a long ride with her across the hills. To be sure, she had refused his company that morning on the pretext, frankly given, that there was work to be done and that he would be in the way. She had gone before he had finished breakfast.

So Bert Atchison had taken the trail and within the hour was badly lost in the hills. The sun and wind were peeling the skin from his nose; he was tired, dusty, and horribly thirsty. He merely grinned at his own discomfort and kept on. He might have his faults, but certainly no man could claim that he was lacking in courage.

113

Bullard, who had arrived at his point of ambush and lay in wait for Bruce and the girl, made an ugly grimace as his trained ears told him that someone was approaching the spot from the direction of the Laughlin ranch. Bruce and Jerry were due any minute now. The coming of this third person, granting that the rider belonged to the Laughlin faction, threw the odds against Bullard.

Inwardly seething with rage, he waited for the rider's coming, thumbing the hammer of his six-shooter. A chance remained. He could kill this rider. Bruce McTavish, thinking his help was needed, might rush blindly into the trap. Bullard had seen him brave squarely spitting guns. So — an ugly light in his narrowed eyes — he waited.

The sound of a song came to him. Bert Atchison, probably in an effort to bolster up his lagging spirits, was singing some popular tune in a creditable baritone.

Bullard scowled. That was no common cowhand singing. He had heard exaggerated rumors of Jerry Laughlin's millionaire guests. Rumor had it that each of those tenderfoot visitors was many times a millionaire. For some reason it made Bullard wild with cold rage. Like most men who stoop to anything to gain wealth, Chick Bullard hated all those who had money. Then, as an idea struck him, he grinned widely.

He was still grinning, though his eyes were red with hate, as he stepped out into the trail, a gun swinging in his hand, to intercept the astonished Bert Atchison.

"Well, I'm damned!" gasped Atchison. "I say, what's the idea? Why the weapon?"

"Pull off the trail into the brush. Then git off. If yuh got a gun on yuh, don't pull 'er, or I'll kill yuh like a coyote. Step fast, my lily-fingered dude."

"As you say," agreed the other, not so badly frightened as Bullard expected. "But I'm telling you, brother, I'm slim pickin's. Haven't a thin dime on me, if that's the game."

"Not a dime on yuh but plenty in the home bank," sneered Bullard, herding man and horse into a brush thicket a little off the main trail.

"I get you, fatty. Ransom, eh? Thanks, big boy, thanks."

"Thanks for what?" snarled Bullard, suddenly suspicious. This man was not showing the proper respect for a naked gun.

"Why, for the diversion. I get a kick out of it. Held for ransom. Do you cut off an ear and send it with the demand for money? I want all the trimmings, big boy. Go the limit, see? And ask for plenty dough. I hope you've got a fancy name. Black Billy, or Eat-'Em-Up Joe, or something. Now what do I do?"

Atchison, arms held high, grinned into Bullard's ugly face.

"You'll keep yore damn' trap shut, that's what." Bullard's voice dropped to a husky whisper. "Folks is comin'. One word outta you an' I'll gut shoot yuh. Git me?"

"Absolutely, old hoss. Mum's the word."

In tense silence the two men waited. Bullard's gun was jammed into the small of Atchison's back. While along the trail, conversing in tones that carried easily to

115

Bert Atchison's ears, rode Jerry Laughlin and Bruce McTavish.

"So you're engaged to this playboy scion of millionaire row, are you, Jerry?" Bruce was saying.

"I am. And he's no sissy, Bruce McTavish. You men out here have some sort of weird idea that any man born east of the Rockies is some sort of mollycoddle, that blue blood is weak blood. What are you grinning at? Bert might be a little out of place among the cactus, but he'd make a chump out of you on his home field."

"Did I say anything against this Ethelbert party?"

"Not in so many words. But I know what you think."

"All I say is that, if this Ethel gent has you hooked, he ought to hang around closer. Some harder rider might beat him out. Now, if I were in his place, I'd ride herd on you till I had you hazed plumb up to the altar."

"Altar or halter? I'm not a bronc'."

"No, but you have a lot of broncho instincts. It won't be the first time that some overconfident boy has been left at the church door all dressed up and the bride suffering from cold feet."

"Are you trying to propose?"

"Just declaring myself in the race. I haven't two bits to my name and no chance of even a decent job. But I believe in keeping home product in the country."

"Another Lochinvar, perhaps," laughed Jerry, as they rode on into the distance, their words dimming. "Well, Kid Lochinvar, shave your whiskers off and take a bath or two, and we'll look you over. I'll decide, then, whether it's worthwhile putting your name on the list."

116

Her laugh, carefree, mocking, came back along the trail. Bert Atchison, his expression one of pained puzzlement, twisted at a small, blond mustache.

"Just who is the lad who rode past, Black Bart?" he asked, ignoring Bullard's belligerent attitude.

"You let one beller outta yuh an' I'll kill yuh."

"Bad Bill, I wouldn't summon him for a million in cold money. He called me Ethel, damn him. I hope he's somewhere near my size. Listen, Curly Wolf, put up the gat and be yourself. How much am I worth? I'll make you out a check right now. Sorry I can't stick around with you a few weeks, but that wise-cracking boy is trying to beat my time, and I've got to be back on the job. Name the price, old son. Write your own ticket. The pleasure has been all mine."

"Jest keep them paws kinda high," snarled Bullard. "You might have a popgun hid away on yuh. A check ain't worth a damn. Green money is my meat. You ain't goin' home today ner tomorrow. Not alive, anyhow."

"Now, listen . . ."

"Dry up. Fork that pony an' ride where I tell yuh. If yuh ever see McTavish, tell him fer me that you saved his life. Now, git goin'.'"

Bert Atchison, after one long look at the gun and the bulk of man behind it, obeyed the command. But behind his smiling, shrugging obedience lay a determination whose strength Bullard did not guess.

"Who the devil is this Bruce McTavish, anyhow?" he asked.

"Black Angus's kid. A four-flushin' coward." And Chick Bullard, with colorful profanity, gave Bruce a

117

pedigree and reputation that would have disgraced a bushwhacking, yellow-blooded craven.

"That bad?" interrogated Bert mildly as he selected a cigarette from a silver case.

"Worse. I ain't got time tuh cuss him out right. He's my meat, hear that? No man kin warp a gun acrost my head without payin' heavy. Ketched me from behind, damn 'im!"

"Ah!" Bert nodded, and lit his cigarette.

Bullard led the way to a deserted cabin where he called a halt.

"I was hoping there'd be the right setting," Bert said easily. "Now, listen, old trapper. I'll write out a check and give my word it will be honored. Be a good sport and I'll add a bonus. I've some . . ."

"Dry up." Bullard undid his lariat. "I'm hog-tyin' yuh fer a spell. Got tuh meet my pard." He approached with the rope in one hand, Colt in the other.

Like a flash, Bert Atchison was on him, fists swinging. But Bullard, for all his contempt of the Easterner, was not unprepared. His gun barrel smashed against Atchison's skull, and the tenderfoot went down with a little moan. Bullard, grinning to himself, tied him hand and foot, and dragged him into the cabin. Then, leading the other's horse, he rode away.

CHAPTER
FOURTEEN

"Ready for Trouble"

Bruce, upon his arrival at the J Bar L Ranch, rode stiffly past the gaping crowd on the long verandah who hailed Jerry with excited questions. Seeking haven in the bunkhouse, he proceeded to shave and scrub off the grime of the trail. He started as the door opened, then grinned when he saw a big man in well-cut riding clothes. Gray-haired, red-cheeked, bulky, he called a hearty greeting.

"Don't shoot, young man. I'm a surgeon. Jerry said there was an outlaw in here that needed attention. Name's Roberts. Yours is McTavish, is it not? Glad to know you. Never mind dressing now. Lie down on that bunk while we fix up that mitt. Fixed lots of 'em. Did all the work for a string of New York pugs. Fighting's hard on the hands. Painful as hell. Hurt? You lie like a gentleman."

He kept up a running fire of talk as he worked. Bruce liked this fellow with his ruddy health and bluff voice. The pain was terrific. Bruce felt things going black, the doctor's voice dimming, dying away. The faint odor of cigar, highball, and antiseptic — then oblivion.

"He needs a week's sleep and some decent food," Dr. Roberts told Jerry when she came in a few minutes later. "He's been going on his nerve. Game as the devil, your friend. Where'd you leave Bert?"

"Bert? Left him here. You mean he's gone?"

"He went out to find you. Love's a great drug. Makes chumps of the best of us. What's the matter, Jerry?"

"Nothing much, only that he's probably riding to his death, that's all. And I'm responsible. Why did I ever . . . ?"

"Here, Jerry," interposed the doctor, "Bert'll come out all right, even if he is a dude. Now tell me what's wrong."

She told him, her words stumbling in an eagerness to share the burden of worry with this man whom nothing seemed to upset. He smiled, nodded, and patted her as a father might calm an alarmed child.

"So, you see," she concluded, "we must send the bunch to town right now. I don't know what it's all about, except it's some horrible feud that's been going on for years. You'll get them in the big car and send them to town for me?"

"Afraid they'll have to stay and see the thing through, Jerry. Young Van Duzen took the big car not an hour ago and went to town for a couple of cases of champagne he had shipped from home. You know Van. He'll get potted, and it will take him two days to leave town, providing he doesn't wreck the car. But don't worry, Jerry. This bunch may be a frivolous lot, but they'd rather die than not be game. Part of their young idiots' code. Sportsmanship and playing the game. Whether it's poker, love, or life. Don't worry. They'll call it a thrill. Now, go take a bath and get some hot food under your belt."

"You're a brick, Doc, a perfect brick."

"Quit it, you young heart-buster. I'll tell my wife."

"You say Bruce is all right?"

The doctor gave her a searching look, and she flushed under the frankness of his scrutiny. "He's tough, Jerry, and game. You couldn't kill him with an axe. Now, get out of here, and do as I said. Leave the bunch to me. I was a major in the Spanish-American War, and this stuff is kids' play by comparison. Beat it. Be a good soldier."

When she had gone, he looked with renewed interest at Bruce. As he had lost consciousness, Bruce had talked a little, the babbling of the unconscious. Mixed in the disconnected sentences was the name of Jerry Laughlin.

After all, *the doctor nodded to himself*, you're more her own kind. But Atchison will fight to keep what he loves. Blond Britisher. Black Scot. And a prize that any man would battle for. It'll be a game worth the seeing. Hard fought. Clean fought. May the best man have her.

And humming a half-forgotten love song, Dr. Roberts, who was *the* Dr. Roberts of New York, strode out to break the news of approaching danger to the laughing, carefree crowd on Jim Laughlin's verandah. Instinctively his shoulders straightened. Again he was the army officer, organizing his forces, and, down in his heart, enjoying the thrill of it.

Because he was a man to invite confidences, he had heard quite a little of Jim Laughlin's past life. There on the verandah, after the others had retired, the two men had spent many hours with cigars and good bourbon and between them had grown an understanding. So the news of approaching danger did not catch the doctor unaware.

Bluntly, he told the loiterers what they might expect. True to his predictions, they took it as a lark, spiced with the thrill of danger. This was a crowd that had ridden to hounds, raced automobiles, flown airplanes, and taken life as one huge game to be played according to the code of the sportsman and sportswoman. They made a clean-cut lot in their flannels and gay silks — healthy, athletic, well bred, a little bored. They greeted the news with typical calm.

"I say, splendid, what?"

"Glad we came. A prize for the first chap to get a notch on his gun. Hang it, Diana, where'd you put my rifle yesterday?"

"The girls can do the nursing, eh, Doc? Put 'em in white. It'll be a pleasure to get wounded."

"I thought feuds belonged to Kentucky, Doc," called a leggy blonde who had been playing tennis, "feuds, liquor, and horses."

"Van'll turn green when he finds out what he's missed. I say, where's Jerry? What a dear she is to provide a real feud. Like her, isn't it? Has Bert come back? He'll eat this up in gobs."

"What of the chap she brought in? Is he a real outlaw?"

"Real, my eye. Ever hear of Stew McTavish? Picked for All-American in his day. Had it straight from Jerry."

"He looked like the real goods. Did he die, Doc?"

"Does he need a sweet, blonde nurse?"

"Did he kill somebody?"

"Will you pipe down? All hands hit the deck and listen to Doc. He's the skipper."

"Go eat a snake, Ted, you're not aboard your silly yacht."

"Know discipline, afloat or ashore," complained a sun-burned, bleach-haired youngster in white flannels. "Pipe 'em down, Doc. Need a first mate?"

"Need a megaphone," roared Doc. "Here comes Jim Laughlin and some men. Quit acting like kids. Do as Jim says and no funny cracks. Ladies in the house. Men wait here. I'm going over to the barn to meet Jim."

As Laughlin and his men rode toward the barn, silence fell over the crowd. Something in the silent, grim-lipped bearing of these men brought home to them the stern reality of the situation. Behind them came the black horse that bore the body of Ed Hardin. There was no mistaking the nature of that burden. These idlers now saw crude, unadorned life as men play the game of primitive, coded living, regardless of law.

Other riders, singly or in little groups, rode in and stabled sweat-streaked horses. Twilight found twenty-five men in the bunkhouse where Jim Laughlin remained. Dr. Roberts took command at the house, ably assisted by Lige and Jake. Jake, of whom they made a hero, was not ill pleased with his lot.

"Danged if they ain't plumb human," he confided to Lige, "an', man, them's the slickest females a man ever laid eyes on. Look at the tall 'un with her yaller hair cut like a boy's. Reminds a man of a race mare."

"Can't a one of 'em touch Jerry," maintained Lige stoutly.

"Dunno, dunno, Lige. That yaller-haired 'un picks up my marbles. That black-haired little gal yonder with the ridin' britches on is shore easy on the eyes, too."

"Yuh's orter see her shoot. Had her quail huntin'. She gits 'em where they ain't, as well as where they are. Savvies the hoss, too. Dunno when I taken to pilgrims like I do these folks. Rich as hell, too."

"That 'un that he'ped the doc tie up my head is shore common as any squaw. Me dirty an' bloody. Her gittin' blood on her white dress an' callin' me Jake like she was kinfolks."

"Yuh didn't expect Jerry Laughlin to be runnin' with a pack uh la-de-da sissies, did yuh?" snarled Lige with prideful air. "The yaller-haired 'un gimme this hat."

"Where's this feller Jerry's gonna marry?"

"Lost, I told yuh. Went out ridin' an' ain't come in. I reckon one uh the boys'll find him an' fetch 'im home. They bin gittin' lost thataway ever since they come. Kep' a crew busy, huntin' pilgrims. They got a rule that the one as gits lost has tuh pay a forfeit. The last 'un had tuh set on the corral all night an' sing. Then they'd heave shoes at him. But he'd took a bottle with him an' kep' hittin' 'er. Directly he fell off the corral on his head. There he was in the mornin', his lavender perjammers all dirty. His name's Van. He owns half of Boston. I learnt him tuh chaw. Yeah, they're real folks. But I dunno how they'll act about midnight when Pat Green an' Bullard opens up the fireworks. Somehow I don't look fer no roarin' fight. Jeff Frazier has some kind uh ace up his sleeve. I hope we ain't done wrong, Jake, givin' him this chanct."

"If he turns sour on us, I kills him, personal. Now I gotta have this here bandage fixed onct more. She's done slipped. What the hell yuh grinnin' at, anyhow?"

"Nothin'." Lige's chuckling grew more audible as he moved off. "Nothin' a-tall."

CHAPTER
FIFTEEN

"Bruce Plays the Game"

Not so much as the glow of a cigarette lighted the buildings of the J Bar L. Men, grim-lipped, slit-eyed, peered into the night. Silence, like a pall, hung over the place.

"Dashed spooky, what?" whispered a voice. "Some idiot coughed. Had me all goose pimply. One should be careful about coughing, time like this."

"Shut up, you ass. Bert's no baby. Where's Jerry?"

"Said she'd be back soon. She took some broth or something to the McTavish camp. Doc said he never saw such nerve."

"Like Jerry's?"

"No, cutie. McTavish's. Never batted an eye when Doc fixed him. Doc offered him a drink, but he wouldn't touch it. Said he'd rather not."

"Then he's changed these late years. Used to train on hooch. He was fired for being soused just before the big game. Not very sportin' of him, considering his . . ."

"Oh, I say, quit bein' catty, Dick."

Over near a window, someone lit a match. For a moment the flame, cupped in a hand, lit a cigarette. It also revealed the features of Bruce McTavish. Then the match went out. Jerry Laughlin, crouched at the window beside him, touched his bandaged arm.

"I'm sorry, Bruce," she whispered.

"What about?" he replied, laughing unpleasantly. "Your friend spoke the truth."

"But you're not like that now. Don't be bitter, old boy. Play the game . . ."

The words died as Bruce's gun crashed. Tinkling glass. The stifling fumes of powder. Outside, the startled cry of a wounded man. The next instant Bruce's big form shot headlong through the window. From the dark ground below came the muffled thuds of a terrible struggle. Then Bruce passed a black keg through the window, and climbed after it.

"Powder, by the looks of it. Jake, watch sharp on your side. They may try it from there. If you'll show me where there's a tub and water, we'll ruin about fifty buck's worth of giant powder."

"That man outside?" questioned Jerry. "You killed him?"

"Tried to. Afraid I got him a little high. But we got the powder. There goes the fireworks."

"Keep away from the windows," cautioned Lige. "Dang it, Jerry, why ain't you in with the other women?"

But Jerry was guiding Bruce to a water tap where he was pouring the powder into the water.

"And some idiot said that Bruce McTavish wasn't sportin'," chuckled a voice.

"I said it," volunteered another voice. "I'm eatin' my words now."

"I say, Lige, when do we shoot?"

"Whenever yuh see somethin' wiggle out yonder, son."

"Fair enough." And the speaker punctuated his words with a rifle shot that brought an answering fire from outside.

Pow! Jake's rifle was roaring. He jerked at his Winchester lever and fired again. Windows sprayed shattered glass about. The darkness of the room was slit by yellow fire. Over at the bunkhouse, the fighting was hot and furious. From the corrals and trees outside came the belching fire of rifles. The siege was on.

"They might set fire to the buildings, what?"

"'Dobe don't burn," came Lige's dry comment. "Who's got a chaw on 'em?"

"Here you go, Lige, and welcome," called a voice. "I'm afraid I'll never learn the knack of it."

Lige chuckled. "Nothin' like it tuh steddy a man's sights."

"I find it quite the opposite. You'll have to come for it, though. One of my damned legs is . . ."

"Here," called Lige, "one uh you boys lend a hand. This gent's hit. Easy, now. We'll turn him over to the nurses."

Jim Laughlin had built his house after the frontier pattern. There was one room whose thick, windowless walls were bullet-proof. In there were the women. Lige and another man carried in the wounded man. White faces stared in the dim lamplight. Dr. Roberts appeared

128

from somewhere. Then Lige and his helper returned to their fighting.

"Game cuss," Lige told Jake. "Hit twict. But he never squawked."

"Let's have the use uh that chawin'."

"It's all blood, dang it."

"If that ain't like a dad-burned pilgrim," grunted Jake, "gittin' hit in his terbaccer pocket. Reminds me uh the time Piegan Charlie was packin' a flask uh licker on his flank when. . . ." Jake broke off to squint along his sights. His gun roared. "Got the varmint!" And the tale of Piegan Charlie was forgotten.

Bruce, having left Jerry with Dr. Roberts, was back in the room with the others.

"How's everything, kid?" asked Jake when he recognized McTavish.

"Not so bad. Not so good, either. Women are sure a puzzle."

"That's what's worryin' yuh, huh? It don't matter a damn that there's a cow war goin' on. Now ain't that jest too bad fer words. Yo're sickenin', Bruce McTavish, plumb sickenin'. Got a chaw on yuh?"

"Don't use the stuff. Never did."

"Nothin' like a jawful uh fine cut tuh steddy yore sights. Green has kinda slacked off firin'. He'll be askin' fer a pow-wow directly she comes daylight. Pat always was thataway. Long on these medicine talks. Too bad ol' Angus ain't here tuh sling psalms at him. He usta make Pat shore ringy when he sprung Bible sayin's on him."

"When was that? Don't you think it was about time you told a man something about this business?"

"Angus'd shoot me, but I reckon yuh got a right tuh know. Him an' Jim Laughlin was pardners onct. They worked for Green an' Ed Hardin, takin' trail herds north from the Staked Plains tuh Montana. Me'n' Lige an' Jeff Frazier, who went mostly by the name uh the Gila Bend Kid, usta work fer Angus an' Jim. Angus works jest long enough tuh learn the cow game, then draws a wad uh money outta the bank an' goes into business fer hisse'f, takin' Jim as pardner. They locates close tuh Green's an' Hardin's place, which makes Pat shore mad, fer he calls hisse'f king uh the cow country.

"Pat's cute, dang cute. He don't show no outward sign uh being mad. Not him. Fact is, he pretends tuh he'p Angus an' Jim git a start. But his heart is bad, an' he's waitin' till the sign is right. Inside hisse'f, he hates Black Angus like pizen. There's a few of us boys that's workin' fer Angus an' Jim that ain't so dang pure. As the sayin' goes, we've heard the owl hoot. But them days there's few boys ridin' trail that ain't busted some fool law or another, somewhere, sometime. So we don't worry much. That is, we don't act like coyotes.

"Green is cute like a fox. He noses along our back trails, gits our pedigrees down in black an' white, an' waits his time.

Then he gits Ed Hardin an' some others made into law officers. Ed's a snake, but I'll say this fer him, he declares hisse'f at the start. Wears his badge where it shows an' tells the cow country he's gonna clean the range of all rustlers. Him an' Green had kinda split up over it, Pat bein' in favor uh goin' at it quiet.

130

"About that time, Angus an' Jim gits ready tuh trail a herd north tuh Kansas City. They needs more men an' hires some boys that's drifted to the ranch ridin' grub line. About the time we gits a herd gathered, Green rides over to the ranch. He 'lows he has a thousand head uh stuff he'd like tuh sell at Kansas City an' offers tuh pay cash, so much per head, if Angus an' Jim will take them steers into our herd. He's offerin' big pay fer the job an' seems friendly enough, so Angus closes the deal, an' Green tells us where tuh pick up the cattle. Which we does. As it's the law them days fer all cattle tuh be put into one trail brand, we lays over at the McTavish pens an' puts all these Pat Green-Hardin steers into our trail iron. Then, come a run an' a scatterment, we kin pick up our stuff under one brand. But right there is where Pat Green begins makin' his snake tracks. I'll tell a man.

"We've got these new men, like I says. Mexicans, mostly. An' among the lot is a feller that Jeff Frazier, who works fer Jim then, has taken to mighty strong. An' a man don't need specs tuh know why. It's Jeff's twin brother, an' they look much alike. That's easy seen, even if they do go under different names. What we don't know is this . . . Jeff Frazier's brother is a stock detective sent out tuh get information regardin' stock that turns up missin' about the time some big trail herd starts north. Fer there's many a steer gits rustled jest thataway.

"We're two weeks on the trail an' things rockin' along nice when Pat Green plays his cards. Up rides Hardin an' ten, twenty men, all deputized. They tell Angus that they come tuh inspect the herd. Jeff's twin is one uh the bunch. He's slipped off the night afore an' met 'em, savvy?

"Well, Jim an' Angus begins tuh see daylight now. There ain't one solitary scrap uh written paper tuh prove that them Pat Green steers is come by in an honest way. Pat has paid cash. A man's word them days was as good as ten contracts on paper.

" 'We're combin' this herd,' says Ed Hardin, 'with a fine-toothed comb. It's gonna go damn' hard with you two gents if yuh can't prove ownership to every hoof uh cattle in this herd.'

"By which sign Jim Laughlin an' Black Angus McTavish knows that Pat Green has 'em foul. Jim falls back on his gun an' good, plain, honest cussin', but Angus pulls his Bible an' is fer pacifyin' Hardin. Things look tight fer a few minutes there at the herd while we each sizes up a man on Hardin's side an' waits fer the word tuh cut loose. It's that quiet that a man kin hear a gnat tromp on his horse's ear.

"Then she happens. Angus, shovin' his Bible in his pocket, hits Hardin with his fist. It's like a mule kickin', an' Ed goes outta his saddle like somebody's roped him an' jerked him off. Then hell busts, an' it's devil take the least fit. Shootin', cuttin', bawlin', an' bullets thick as hailstones.

"Ed Hardin has John Law behind him. He's packin' warrants fer me 'n' Lige an' some more boys. The best us boys kin hope fer is the wust of it, but we plays our strings out then an' there. It's root, hog, er die. Yeah, an' there's some that dies, then an' there, fer guns is poppin' loud an' frequent.

132

"Amongst them dead fellers is this twin brother uh Jeff Frazier, but we don't know about it as we whips our ponies down the hind laig, an', leavin' the scattered herd, we drifts yonderly.

"Two, three of our boys is killed. Every man in our outfit has at least one bullet somewhere in his hide. When we rides into the hills, John Law has put us on his Injun list, an' we're wanted dead er alive. Black Angus is bleedin' like a stuck pig. Laughlin's hangin' onto his saddle horn, hit bad. An' as we heads fer the tall timbers, down comes a second posse with Pat Green headin' 'em. They got us, goin' er comin'.

" 'Boys,' says Angus, 'you drag it. Jim an' I gives up here. We ain't done no law-breakin' regardin' that herd, an' they can't do nothin' to us. All you boys that has indictments out ag'in' yuh, run fer it. Me 'n' Jim'll hold 'em off while yuh drag it.' Which they shore does. Them two holds up the posse while us boys drifts outta sight. Then they surrenders."

Jake, as he talked, kept up an intermittent firing. Bruce listened interestedly, his own gun belching fire now and then. But the fighting had simmered down to occasional snap shots.

"Hardin an' Green proved their case," Jake went on. "Jim went to the pen an' so did Angus. Jeff Frazier's evidence he'ped send 'em up. Jeff bein' a Laughlin-McTavish man, his word went big at the trial. He was dead ag'in' Jim an' Angus because it was proved that Jim killed Jeff's twin brother. Only fer Jeff Frazier's evidence, Jim an' Angus might've got off easier. Hell, they'd still be doin' time if they hadn't got pardoned."

133

"No wonder Laughlin hates Frazier," said Bruce. "Why didn't Dad ever tell me about that deal, Jake?"

"Scared it might have a bad effect on a kid, I reckon. He wanted yuh to be honest an' sober. The Bible-readin' ol' rascal usta condemn hisse'f a-plenty fer that temper uh his."

"How come they got pardoned, Jake, if the evidence was so strong against them?"

"Well," drawled Jake, "us boys had bin treated right. We wasn't the sort tuh set aroun' idle while Angus an' Jim laid in the pen. So we makes arrangements with certain folks fer their pardon." Jake grinned dryly and dug a hard lump of plug tobacco from a dusty pocket.

"Now that's what I calls luck. I bin needin' a chaw fer hours. You an' that gal uh Jim's seems tuh be gittin' right well acquainted, kid. When's she gonna marry that dude uh hers?"

"Not today, anyhow," grinned Bruce, "you darned inquisitive old woman."

"He run off huntin' her, then gits hisse'f lost. Looks like now was yore time tuh cut in on his game."

"That's all you know about it," growled Bruce. "Looks like it'll be up to me to go hunt him."

"Go . . . what?"

"Hunt him. Bring him back. The damn' fool's lost."

"An' will yuh tell a man jest what's the sense in fetchin' that dude back?"

"It's not a question of sense. It's what the dude and his kind call sportsmanship. Jerry and her gang have the idea that I'm yellow. Get the idea?"

134

"Yaller, eh? Yaller. Well, I'm damned. Yaller!" Jake's voice was heavy with disgust for no man could ever call Bruce McTavish cowardly, and Jake, of all men, knew it. "When yuh start on this dude hunt, young 'un?"

"Darn soon."

"No holdin' yuh, I reckon?"

"No, Jake."

"Then I want tuh say suthin' afore yuh drift. Yuh may get killed, an' I reckon yuh orter know. That gent you shot up home never died. I knowed it, an' yore dad knowed it the night we pulled out."

"Then why did Dad let me run off like a . . . ?"

"He wanted that I should show yuh some real tough gents. Kinda to shame yuh into actin' like a man when we got back home. Ol' Angus was damn' bad scairt about yuh, son. Don't mistake that. So he give yuh a letter tuh Jim Laughlin, his ol' pardner. Yuh give Jim the letter, Bruce?"

"You know damn' well I didn't. I didn't need his help."

Jake chuckled. "Angus was hopin' yuh'd burn it. He's long-headed, is Angus. The letter was more of the test. Fact is, the letter was a sheet uh blank paper."

"Well, Jake," Bruce laughed shortly, "you sure have made a damn' fool out of me." He moved as if to rise, but Jake halted him.

"Reckon not, Bruce. Angus loves yuh, son, as few men love their kids. But he has pride, an' he wanted tuh make a real man outta yuh. Don't be too hard on us."

"Jim Laughlin and Jerry were in on the deal, too?"

135

"Shore thing. Leastways, Jim was. Angus wired him er wrote him you was comin'. None of us figgered on this mess, though. I'm hopin', son, that yuh ain't goin' tuh hold no hard feelin's about this. We was all tryin' fer yore own good."

Bruce was silent for a long time. Then he laughed softly and found Jake's hand in the dark.

"Hard feelin's, you darned old he-woman? Not by a darn sight. It's done me plenty good. Now I'll be going."

"Tuh fetch back the dude?"

"To fetch back the dude, Jake."

He moved away in the darkness.

"Good luck, Bruce." Jake's voice was a little husky. "Good luck."

CHAPTER
SIXTEEN

"Jerry Decides"

A shadow stirred in the half light of the coming dawn, the shadow of a man, creeping along the wall of the barn. A crimson shot ripped the silence, and a bullet missed the crawling shadow by a matter of bare inches.

"The danged young fool," swore Jake Raine. "He'll never make it, even if he gits his hoss. They'll kill him. All because of a dang woman that ain't worth the powder tuh blow . . ."

"Take 'er back, yuh dang varmint!" Old Lige snarled the words in the darkness of the room. "Take 'er back, er I whup yuh, here an' now! That Jerry gal's wuth ten McTavishes. Look yonder if yuh don't believe me." Lige pointed to a second shadow that moved along behind Bruce. "That's her. That's Jim Laughlin's kid. Bound and determined she was goin' with Bruce. They'll both git killed afore sunup. All because uh the moonstruck locoedness folks calls love."

"Love, eh?" Jake snorted disgustedly. "Bruce is goin' tuh fetch her dude lover back to her. What's he git, huh? A Thirty-Thirty bullet in his hide. Gone tuh fetch her pilgrim lover. What yuh haw-hawin' about, yuh ol' fool?"

"Nothin', bonehead. Only that Jerry Laughlin don't give two bits fer the lost dude, that's all."

"Then will yuh tell a man what the . . . ?"

"I'll tell yuh, directly yuh dry up. Seems like Jerry's bin stuck on Bruce McTavish fer several years, but he kinda high-toned her. It made her kinda mad, an' when that young 'un gits mad, watch out. Now he's plumb gone on her, an' she's makin' him crawl a-plenty afore she gives in an' tells him she loves him. I heered the two of 'em talkin'. Jerry tells Bruce that this Atchison dude is a better man than him. Bruce 'lows he's gonna go out an' fetch the dude home, then whup him fer gittin' lost."

"The two young fools. Danged if they ain't made it into the barn, Lige!"

For Jerry and Bruce had slid out of sight and into the black maw of the huge barn.

Bruce, crouching, led the way. Suddenly he halted, tense as a striking rattler, every nerve bristling. Some sixth sense told him that someone stood before him, there in the inky blackness. He fancied he could hear the man breathe.

Without hesitation, Bruce sprang. Arms spread, he hit the man with a low tackle that sent him sprawling. The struggle, while short, was terrific. Blows thudded. One of them grunted with pain. Horses in nearby stalls danced nervously, snorting. Then Bruce's hoarse whisper came out of the dark.

"Jerry!"

"Here." The girl's voice was a little shaky and weak.

"Bring a rope. He's out like Nellie's eye. But he sure went sweet for a minute. Hurry!"

Jerry found a rope and handed it to Bruce in the dark. Their groping hands met, clasped for a moment, then parted. Bruce grinned happily as he began tying the man's feet. Suddenly he paused.

"Something odd here, Jerry. This ain't one of the Bullard men. Cowpunchers don't wear polo boots and English breeches." He chuckled softly. "Bet a hat we've found Ethel."

"What?"

"See for yourself. Feel. Can't strike a light."

Jerry knelt beside the unconscious man. Then she laughed a little nervously.

"It's Bert, all right. But how the dickens did he . . . ?"

The unconscious man groaned, then sat up.

"Bert," Jerry whispered hoarsely.

"Jerry, old girl. I say, what happened?"

"*Shhh!* Not so loud. You had a fight."

"So I recall. But with whom? They're all gone, you know. Quite. All but Black Bart . . . the Bullard chap. I have him trussed up and locked in the grain room. Who attacked me?"

"You say they're gone?" It was Bruce who spoke.

"Ah! You, eh? I say, you're the chap who called me Ethel, what? I take it that you're the same duffer who knocked me blotto. Jolly war, eh? You won it, dash it. I don't mind shaking on it. Best man won and all that sort of rot. Shake? Right-o."

Bruce grinned in the dark as he took Atchison's hand. Theirs was the grip of clean sportsmanship.

"But what's this about them all being gone?"

"All gone, old chap. Quite. Bullard locked in the grain room. I heard them talking. They deserted, understand. Mutinied. I'd gotten loose from the cabin where the Black Bart chap had me prisoner. Luckily found my way back. I heard firing here and crept into the barn quite unseen. I was among them and heard them plan their desertion. Having an old score to settle with the Bullard person, I pounced on the duffer as he followed the others. They went off ignorant of the fact that I had effected his capture."

"But there's somebody out there in the brush," said Bruce in a low tone. "He took a shot at me."

"That's the Green fellow. The one they all deserted. He's quite alone out there and knows it. But he won't leave. Gad, how he cursed when he discovered their treachery."

"Green out there alone?" Jerry's voice was husky with emotion. "He's a killer. He'll pick off anyone who leaves the house. Something must be done, Bruce."

"Stay here a minute till I take a look." Bruce thrilled at the knowledge that she had turned to him for advice. He stepped to the door and looked across at the house. All was silent over there. No sound came from the brush that hid Pat Green, cowman and killer.

Bruce flattened himself against the inside wall of the barn from where he commanded a view of the house, yet remained hidden from Green's position. Then he whistled a signal used by Jake and himself since Bruce was a youngster. After a short pause, an answering signal came from the house.

"Hi, Jake!" he called.

"Yeah?" There was a note of relief in Jake's tone. "What's up?"

"Don't show yourself. Green's out in the brush, laying to kill somebody. The rest have pulled out."

From the brush where Green lay hidden came a string of cursing. Bruce grinned and called out again.

"We're all right out here. If we get hungry, we'll eat hay."

"Give up the dude hunt?"

"Found him here in the barn. He's got Bullard locked in the grain room."

"The hell?"

"Exactly."

"He ain't so danged harmless, after all, eh?"

"Just who," cut in Atchison, "is the complimentary chap?"

Bruce turned to face the man from the cities. He saw him smiling, there in the dim light a trifle disheveled and bruised, but withal the picture of a clean-cut sportsman.

"I reckon, Atchison, that I owe you an apology, both for myself and Jake. You're a man and a clean one. Makes me feel like a bum."

"Bum? Not at all, old chap. Quite the opposite. I say, now, what goes on?" He pointed to the figure of a man that stepped from the brush and out into the open. A gray-haired, wolf-like man, with a six-shooter dangling in his hand.

For a moment Pat Green stood there, unafraid, an old he-wolf at bay.

"I'm licked!" Green's voice cut the dawn with the clearness of a steel blade. "Whupped because my pack was skunks instead uh wolves. You got me, Jim Laughlin. Got me where yuh want me. You killed Hardin. You licked me. But if yo're any part of a man, you'll step out an' fight here in the open, man to man."

"You want the man that killed Ed Hardin?" came a grating voice from the house.

"I'd be proud tuh look at him acrost a gun barrel."

"Then I'm comin', Pat Green!"

The door of the bunkhouse opened slowly, and Jeff Frazier stepped out into the clearing, gun in hand.

"I want Laughlin." Green's voice gritted with hate.

"You want the man that killed Hardin, Green. I killed him. Want tuh know why? Because Hardin killed my brother, an' you paid him tuh do it. Lige knowed it, an' Jake knowed it, an' Lige told Jim Laughlin's gal. Lige was scared tuh tell on account uh the old charges ag'in' him an' Jake. So they kep' quiet till this row come up. Then Lige tells Jerry Laughlin, an' she makes Lige tell me. So I killed Ed Hardin, fair an' square."

"Then yo're the man I'm after."

"I'm the man, Green. Fill yore hand!"

Across a twenty-foot space two guns crashed. Green swayed in his tracks, his gun roaring again. Frazier was down, shooting from a kneeling position. The rattle of their emptying guns blended in the gray dawn.

And when their guns were empty, the souls of Pat Green and Jeff Frazier were riding together across the Great Divide.

"I say, McTavish, she's fainted, old man."

Bruce, his eyes still filled with the swift tragedy of what he had seen, turned to see Atchison, pale but holding himself in hand, with Jerry in his arms.

"Your job, old chap," he smiled gamely into Bruce's eyes. "She told me a bit ago. Said she loved you a long time. I wish you all that a man can wish another. My hand on it, Bruce McTavish."

And so the man from the East gave a girl into the keeping of the man from her own country.

That night a telegram went to Angus McTavish in Montana. It was brief and to the point and ran as follows:

Dear Dad:
Have heard the owl hoot and thereby learned a lesson. Marrying Jerry tomorrow. Checking on you for honeymoon cash. Will be home next month to work it out. I reckon that from now on, we'll both savvy each other. Love from us both.

Bruce

The Badlands Buckaroo

This short novel was Walt Coburn's only story to appear in a Fiction House magazine in October, 1930. It was published in *Action Stories* and, curiously, is one of the few short novels he wrote for this publisher that was never reprinted in a later issue of a Fiction House publication. Although there is constant forward progression in so much that he wrote, the "action" content of Coburn's fiction usually occurs only as the surface of events. What his stories so often are really about is the moral drama beneath the surface action, a drama that grips his characters and in which men and women are rewarded for the good they do and frequently destroyed, sometimes in devious, ironic, or prolonged ways, for the evil they do. Reading character, arriving at human truth, is the eternal quest that runs through so many of his stories, and it certainly was his pre-occupation here.

CHAPTER
ONE

"Brother Matthew"

His real name had been lost long since under his aliases. He had used many names in the many places where he had engaged in his various deals, none of them lawful. Just now he waited at Los Gatos with his wagon train of zealous followers, men, women and children. He told them that, when the awaited sign appeared written in the stars, he would lead them across the mountains and the desert to a city of gold. And there, in prayer and righteous living, they would await their Day of Judgment. The women all believed him. And if there were doubters among the men of his following, their biased opinion of Matthew, as he was called, had been smothered under the indignant fervor of their women.

He was a giant in stature, this self-styled prophet with a deep, resonant voice, sunken black eyes, bold features, and fiery red beard and hair that fell to his shoulders. He possessed a remarkably keen brain and a powerful personality. His sermons, however fanatical, were worth hearing, even if you did not believe.

On Fridays, which day the followers of the House of Matthew observed as their holy day, he wore a loose, white robe of rough material, girdled by a knotted rope. On his feet were sandals made of bullhide, and he carried a heavy staff. Many sun baths had given his entire body a deep bronze hue. Often, when he "meditated," he could be seen standing on some elevated rock, naked, save for a loin cloth, his powerful muscles rippling like living bronze in the sunlight.

Now Matthew and his hundred or more followers with their heavy wagons, their household goods, and their livestock waited at Los Gatos, on the edge of the Southwest desert. They waited for the sign that Matthew would see written in the stars. When the sign came, he would lead them into Mexico.

Los Gatos was divided between ridicule and pity for these followers of Matthew. Los Gatos, man and woman, knew the danger, the hardships, the heat and thirst and desolation of the desert to the south. Hardy prospectors had died out there. Cowboys gathering wild cattle in the rough hills beyond the sand wastes told grim tales of the wild Indians and renegade Mexicans and white men who dwelt in those hills. What chance, then, had this Matthew and his band of zealots? Even if God let them cross that desert, they would fall prey to the lawless men of the hills beyond.

Whatever the coming was for which Matthew waited, it was delayed in its arrival. They had been camped on the edge of Los Gatos for two weeks. And Los Gatos had fallen into the habit of strolling to the camp of Matthew of an evening to hear him preach. Saloonmen, gamblers, cowboys, desert rats — and the women of Los Gatos, good and bad, the latter making up the

148

majority — were never niggardly when the collection box was passed. Here, so figured Los Gatos, was a new form of amusement. And these people of Los Gatos were of a breed that paid for what they called amusement. These evening collections were, therefore, netting the eloquent and keen-brained, self-styled prophet an ever-increasing bankroll.

There was also the girl who played the little organ and led the choir. Ruth, they called her. When she sang, even the roughest of the rough men of Los Gatos took off their hats and listened. This girl was as beautiful as her songs — hair like flashes of spun gold, steadfast eyes of smoky gray, delicately chiseled features. The children followed her, and older women came to Ruth with their sorrows. Men respected her and trusted her with secrets they never told their wives. Even in the shapeless dresses that the women of the House of Matthew wore, Ruth was beautiful.

To Lin Rawlins from the Pecos country, this girl was the most beautiful living thing he had ever seen. Lin had drifted into Los Gatos to celebrate after a three-month roundup across the Mexican border. Lin had been working for the Circle Dot down there, gathering the remnants of an outfit they had bought from a Mexican cowman who could no longer live down there for political reasons.

Since the first night when he had pulled up his horse at the Matthew camp, pausing in wonderment at the sound of a woman, singing a song, Lin Rawlins had been a regular attendant at the evening services.

149

The bellerin' of that big red bull don't buy no chips in my game, *Lin told himself,* but I'd ride across a lot of country to hear that lady sing and just set and watch her. She's just about the nearest thing to an angel that this cowhand will ever see. But what business has a swell little lady like that got a-herdin' with that bunch of locoweeds?

The more Lin Rawlins thought it over, the more puzzled he became. He'd never gotten near enough to her even to lift his hat. She was always surrounded by a pack of kids or women, or else she was walkin' with that big red bull. Somehow Lin learned that the girl's name was Ruth. He thought that name plumb suited her. She wouldn't fit many names.

"When's the big red bull trailin' his weeds across the burnin' sands to wherever he thinks he's bound for?" Lin asked the sheriff of Los Gatos.

"Quick as he gits this here sign he's a-waitin' fer, Lin."

"What kind of sign?"

"Join up with 'em and find out. Me, I don't know."

"Even if they died off out yonder in the desert," said Lin Rawlins, "they'd be a heap better off than if they got into them Blanca Mountains beyond . . . especially the women folks." Lin's puckered blue eyes hardened as if he were remembering something he had seen.

"You boys worked down in there, didn't yuh, Lin?" the sheriff asked.

"What there was left to work for. Those jaspers have been whittlin' on the beef down there fer five, ten years.

150

Not much left worth gatherin'. What we did gather, we had to fight for. It's no place to go for pleasure."

"So they tell me. Bad as I want some uh the sons that hides out down there, I'll never be fool enough to make a pass at 'em. That ain't any man's land. I bin tryin' to find some way to keep this big, red-maned psalm-shouter from takin' this outfit down there. But my hands is tied. No law kin stop him."

"Couldn't the Mexican government keep 'em out?"

The sheriff of Los Gatos gave Lin a withering look. "Son, they got their own troubles. Another revolution in the kettle about tuh boil over, none uh the *jefes* knowin' what color ribbon tuh wear on his arm, till the fight goes one way or the other . . . Mexico hollerin' fer folks to move down there and settle the country. Nope, Mexico's willin' to let these locoweeds in, if they're fools enough tuh tackle the trip."

"It's worse than plain murder," protested Lin, "and I bet, if they get into a tight, that big red bull will be the first bunch-quitter."

"Hard tuh tell, Lin. Say, yo're takin' a almight' interest in this layout, young feller. Yuh nibble at yore likker like yo're ailin', and yore poker game is somethin' disgraceful. Are yuh gettin' religion or have yuh got a good look at the yaller-haired gal as sings them psalm songs? Dawg my cats, if yuh ain't blushin'."

"Aw, dry up." Lin grinned confusedly. They were standing in front of a saloon. Now, as a man on horseback came up the dusty street, Lin's eyes narrowed. "Well, I'll be . . . hmm."

151

The sheriff followed Lin's scowling gaze. "Know 'im, Lin? He's a stranger to me. Who is he?"

"I don't know who he is, Sheriff, but he ranges down in the Blanca Mountains, and he draws water amongst them renegades down there. He's heap bad medicine."

Lin Rawlins was not the only man who saw something familiar about the straight-backed, darkly handsome horseman who rode into Los Gatos. Matthew had also seen the horseman, and a strange glint, almost a look of fear, had come into the deep eyes of the pseudo-prophet. He was standing talking to the girl, Ruth, at the moment, and she wondered why the cult leader had left her without a word, stepping out of sight into his private tent. Then she, too, saw the man on horseback.

He was smiling queerly as he pulled up. With elaborate courtesy he lifted his big, silver-crusted Mexican sombrero. He was almost dark enough to belong to Mexico, save for a pair of steel-colored eyes and an indefinable something that labeled him as a half-caste.

"I have ridden far, *señorita*. The day has been warm, and I have tasted no water since early morning. Could I beg a dipper full of water from your pail?"

The girl, Ruth, flushed a little under his bold eyes. Without speaking, she handed him a dipper filled with water.

"You folks are traveling far?" he asked, his white teeth flashing under the slender, carefully trimmed black mustache.

"We of the House of Matthew," came her stilted reply, "are forbidden to talk with Gentiles."

"I beg your pardon, *señorita*." There was a shading of twisted mockery in his voice. "I did not know. For the water and the pleasure of looking at one so beautiful, I thank you. *Adiós*."

When he had bowed and ridden on toward the town, Matthew came out of his tent. He was scowling blackly. The girl's cheeks flamed crimson, and she picked up her pail of water. There was a sort of possessiveness about the giant's anger that confused and frightened her. He seemed about to speak, then he turned and went back into his tent.

Ruth carried the pail of water to the covered wagon where her mother, a frail woman with blue-veined hands and the eyes of a religious fanatic, sat mending one of Matthew's white robes. Time had been, perhaps, when the mother of Ruth had been beautiful, but never with that beauty that was the girl's. There was a tightness to the mother's lips, accusation in her eyes.

"You talked to that man on horseback!" she said in a voice that had long ago lost its sweetness. "You, chosen of Matthew's chosen people, talking to a Gentile! Have you no shame?"

"He asked for water, that was all." The girl's tone was quiet, respectful, but lacking in meekness. For a moment Ruth's gray eyes seemed to grow darker. Then she put the pail of water in the shade and joined the group of small children who sat in the shadow of a wagon.

Matthew joined Ruth's mother after a time. He had regained his self-composure. In passing, he had laid his hand on the heads of one or two children. When he spoke to the girl's mother, his voice purred gently. He addressed her as Rebecca. For the followers of Matthew had only given names. In many cases these names were given them by the cult leader — Biblical names, for the most part.

From another covered wagon a pair of dark, smoldering eyes had seen the little drama from its beginning. The owner of the dark eyes had passed those years so dear to every woman who dreads the approach of middle age. A handsome, rather statuesque woman, almost swarthy, almost coarse of feature, yet retaining a certain beauty. The ugly dress she wore could not hide her beautiful figure. She carried herself with a queen-liness and a panther-like sinuosity. The fires of passions had burned there in her eyes. She should have been clothed in a tight sheath of crimson silk. Her hair was as black and sleek as a crow's wing.

Now, as Matthew passed her wagon to stop at the wagon of Rebecca, the dark-eyed woman smiled twistedly. For she was Carlotta, wife of Thomas; Carlotta, who had known Matthew before ever he had become Matthew and who had loved him and been given a sort of love in return. Thomas was a man of soft flesh with a petulant, womanish mouth and weak blue eyes, the unwilling slave of Carlotta's whims and moods. He had been a manufacturing chemist of considerable means in a small town in the Middle West when Carlotta, traveling with a road show that played

"East Lynne," "Uncle Tom's Cabin," and "Ten Nights in a Bar Room," had found him and married him before his plastic ardor had had a chance to cool. Then she had persuaded him to sell out his business and join the House of Matthew. He had balked a little when it was explained that he sign over all his worldly goods to the prophet, for such was a ruling of the cult. But pitted against the fiery and bitter passion of Carlotta, Thomas had been helpless.

Now, after six months, he hated Matthew with all the flabby, weak-spined hatred of his kind. He prayed for the strength to kill the giant. Once, when he had sought solace in drink and had grown so bold as to voice that desire to Carlotta, she had ridiculed him, then had taken his flabby face in her long-fingered hands. "Perhaps some day you shall be given the chance, Thomas," she had said, and kissed him on the mouth.

CHAPTER
TWO

"Blood-Stained Gold"

Lin Rawlins nodded coldly to the rider from the Blanca Mountains as that resplendent gentleman drew rein and dismounted. The man smiled, but his steel-colored eyes held no light of warmth.

"We meet again, *señor*."

"Yeah." Lin's soft Texas drawl was unfriendly. "This time we ain't in the Blanca country, either. And you haven't your gang with you."

"That is so, *Señor Tejano*. Do you expect me, perhaps, to be afraid because I am alone?"

"Suit yourself about that. You don't look like the kind that scares easy."

"Yonder's the feed barn," said the sheriff. "There's the hotel. Hop to it."

"Thank you, *señor*." The man mounted his horse and rode down the street.

"Said his horse was tired, didn't he?" mused Lin Rawlins aloud, his eyes following the man and horse. The horse was a mahogany bay with good points, a mixture between Thorough-bred and range horse. Fast, game, tough.

"If he's come from the Blanca country, Lin, I reckon that bay geldin' is laig weary, no mistake."

156

Lin nodded. "That's where he's come from, all right, but he stopped somewhere on the way where there was feed and water."

"There's no feed, no water on that desert, Lin. That Yaqui desert country is dry as a bone."

"Just the same," argued Lin, "that man and horse have had feed and water between here and the Blanca Mountains. It proves what I've heard down there, about a well on the desert. Of course, there are some stories told down there that are hard to swallow, not only of hidden water but of lost mines, of hunks of gold, big as a man's fist, there for the taking. They say it's guarded by evil spirits of dead men that were killed there a long time ago, men who killed off a little band of *padres* that was the first to find the gold.

"I've had a hankerin' for some time now to make a hunt myself for that place. The old Indians that claim to know about it won't go near there, and they won't tell where it is. Many a desert rat that hunted for it never came back. I've seen tracks that slanted off to the westward of the main trail. Tracks of a horse that went that way and returned to the trail farther on. The heat waves hide a lot of that country to the west of the trail where the sand hills are spotted with cactus trees. Twice I've seen a mirage of a little blue lake and trees around it, upside down in the air, there to the west. I'd like to try to find that place some day."

"Better stick to punchin' cows, Lin."

Lin Rawlins grinned and took something from the pocket of his Levi's. It lay on his opened hand. A gold nugget, almost the size of a hen's egg. The sheriff gaped at it.

"Where'd yuh git it, Lin?"

"I backtracked that horse that had been ridden off westward and then back onto the trail. Along that trail I found this."

Lin's voice held the tremor of excitement that raw gold brings into the voices of men who seek it. The sheriff took and examined the nugget in nearly the shape of an egg, its surface polished smooth. So intent were the two with the bit of gold, they did not notice the stranger from the Blanca Mountains until he was almost upon them.

Lin pocketed the nugget hastily, but not before the man had seen it as it lay in the palm of the sheriff. There was a queer glitter in the steel-colored eyes of the man from Mexico. His smile was but a grimace of hate, but in the fraction of a moment he regained his composure.

"I would be pleased to have you gentlemen join me in a little drink. *Señores*, I seek no quarrel here in Los Gatos. This gentleman, who speaks with the softness of the *Tejano*, and I have met before. His impression of me is, I am afraid, none too good. And yet, *Señor Tejano*, men have fared much worse down in the hills than you and your *compañeros* found it. There are some evil men down there. When we met, *Señor Tejano*, I warned you to leave the hills, no?"

Lin grinned crookedly. "I'll say you did. And about a hundred of the ugliest-looking *hombres* I ever saw were backing your play."

The other man smiled. "They are not so handsome, those *hombres*, that is true. But there are men in the Blanca cañons who are far more ugly. Lucky for you that you met us before those wolves gathered for the attack. They would kill a man for his boots, those Blanca wolves." He smiled and shrugged. "Shall we drink, *señores?*"

At the bar the three men and the bartender stood with filled glasses.

"*¡Salud, señores!*" smiled the stranger.

"Here's how, mister," said the sheriff.

They put down their empty glasses, and the bartender pushed back the gold piece proffered by the stranger. The man smiled, as if pleased by this gesture of hospitality on the saloonman's part.

"Could we find some cool place, *Señor* Sheriff, where we might talk without interruption?"

"My office is about the coolest place in town."

"*Bueno.* It is a matter of some importance. A private matter. The *Señor Tejano* will excuse us?" There was cold mockery in the man's steel-colored eyes.

"The pleasure," grinned Lin, "is all mine."

When the sheriff and the man from Mexico had gone, the saloonman lit the cold stub of cigar he held between teeth that were mostly gold.

"Now I wonder what that son-of-a-gun is doin' here in Los Gatos? He's up to somethin' that'll stand pryin' into."

"You know him, Joe?" asked Lin quickly.

"I was in Juarez the night he shot three gents quicker than you could chalk your cue. And they was all three

159

tough birds, too. Gun runners and hop smugglers. They claimed he was crookin' 'em in a card game, though I always did think they just used that as a stall. There was somethin' else back of it. They all three jerked guns, but this smooth *hombre* got 'em all."

"Who is he, Joe?"

"I heard him called Pablo. Pablo Jones. But I don't have any notion that's his real moniker. Because, back in Colorado where he run a gamblin' house and a good 'un, he went under the name of Sanchez. Monte Sanchez. And over at Greenfield where he was in the minin' and gamblin' business, where he played 'em high, wide, and handsome and killed his pardner over some woman, his name was Jack Durango. And like as not none of them names is his real name.

"He's a gambler and a killer. Cold blooded as a fish and quick as greased lightnin' with a gun. He's killed men from the Yukon to Juarez, and killed 'em all in fair fights. I'll bet a new hat he recognized me, though he never was any hand to line up at a bar, and never took notice of us boys behind the mahogany. But we all knowed who he was, and that he was a good gent to let alone.

"He's a high roller, Lin. Whatever his game is, it's no Piker's layout. He used to pack around a gold nugget big as a hen's egg as a lucky piece. He'd lay it alongside his chips. In Goldfield one night I seen him turn down a plenty big roll of yellow-backed bills that a San Francisco gambler offered for that egg."

A look of disappointment clouded Lin's eyes. He reckoned now the nugget that he had used to conjure up visions of fabulous gold mines was just this gambler's lucky piece that he had dropped.

Lin laid the big nugget on the bar. "This it, Joe?"

The man behind the bar examined the nugget. He got a magnifying glass that he had probably carried in his travels from the boom towns he had been in during their heyday. Under its powerful lens he studied the gold egg. Then he handed the glass to Lin.

Under the magnifying glass, Lin could make out minute letters that had been engraved on the nugget. Time and the friction of years had all but obliterated the lettering. No whole word remained. Lin handed back the glass to the bartender.

"Some said it was the Lord's Prayer he had on the egg," explained Joe. "Others claimed it was the location of a lost mine that only he knowed about. While still more used to say he tallied on it the names of the men he had killed. Nobody knew for certain, and now whatever was on there has bin rubbed off from packin' it around. But where the devil did you get hold of it, Lin?"

"I found it between here and the Blanca country. Thought I'd run into something that spelled gold. Dog-gone the luck. Well, being as it's his lucky piece, he's welcome to it. Me, I pack a rabbit's foot, which is a heap lighter in a man's pocket than this. Yonder he comes from the sheriff's office."

The ornately garbed man from the Blanca Mountains came into the saloon. Lin held out the gold egg.

"Joe tells me this is yours, mister."

161

The gambler took it, an odd light in his eyes, as those eyes probed the cowboy's face with a cold scrutiny. Suspicion was in that stare. Then he smiled.

"For many years I carried this. It was stolen from me in El Paso, more than a year ago. For its return, señor, I am more deeply in your debt than you can ever know. Is there some way in which I may reward you?"

"I reckon not. I found it out on the desert." Somehow Lin thought that the man lied about the nugget's having been stolen.

"The thief who stole it must have lost it there." The stranger opened his shirt and showed a buckskin sack hung about his neck by a thong. Into this sack he dropped the egg. The buckskin fitted it like a sheath. Now he looked searchingly at the bartender, nodded, and smiled. "Our trails have crossed before, no? Several times. And each time you have known me by a different name, no? When a man has many enemies, it is well to change the name often and be always moving. Señores, amigos, I ask you to have a drink with Keno Kinkaid. Oddly enough, Kinkaid was also the name of my father. It is the name carved on his headstone down there in Mexico where he was murdered.

"This egg-shaped nugget was part of the gold that cost him his life. On it was once engraved the names of the men who banded together to rob him of his hidden mine and kill him. They killed him, but they did not find the mine. Their names are no longer visible on the nugget. Time has rubbed out their names, even, señores, as my gun has rubbed out their scurvy lives. ¡Salud, señores!"

CHAPTER
THREE

"Gun-Toting Pilgrims"

It was some time after the evening services, some time after midnight but before dawn, that Matthew saw the awaited sign that was to be written in the stars. Since Matthew had seen the man who called himself Keno Kinkaid, he had been strangely upset. He had suggested to Rebecca, mother of Ruth, that perhaps it would be better, after all, if he and Ruth be bonded in marriage before they began the journey across the desert.

"I have chosen Ruth to be my wife, the mother of my children. As I have told all of you, the command was given me in a vision that came to me one night on a mountain top after a period of fasting and prayer and meditation. There is no reason for further delay. We can be married according to the laws of the House of Matthew, here at Los Gatos. After the evening services, you and Ruth and I shall climb to the top of that hill yonder. You, Rebecca, mother of Ruth, shall give her into my care forever. I shall pronounce the words that forever bind us. The others need know nothing about it until we begin our journey across the desert to our land of promise."

Rebecca was vastly pleased and flattered that Ruth should be so chosen. Her eyes were bright with a zealot's joy.

"You have spoken to Ruth?"

"No. I leave that most pleasant duty for you, Rebecca. You shall tell her."

He smiled down at the woman, and whatever was in his heart, he hid behind that smile. He flattered himself that he could handle these fools who had given him their all and followed him like sheep wherever he chose to lead them. The only rebel among them was Carlotta. Carlotta, who had known him in days long past. There were times when Carlotta became unruly. Matthew had racked his brain for means to rid himself of her and the soft-muscled Thomas. He had their money, even as he had the money that belonged to all the others. That money was safely banked under a certain name, waiting to be withdrawn by him when he returned from this journey across the desert.

Matthew planned to return. With him he would bring Ruth. They alone would return across the desert. So he had written it into his scheme of things. Somewhere, in some distant land, he and Ruth would live on. And the desert would forever hold the terrible secret of that journey's end.

It must be said for Matthew that the man, like so many another good actor, had been carried away by his own flowing words. He hoped to find, beyond that desert, a fertile land where these poor, ignorant folk could find some measure of happiness. True, there lay a fertile country beyond — green valleys with an abundance of water, farm lands, waiting the plow. The Mormon church had a colony down there somewhere. He had heard of it. A substantial village with solid brick buildings, streets, farms where fruit grew in abundance. A farmer's paradise. Cattle and horses, grazing on land that cost a few cents an acre to lease.

The followers of the House of Matthew could build a similar colony. He would stay with them long enough to see them settled. Then he would put Ruth in his light rig, to which would be hooked a span of stout mules. And they would return to Los Gatos. And from Los Gatos they would travel on.

Matthew left Rebecca and strolled through the camp, pausing now and then to talk to the men and women. Past the edge of camp he found a secluded spot where no one was likely to come upon him. And here he sat down. He was clad in the conventional garb of the frontier. Boots and corduroy and flannel shirt, though he wore no hat. Sitting here, he carefully examined two small Derringer pistols, then shoved the twin weapons back into his pockets.

From behind the screen of nearby brush came a woman's soft laugh. Matthew scowled as Carlotta stepped into view.

"Expecting trouble, Matt?"

"What are you doing here?" he growled.

"Keeping an eye on the prophet. Something tells me that he'll stand watching. You may be able to bunco these poor yokels that think you're some kind of a tin god, but I 'knew you when,' Brother Matthew. And I smell the sign of the old double-cross. You've stalled me

165

about long enough. You've trimmed these suckers, and you've cleaned up a traveling stake from the collection box at the evening shows. I'm sick of livin' in a wagon, sick of watchin' you soft soap these poor saps, sick of your so-called sermons. And I'm more than sick of watchin' you spread your trap for that blonde-headed gal. Tommy is like a kid that's lost his marbles, and I feel sorry for him. He may be just another sucker to you, but he's kinder to me than any man ever was."

Matthew smiled and reached out to take her hand. She stepped back, her lips curling with scorn.

"No, you don't, Matt. That's out. This is gonna be a cold business proposition between you and me. I did my part in ballyhooin' this show. I helped get these suckers to follow you. I even talked Tommy into droppin' his pile into the jackpot. And you promised me a cut of the proceeds. I want what Tommy and I put into this. And I want my cut of what these suckers dropped into the pot. Then I'm takin' Tommy to Paris where we can see how the other half of the world gets by. Gimme, brother. Kick through. There's a train that leaves here tomorrow, and I'm gonna be on it. No desert picnics for me. Pay me off, deacon."

Matthew smiled and stroked his red beard. "When I get back to my tent, Lottie, I'll write you out a check. You can take your precious Thomas and fade away."

"Your check? You think I'd be sap enough to take a check signed by you? It's green money I want, and it'll be green money I get."

"Be sensible, Lottie. You don't think I'm packin' around a hundred thousand dollars in my pocket. I swear my check's good."

"Swear your head off, Brother Matthew. I wouldn't believe you under any kind of oath, if you swore it on every Bible ever made and threw in the Koran and the Chinese Proverbs. Green money, brother, or I'll tell these nuts who you are. I'll blow you up right and . . . God! Don't! Don't kill me!"

His face suffused with terrible anger, Matthew's strong hands gripped the woman's throat. A grin spread across his bearded mouth. Though she fought like a wildcat, her strength was a puny thing against the giant leader of the House of Matthew. He forced her to her knees, grinning down at her twisted face. Then his fingers relaxed their terrible grip. Carlotta crouched, her hands against her bruised throat. Fear was in her eyes now.

"You'll do as I say," smiled Matthew. "You'll take what I choose to give you. And no matter what you told these fools, they wouldn't believe you. Remember this, and don't let it slip your mind. That if you do any funny talking, I'll finish the job I just left off. Get that?"

"I get yuh, you big bum. I get yuh, plenty." The woman was on her feet now, and the fear was fading from her dark eyes. "Pick up the marbles, Matt. You win. I bet you can lick any woman or sick man around here, can't yuh? But some of these days you'll meet some man that's half your size, and you'll dog it like a yellow cur.

167

"Touch me again, you big tramp, and I'll begin yellin'. And they'll hear me over there at town. And what these cowboys would do to a big bum like you for hurtin' a woman would be plenty. They'd swap you a coat of tar and feathers for that white bathrobe you sport around. And the House of Matthew would lose its tin god. Back away from me, you big ham."

Matthew stepped back. Within shouting distance was the town. And in the blazing eyes of Carlotta was a desperate sort of courage. He turned away and strode angrily back to camp. For a long moment Carlotta stood there. Then she sank to the ground and sobbed brokenly, her body quivering as if under the lash.

CHAPTER
FOUR

"A Hot-Headed Prophet"

It was at the close of Matthew's evening services that the man who called himself Keno Kinkaid, who had listened to the preaching and to Ruth's singing, stepped quietly up to the white-robed cult leader.

"I will wait for you, *Señor* Matthew, at your tent, no?"

Matthew had prepared for this meeting. Yet his eyes shifted fearfully about and his face was a little white under its bronze.

"*Shh*. Not my tent. At the big tree below the camp."

"That suits me, *señor*."

Keno Kinkaid's white teeth were bared in a cold smile. He walked away, humming softly under his breath.

Five minutes later Matthew, his robe changed for conventional clothes, faced the gambler.

"Well, Sanchez?" he growled, "what do you want of me?"

"The name is Keno Kinkaid . . . no longer Sanchez. What is it I want of you? I have not decided that. Keep the hands out of the pockets, *mi amigo*, or you will force me into an unpleasant task. That is better.

"Now, *señor*, you shall talk, and I will be a good listener. You are going to tell me just what this game is that you play with these people who think you are some sort of priest who is to lead them to Utopia. I take it for granted that they are not aware of the fact that you are a swindler, a sneak thief, a cheater, and a murderer.

"Easy, *hombre*, or I shall shoot you just the same as I would shoot a mad beast. The hands where I can watch them, always. Now, tell me about this graft game you are playing."

"Blast you, Sanchez, name your price and I'll pay it!" gritted the big man.

"Did I mention a price?" The gambler's voice lost something of its softness. "If I have a price, *señor*, no man has ever found it. Granted that I have one, it would run into figures that no man of your small caliber can meet. Talk, red one."

Matthew talked, his voice having dropped to little more than a whisper. For almost an hour he talked while the other man listened. And though the night was not warm, the prophet kept mopping sweat from his forehead. Always those cold, steely eyes of Keno Kinkaid watched the other man, there in the moonlight, reading every changing expression on the bearded face.

After an uneasy silence, Keno Kinkaid spoke: "What of the girl who sings? The girl you call Ruth? You say you are taking these pilgrims to a land of promise. That, when they are located, you will return to the States. Providing they find this fabled, promised land and you return, do you return alone?"

170

For a long moment the eyes of the two men gripped and held. Then Matthew's eyes fell under the intent gaze of the gambler. His voice was barely audible when he spoke. "Yes."

Keno Kinkaid smiled contemptuously. "You are a bigger coward than I thought, my red one. You have not even the guts to fight for the woman you want." He rose from where he sat and brushed the leaves and dust from his clothes. "We leave in the morning, señor."

"We?" echoed Matthew.

"I am going along with you. Charmed by your eloquence, I am joining this House of Matthew."

"You . . . you join us? You can't! These people would suspect something queer if I took a man like you into the House. You, a gambler, a killer, an adventurer!"

"And you a sneak thief, a robber of women, and a murderer." The gambler smiled. "What of you?"

Matthew groaned, his big hands clenching and unclenching.

Kinkaid spoke again. "I repeat, señor, I was quite over-whelmed by your eloquence. And by the most beautiful voice of the young lady you call Ruth. I have, so you shall tell your flock, gotten religion. Buenos noches, Señor Red One."

Matthew walked with dragging steps back to the camp. There was a light burning in the covered wagon that belonged to the girl, Ruth, and her mother. Matthew paused there. His voice sounded hoarse and unnatural when he called softly.

Rebecca, tight-lipped, strained-looking, stepped down from the wagon.

"Ruth has been carrying on like she's lost her senses, Matthew. But I made her put on her wedding robe."

"I have been meditating, Rebecca. That is what has so delayed me. A voice has told me that the wedding must be postponed. There, there, Rebecca. Do not weep. We must obey that stronger voice. I go now to look for the sign that will be written in the stars."

He planted a bearded kiss on the woman's forehead and gently pushed her, weeping, back into the wagon. Then he strode quickly away, his big fists knotted, his lips moving in soundless words that had little to do with prayer.

At the sunrise prayer, Matthew announced to them that he had at last seen the sign written in the stars. They would start right after breakfast on their journey to the land of promise.

The loud hallelujahs, the shouting, and rejoicing awakened Los Gatos. One of the men of the House of Matthew, Thomas to be exact, brought the tidings to the townspeople. Thomas had slipped into the saloon by way of the side door. After he had gulped down several big whiskies, he gave Joe, Lin Rawlins, the sheriff, and several other men the news.

"We'll all die out there on that desert. Matthew will be our murderer as sure as if he used a gun to kill us. God, is there no way to stop him?"

"Yo're free, white, and of age," said the sheriff bluntly, annoyed by the man's blubbering. "There's no law that kin make yuh foller him."

"He's got all my life's savings!" wailed Thomas, thus violating by his confession his oath to the House of Matthew. "Then, there's the wife. She's set on following this man, even out there across that hot desert. I never could stand heat. The summers back in Iowa used to nigh prostrate me. Give me another drink."

Nobody noticed Lin Rawlins slip out the door. He made his way to the stable where he found Keno Kinkaid, saddling his splendid bay horse.

"Good morning, señor."

"Leavin' us, Kinkaid?"

"There is nothing to keep me here. We will meet again, perhaps?"

"You never can tell."

"Adiós, señor."

"So long, Kinkaid."

When the gambler had ridden away, Lin saddled his horse, a rangy dun, and rode over to the camp. He found Matthew without difficulty — Matthew and, to Lin's surprise, Keno Kinkaid. The gambler smiled thinly.

"We meet so soon, señor."

Matthew looked up at the cowboy, his bushy brows scowling.

"I rode over to see if these folks didn't need a wrangler for their loose stock, or mebby a guide."

"We have our men," was Matthew's curt reply.

"They're all pilgrims, though," said Lin, "and kind of weakish-looking. I'd be proud to get a job with you."

"We hire no Gentiles."

"I think," said Keno Kinkaid, still smiling, "that you could make this an exception. Rawlins knows the trail. He just came from down there. I would make the suggestion, *Señor* Matthew, that you hire this man." And the gambler's cold eyes mocked the head of the House of Matthew.

"Very well. But you will camp apart from us. You will hold no conversation with any man, woman, or child here. Is that understood?"

"Sure thing," Lin agreed. "I'll go back to town and get my bed and pack horse."

"We ride back together, *señor*. I forgot a message I meant to leave with the sheriff."

When they had ridden beyond earshot of the camp, Kinkaid looked at Lin with hard eyes that seemed to read the cowboy's thoughts. "Remember, *señor*," he smiled mirthlessly, "you talk to no man, no child . . . no *woman* of this pilgrim party."

Lin's jaw muscles tightened. "Just what have you got to say about it, Kinkaid?"

"I am one of the House of Matthew. I joined last night. And Matthew has given me authority to act in such matters. You'll take orders from me, *señor*, or you'll remain here in Los Gatos. Do we now understand one another, *Señor* Rawlins?"

"Plumb." Lin's blue eyes were as hard as those of the gambler. His smile matched Kinkaid's for coldness.

They rode on in silence. Kinkaid went to the sheriff's office. Lin caught his pack horse and led it around to the cabin where he had been staying with two other cowboys. He was glad they were not there to hooraw him. It was Lin's intention to slip out of town without seeing anyone he knew. But in this he was defeated. Before he had the bed loaded on his pack horse, the sheriff came up.

"Just in time to help me throw this diamond hitch, Sheriff."

"Yeah. And likewise in time to tell yuh what a danged fool yo're a-makin' of yorese'f, herdin' with them weedies. All because a gal with yaller hair sings songs. Now don't git hot under the collar, Lin. I knowed you when you was knee high to a burro. I'd hate tuh see yuh murdered out yonder."

"Murdered?"

"Exactly."

"Listen, Sheriff, that big red bull may beller loud, but he don't look no way dangerous."

"No? How about this Kinkaid gent? I reckon you kin take on ten like him before breakfast?"

"Kinkaid's dangerous," admitted Lin.

"Yeah. And Kinkaid is the man yuh'd have to be watchin'. The way I figger this, him and this Matthew gent is pardners. Kinkaid rides here from the Blanca country. What for? Matthew has bin hangin' around here, waitin' for the sign to start. Directly Kinkaid shows up, Matthew 'lows he's seen his sign in the stars. Them two has met before. They're in on this together. And God he'p them pore, ignorant folks that follers them two crooks into the desert, on into the Blanca Mountains."

"All the more reason, then, why I'd better trail along with the spread."

"What kin you do against them two? Kinkaid's a killer and a bad 'un, so Joe tells me. He's got friends down in that country. If it's the yaller-haired gal yuh want, forgit it. She ain't the kind as 'ud make a good wife fer a roamin' cowboy. She don't talk our kind uh language, son. She's got her sights lined on heaven while you don't know no more about religion than I know about shearin' sheep. Draw outta this fool game, Lin. Go git on a drunk and forgit it."

Lin shook his head. "No can do. I've drawn cards, and I'll play 'em, even if they've cold-decked me."

"Yo're a plumb fool, Lin."

"You ain't the first man to tell me that, sheriff. Help me get this hitch tied, will you?"

"Just one thing more, first. Kinkaid had a medicine talk with me yesterday . . . about a gold mine out there on the desert. A lost gold mine. The same lost mine that yuh talked about. He claims it belonged to his father and that it is his now, providin' he can locate it exactly. His father, knowin' that he was follered, hid the map before they killed him. Now this Keno Kinkaid thinks that somebody has found the map and is goin' after the gold. And while he never come out flat-footed and said so, I think he figgers that yo're the gent that found the map. Lin, that son will kill yuh if ever yuh go back down there. I reckon he seen yuh show me that gold egg and that give him the idea that yuh had the map. And I wouldn't be su'prised if he thought me and you was in cahoots on the deal.

176

"Joe said he acted danged queer when yuh give him the gold egg. Told a scary yarn about killin' the men as killed his daddy, and so on. Lin, yuh loco fool, stay outta that country down there. You'll git killed."

"A man can die only once," grinned Lin. "Here, catch the end of this rope."

"Fool!" grumbled the sheriff, and grabbed the rope.

CHAPTER
FIVE

"Sands of Peril"

Dust. Thirst. A blazing sun in a cloudless sky. The creak of wagons, the rattle of chain harness, the cry of a feverish child. The wagon train of the House of Matthew was crawling across the sand wastes.

Their leader, in his canvas-topped buckboard drawn by stout, grain fed mules, was in the vanguard of the train, although ahead of his rig rode Keno Kinkaid and Lin Rawlins, side by side. Matthew's brooding eyes followed them as they piloted the way across that tortuous sand waste. In the cult leader's mind was the conviction that the two pilots were together in their plan to rob him of everything — his power, his wealth, his life.

The last wagon in the train was that of Carlotta and Thomas. Defeated in her attempt to get money from Matthew, Carlotta was determined to follow along, hoping in her desperation that something would give her the advantage over the red-bearded giant whom she had once loved but now hated. Thomas nibbled furtively at his bottle.

"Get as tight as you please, Tommy dear," she smiled grimly, "but keep your yap shut."

"We're ridin' to our own funeral," he moaned.

178

Something heavy slid from his pocket to the bottom of the wagon. He retrieved it hastily, but Carlotta had seen the thing.

"Where'd you get the cannon, Tommy?"

"I bought it off the bartender at Los Gatos."

"Ever shoot a gun?"

"No, but I won't miss, because I'll be close to him, and he's big."

"Give Mama the pistol, dearie. You'd just get yourself in a mess with it. Is it loaded?"

"I didn't notice."

"As an assassin, you're a good chemist. Stick to your test tubes and pill rolling, baby." She took the gun. "Just as I thought, the thing's empty. And I bet you didn't buy any cartridges."

"I never thought about the silly cartridges, Lottie."

"Of course you didn't, Tommy. Well, I'll borrow a few from that cowboy with the nice eyes."

"The one with the silver on his hat?" Thomas's tone flamed with jealousy.

"Heavens, no. The younger one. He's on the level. That black-haired sample of the Mexican fashion plate looks like a snake to me. And he has something on . . . well, take another drink, Tommy, and then have a nap. Mama will skin these mules."

"Matthew will raise a fuss if he finds you talking to that cowboy."

"He won't catch me, Tommy dear."

"How about swinging across there, Rawlins?" the gambler asked, smiling crookedly.

"You savvy this country better than I do, Kinkaid. Is there water out there?"

"You know there's water there, *mi amigo*. Because you've camped there."

"I reckon you've got me mixed up with somebody else, mister. I've been about five miles in that direction, and it was dry as a rock."

Kinkaid smiled and shrugged his trim shoulders. "You knew, did you not, that this wagon train had no chance of ever crossing the desert by following the main trail? Twenty miles a day is good time for the wagons in the sand. And it's fifty miles by the trail to the first water. A good horse, traveling at night, can pack a man across. But a wagon train like this, starting in the morning and traveling in the heat of the day, could never make it. You knew that?"

"I figgered 'er thataway."

"Then why did you think we'd keep on to certain death, *mi amigo?*"

"I figured that, when they saw how hopeless it was, we could mount the layout on their mules and herd 'em back to Los Gatos."

"I would like to believe that, *señor*," smiled the gambler coldly.

"Kinkaid," said Lin Rawlins grimly, "it doesn't matter a hoot to me, one way or the other, whether you believe me or if you don't. I came along with this locoed outfit to try and save these kids and women from dying out here. I don't trust that big red bull. He's about as big a crook as ever took the last dollar from a widow. I think I heap savvy his game. And if I'm right, killing is too good for him. But if he tries out anything raw, killing is what he'll get."

"Ah! And is it all women and children, or perhaps just one, that the *Señor* Rawlins so champions?"

"One in particular, Kinkaid, but likewise the others."

"An honest reply, *señor*. So I shall also lay my cards on the table. I am also interested in this one lady. And to a certain extent, likewise interested in keeping the others from a horrible death on this desert. So I suggest that we turn westward."

The two rode back to the train. Matthew looked at them from under scowling brows. "Well?" he growled.

"We turn to the westward here," said Kinkaid.

A glint of suspicion crossed the cult leader's eyes.

"Why?" he asked harshly.

"Because I do not stomach the sight of fools dying of thirst out here. There's water where I'll take you. And at the end of the trail there is your land of promise that you've lied to them about."

"It's a trap" rasped Matthew. "A damnable trap. We'll stay on the main trail!"

"Listen, my red one," said Kinkaid, and his hand was on his pearl-handled gun as he spoke. "You'll follow me, or I'll kill you where you sit. I'm dealing this game. Do you fully understand what I mean, my red one?"

"Yes. You mean to murder us all."

"You wrong me, my red one. The *Señor Dios* has sent you a pilot who leads your pilgrims to their land of promise. I have killed, yes. But I have never done a murder. And I have never killed a child or a woman. Can you say as much, *señor*?"

181

Matthew threw up one arm as if to ward off a blow.

Kinkaid laughed softly. "Follow us, my red one."

Now, as the wagon train quit the trail, Kinkaid rode back along the wagons to tell them that they would camp on water before sundown. And that they might make free use of the water in the barrels they had filled before leaving Los Gatos. Rebecca eyed the resplendent Kinkaid with open suspicion and animosity, but Ruth favored him with a furtive smile of thanks.

Kinkaid rode on down to the last wagon. His news brought an incredulous smile to the red lips of Carlotta.

"You wouldn't fib to an old trouper, would you, handsome?"

Kinkaid chuckled. Carlotta spoke a language he could understand. "Lady," he said, lifting his hat, "I wouldn't lie to you on a bet. If we are not camped on water by sundown, the followers of the House of Matthew may hang me to the nearest limb."

Carlotta looked out at the treeless desert and smiled. "That is a safe statement, brother."

Thomas, awakened by voices, poked his head out. His eyes were bloodshot and his sparse hair awry. "Oh, it's you. Have a li'l' drink?"

"It might help."

"Better ride around behind the wagon, then," suggested Carlotta. "Matthew doesn't believe in likker."

"No?" Kinkaid smiled. Carlotta winked broadly.

"I don't want to rob you," said the gambler, as Thomas passed the bottle through the opening at the rear.

"Plenty more where it came from. I loaded up before I started. Like I tells Lottie, if I'm going to die out here, I'll die happy. Where's the big false alarm leadin' us now?"

"To the land of milk and honey, *señor*."

"Beer and pretzels would suit me better. Have another snort. What's the name?"

"Kinkaid. Keno Kinkaid."

"Ever hear of Zingo? Cures corns, dandruff, hay fever, toothache, rheumatism, and eczema. Ever hear of it?"

"Many times," lied Kinkaid.

"I make it. That is, I used to make it, till Lottie talked me into selling out and traveling with this circus. Yes, sir, I'm the man who found that marvelous formula. Got a case of it with me, too. I'll give you a bottle if you drop around this evenin'. Sniff it, drink it, or rub it on. Greatest thing ever put on the market. My life's work, sir. And I sold it to follow that red-headed windbag out here." Thomas sniffed. Tears welled in his pale eyes.

Kinkaid made a hasty excuse and rode off. "At any rate," he mused, smiling, "there are two human beings in this band of sheep. Zingo. His life's work. The poor sucker."

That evening, an hour before sundown, Kinkaid led them to a small lake fringed with gnarled mesquite trees, the largest Lin had ever seen.

CHAPTER
SIX

"Prowler's Lead"

Lin spread his bed some distance from the main camp. He turned his pack horse into the cavvy of mules and horses belonging to the followers of Matthew. His dun saddle horse, that he called Yellowhammer, he staked where there was fairly decent feed. Then he made a little fire and started his supper of bacon and coffee and bread.

While he was some distance away, the voices of Matthew, Kinkaid, and the others came to him clearly. One of the men had come upon some human bones, half buried in the sand. The others were jabbering excitedly. Now the cold, sinister voice of the gambler cut through their chatter like a steel blade.

"If you'll hunt further, *mis amigos*, you will no doubt find plenty more bones. More than one luckless *hombre* has died here. This water hole is not always here. Now it is filled. Tomorrow, the next day, it may be empty. Why? *¿Quíen sabe?* It vanishes. Then, in a day, or a week, or perhaps in six months, it will again be filled as if by some magic hand."

"But the skeletons?"

"Are those who found the water hole empty."

"It was not thirst that killed this man," said Matthew's deep voice. "Look at this skull. A bullet hole between the eye sockets. This man was murdered."

"Murdered?" Kinkaid's voice was edged with grim mockery. "Might it not have been that he was a second slower than some other man, no?"

Lin Rawlins grinned to himself. This Kinkaid sure had a way of putting things. His last remark had silenced Matthew and the others.

As the bacon sizzled in the skillet, Lin turned over in his mind all the strange stories he had ever heard about this water hole that vanished and reappeared. Stories of the gold that was within a day's march of this water hole. Of men who had died searching for it. Grisly tales, to be sure. And there were other yarns more sinister. How men who had found gold had fought to the death for it. Black murder. Duels that ended in red death. Even now a buzzard swung like a black speck against the evening sky, as if waiting for death to feed him.

Plainly, Keno Kinkaid had been here before. And the gambler was of the opinion that Lin had likewise visited this water hole. Memory of the sheriff's warning made Lin's eyes harden as he watched the gambler now. It was not yet dusk, and he could see Kinkaid, talking to the girl, Ruth, who had gone for a pail of water. Lin could also see the towering Matthew, standing apart from the couple, a menacing figure blocked out against the tinted sky.

If gold was near here, Lin wondered why Kinkaid had deliberately led this wagon train so close to the

185

precious stuff, thus risking the chance that someone might stumble upon the lost mine. What was Kinkaid's purpose in bringing them here, anyhow? The gambler had spoken of a fertile land beyond this place. Had he lied? Or was there, in fact, a fairer land beyond those ragged peaks that now, in the approaching twilight un-marred by the heat waves, looked almost within arm's reach?

What lay beyond those peaks? Lin had never talked to any man who had ever been there and returned. It was part of the Yaqui country and unsafe for white men, so he had always thought. Still, it was not improbable that there could be fertile valleys and flowing water there. Lin had seen spots like that in Mexico. But what was Keno Kinkaid's game? *Whatever he's up to*, decided Lin, *it's no good*.

At the main camp, Kinkaid deliberately blocked Ruth's return to her wagon.

"It is not fair, *señorita*, that one so beautiful should be doing a man's work. Those most beautiful hands were never meant to harness mules and carry water and split wood. Are there no men to do those chores?"

"I do not mind, sir. I've . . . grown used to it."

"I savvy. At home, before you joined this fools' journey, you did not do this heady work?"

"I was at school. A convent, where my father had sent me." Her gray eyes clouded.

The day had been a most trying one. Her mother had wept and fretted and complained of the heat and dust and discomfort. Rebecca had been most bitterly disappointed last night. As for Ruth, she had silently prayed to God because she had been saved from Matthew. Her nerves were frayed now. She was afraid, and that fear had opened her eyes to things she had not noticed before.

"Where is your father, Ruth?"

"Dead. If he were alive, we would not be here, Mother and I. And only because my mother threatened suicide, if I did not come with her, I am here."

"You do not hold with the teachings of our Matthew, then?"

"I?" The girl's lips twisted in scorn. "No, I do not believe in that man. My father was a Catholic, and I was brought up in that true faith, in spite of my mother's protests. No, I don't believe in Matthew. Nor would my mother, if she were in her right mind. She has never been quite sane since my father was killed. The shock of his death unbalanced her mind."

"And so she was a ready victim for Brother Matthew's sales talk, no?"

"She was almost eager to believe. She'd taken up spiritualism, dabbled in two or three other cults, and Matthew's show appealed to her. I was away studying music. A telegram brought me home. Imagine how I felt when she told me she'd signed over every blessed thing we owned to this Matthew, and that we were about to join his band and journey to some distant Utopia." Ruth's laugh was pitifully bitter.

She had allowed Kinkaid to take the pail of water from her hand. The hardness was gone from the gambler's eyes. He looked down at her, smiling a little.

"Would you trust me, *señorita?*" he asked gently.

The girl looked at him for a long moment, smiled faintly, and shook her head. "I'm afraid not."

Kinkaid smiled and shrugged his shoulders. "An honest answer, *señorita*, and a wise one to come from a little convent girl."

"I've been around a little," she said. "I went with my dad a lot, vacation time. He had a string of race horses. We made the different race meets. Sometimes we had money and lived like millionaires. Sometimes we slept in the stable, and I'd pawn my jewelry to pay for oats and hay. While mother stayed home, trying the convince the neighbors that Dad was a traveling man. Well, he was. He traveled high, wide, and, at times, handsome. I'll take my pail of water now and be on my way. Before Mother throws a fit. I've unburdened my load of troubles, and it's done me a world of good. Had to tell someone, or go mad. Many thanks."

"Can't I carry the water?" he asked, a new understanding of the girl puzzling him more than a little.

"That's against the rules and regulations, I believe. The women of the House of Matthew do the work. He's been standing over there, scowling for the past ten minutes. Sometimes I'm afraid of him. Other times I merely despise him."

She made a wry face and walked toward her wagon with the pail of water. Kinkaid smiled after her, then walked over to Matthew.

"Damn you, Sanchez," growled the giant in an undertone, "keep away from that girl."

"You forget, my red one, that my name is Keno Kinkaid and that, if you do not wish to die very sudden, you take the orders from me. And it is you, *hombre*, who must keep away from the *señorita*."

He turned and walked off, whistling softly.

Thomas signaled, and Kinkaid walked over that way. Thomas, quite tipsy, thrust a bottle into his hand. The bottle was adorned with a bright yellow label that described the benefits of Zingo, the wizard cure-all.

"Step behind the wagon," whispered Thomas, "and we'll hoist one. Saw you talkin' to the little Ruth lady. Careful, brother, or Matthew will raise the devil with you. Join us, Lottie?"

"Get some ice and ginger ale, Tommy, and I might. It takes a better man than me, Gunga Din, to lap that stuff straight when it's been a hot day like this." She was fussing over her campfire.

"Have supper with us, handsome?" she asked carelessly.

"I will, and thank you, *señora*. I was wondering where I'd eat."

"Straight up or over?" she asked briskly.

"Excuse me?"

"The eggs, dearie, the eggs?"

Kinkaid smiled. "Straight up, please."

"Don't mind Lottie," apologized Thomas. "She got her manners off the vaudeville stage."

"I don't mind her. Not a bit. Where does Matthew eat?"

"With the queen bee," said Lottie. "Rebecca, mother of the Ruth sketch. The skinny dame with a map that'd sour fresh cream. But there I go, gettin' catty. But I should worry. She gives me nothin' but dirty digs. Whew, this smoke! And I thought I had a tough break when we played one-night, tank-town stands.

"Tommy, wean yourself away from that bottle long enough to bring mother a pail of water, that's a sweet boy. And don't fall down on the way back. Or don't invite any of those human worms over for a shot of corn juice. Not till dark, anyhow. Then you can coax 'em into temptation. Wouldn't it put a sty on Matt's eye if they'd all get soused enough to tackle 'Sweet Adeline'?"

Kinkaid chuckled. Thomas, weaving a somewhat erratic course, was on his way after water. Lottie looked up from her cooking.

"If it ain't a lodge secret, what's on the other side of them hills?"

"Green grass, water, orchards, a truck garden gone to weeds. Some adobe buildings. A vineyard. The crumbling walls of an old mission built two or perhaps three hundred years ago. And not a human being to dispute your right to colonize the land."

"Honest Injun?"

"Honest Injun," nodded Kinkaid. "The *padres* were massacred. The Mexicans and Indians claim the place is haunted and won't go near it. That, *señora*, is what lies across the mountains, though few white men know it. A garden spot, already planted. A year of cultivation and it will be beautiful."

"Give me the big city, thanks."

★   ★   ★

190

It had grown dusk now. The campfires scattered through the mesquite patches were orange spots against a purple-black background. There sounded the sharp crack of a rifle.

Kinkaid fell backwards, rolled over and over into shelter, his six-shooter spitting fire. Women screamed in terror. Men were shouting. Then the shooting stopped, as suddenly as it had commenced.

Kinkaid quit his shelter of the wagon and, gun in hand, walked toward the huddled form of a man that lay at the edge of a mesquite clump. For a moment he squatted beside the still form. His hands searched the dead man's pockets with swift thoroughness. A close observer would have seen him slip something he had taken from the dead man into his own pocket.

He was standing erect, coolly reloading his gun, as Lin Rawlins, Matthew, and some of the others came up. Matthew held a lantern in his hand. He shifted it so that its rays fell on the dead man's upturned face.

For a long moment the cult leader stared at the dead man's face. He looked pale and a little frightened as he faced Kinkaid, who smiled thinly. Lin saw that the dead man was a stranger here among these people. A bearded, heavily armed, rough-looking man. There was a carbine still gripped in his hands. Across Kinkaid's cheek was a red smear.

"Close call, Kinkaid," said Lin.

"A close one," nodded the gambler, shoving his gun back into its scabbard. He faced Matthew. "Better to bury him now, no? The sight of a dead man is not so nice for the ladies. And a chance for you to preach the

191

funeral sermon, eh?" He spoke in a barely audible tone that Lin could scarcely hear.

"Yes, we will bury him . . . now." Matthew's voice was shaken.

"*Señor* Rawlins and I will see if this clumsy one came alone or with friends. Calm your sheep, my red one. They might make the stampede. Come, *amigo*, you and I will see what there might be to see."

Together Lin and Kinkaid searched the brush thickets. Several hundred yards away they found a saddled horse tied in the brush. The gambler smiled as he untied the hackamore rope.

"As I thought, he came alone. But the next time there will be several. Always, that bold one was like the lone wolf, working by himself. A brave man, but clumsy, that one who will be buried by our Matthew. And I remember moving my head a little. Otherwise the tale might have had another ending." He touched the gold egg in its buckskin sheath.

"Who was he, Kinkaid?"

"Among other things equally shameful, *señor*, he was the brother of Matthew, our red one."

CHAPTER
SEVEN

"Rebellion"

Lin Rawlins let his fire die out. When he had finished his after-supper smoke, he took one blanket from his tarp-covered bed and slipped away into the darkness. He had no wish to be murdered while he slept. Choosing a spot that was well hidden in the brush, a place from which he could see his horse, his bed, and the main camp, he lay down. He could see the giant Matthew, standing on a little knoll, his massive, bearded, long-haired head bowed as if in deep thought.

Lin wondered just what thought stirred in the brain of Matthew who had, but an hour ago, buried his brother. What was his attitude toward Kinkaid? Hatred, naturally. Even before tonight's killing, they had been enemies. Perhaps the shooting had but climaxed a feud of long standing. What would happen next?

Kinkaid's handsome figure no longer silhouetted the firelight. He was nowhere to be seen. Suddenly Lin stiffened, his hand on his gun. Off there in the darkness behind him he heard the creak of a saddle. The soft thud of shod hoofs. And for the fraction of an instant Lin caught a clear view of a man on horseback. No

193

mistaking man or horse. Keno Kinkaid was riding furtively out of camp.

Lin had no intention of sleeping much that night. He sat cross-legged on his blanket, watching the figures that showed against the firelight. They were no doubt frightened and filled with dread on account of the evening's killing.

Now Matthew stood in their midst. Lin heard him telling them that there was nothing to fear. Sentries had been posted. But, as it was strictly against the rules of the House of Matthew to carry firearms, the sentries had only clubs to defend themselves and the others.

For once the cult leader's eloquence had little or no effect. Some of the men openly complained of this folly of venturing unarmed into a perhaps hostile country. Among those who voiced complaint was Thomas. He and several other malcontents had been imbibing a little freely. The whiskey had warmed their thin blood.

Matthew paid little heed to the grumblers, passing over their whining with tolerant platitudes. "The Lord will watch over us. He will let no harm befall us."

From somewhere in the circle of men and women came an audible snigger.

"Am I not here to protect you all? Have I not been given the sign that told me to lead you to the land of promise? Come, come, my children. Put all fear from your hearts. Ruth, will you lead us in song?"

"No." The girl's quick negative brought a gasp from the others.

Matthew looked stunned. "Ruth, surely my ears heard wrong?"

194

"Not at all. I'm not singing. Not tonight or tomorrow night or any night thereafter."

"What evil thing has crept into your heart? What devil's work has poisoned you? What has come over you, Ruth?"

"It is that murderer who has done this thing, Matthew!" cried Rebecca. "Forbid her to talk with him again. Forbid her to even look at him. He is a disciple of Satan, that man. How can he, a man who kills wantonly and in cold blood, be one of us who are men and women of God's peace? Matthew, the child is bewitched!"

"Let us all kneel," sounded Matthew's sonorous voice, "and together we shall offer up a solemn prayer for the deliverance of Sister Ruth from this evil spell that has been cast over her."

With an impatient exclamation Ruth turned and walked swiftly away. Rebecca, making as if to follow her daughter, halted at a gesture from Ruth.

"Stay and pray, why don't you, Mother? I'm fed up on all of it. Gosh, if I have to listen any more to that man rant his hallelujah stuff, I'll do something that won't be lady-like."

"Hip, hip, hooray!" shouted the jubilant Thomas, and was promptly silenced by a none too gentle dig in the ribs.

"Hush, you dumbbell," whispered Carlotta.

"I won't hush. I've been shushed long enough. The worm will turn. Come on, boys. A li'l' song . . . Hail, hail, the gan's all here . . . Ouch! Dang it, Lottie, quit pinchin'!"

"Thomas," growled Matthew, standing over him and glowering, "have you been drinking?"

"What if I have? I'll drink when I want a drink, and, when this bottle's empty, there's more where it came from."

"There won't be any more when I've finished destroying it. This is disgraceful, scandalous, terrible! Luke, Stephen, John, go to the wagon of Thomas and destroy all the . . ."

"Be yourself, big boy!" said Carlotta sharply. "Nobody touches anything in our wagon. If you want to bust a few bottles of hooch, look in that big box on Matthew's buckboard. You lay off my Thomas, understand? God knows he's given up enough already. If he wants a drink, he can have it. Let him alone, or I'll make you sorry."

"This is mutiny! This is disgraceful!" cried Matthew, but he made no further attempt to molest the cargo of whiskey that Thomas had fetched along.

Lin, on his feet now, stood in the black shadow of the brush, a wide grin on his face. He saw the girl, Ruth, walking swiftly toward where he was hidden. Lin stepped out of the shadow. The girl gave a startled gasp.

"No need to be scared, ma'am. I couldn't keep from hearing what went on. I'd be proud to help you. I'm Lin Rawlins, kind of a chore man around here. A Gentile, so the big, red bull calls me."

"You're Kinkaid's partner?"

"No, ma'am. I'm playing a lone hand, you might say. I'd shore like to help you."

"I may need help before long," said the girl grimly. "I have a feeling that something is going to happen. Something terrible. Where did Kinkaid go?"

"I'm wondering about that myself. He rode off about an hour ago. Either he's afraid of being killed if he stays, or else he's gone to have a pow-wow with his men."

"His men?"

"This is his stomping ground down here. He's got a crew of renegades that'll balk at nothing. Mostly, they range over at the east end of the Blancas, but I've seen sign around here that tells me they ride this way."

"Is there really a fertile country across the hills?"

"Kinkaid claims so. I've never been there, myself. I've heard the Indians and Mexicans tell yarns about such a country. But supposing there is, there's no market for what they'd raise there."

The girl nodded. "The majority of these poor things who follow Matthew care little about a market. They're religious nuts. They think Matthew is a sort of second Moses. There are a few rebels. Thomas, the discoverer of Zingo, his wife, Carlotta, and a few more. Outside of them, the rest would be well content to colonize here and listen to the preaching of this Matthew burglar. It takes all sorts of folks to make up a world. Yes, they'd be content. Mother would call it paradise. Where she goes, I follow."

"And where you go," said Lin boldly, "I'll be trailing along. Kind of like a hound dog. When you need me, whistle."

"Is that why you've joined this party? On my account?" Ruth's voice was stern.

"I reckon so. It's a cinch I wasn't trailing along to listen to the bellering of the big, red bull. It seemed to me like he was leading you folks into trouble, so I hired out, hoping I could do you some good. That's about the size of it, ma'am."

"And just how do you expect to be rewarded?" she asked.

"I don't know as I'd figured on being rewarded. I've got a good ranch, a bunch of cattle, and some horses. All a man needs, you might say. No, I hadn't reckoned on any kind of reward. A man can turn off the trail now and then to do something just to even up for the ornery things he's done."

"But you say that you came on my account," persisted Ruth. "Men don't come to the rescue of some girl without expecting something in return. Lay your cards on the table, cowboy."

"I reckon," said Lin, his face growing hot, "that I savvy what you're driving at. I don't know what kind of men folks you have been traveling with, but I can name you plenty of boys that can do a lady a decent turn without asking any kind of pay for it. There's some of us that follow the steer for a living and ain't up on manners much, nor can't handle these double-barreled words, that might be ornery and not parlor broke. Our ways are rough ways. But we don't thank nobody for classing us among skunks."

"I'm sorry. I made a mistake, and I apologize. I'm really, truly sorry. Will you shake hands, Lin Rawlins?"

Lin hastily pulled the palm of his hand across his Levi's and gripped the small, tanned hand.

A twig snapped. Lin dropped the girl's hand, and she saw the barrel of his six-shooter in the moonlight. The next moment he had leaped through the brush. There was the sound of a brief struggle. A startled grunt from the cowboy. Then a woman's voice, vibrant with anger.

"What a swell way to treat a lady! Knock the wind out of a person. I thought you was a gentleman, but I take it back."

"I thought you were a man," stammered Lin. "Excuse me."

"Are you alone?" asked Carlotta, for it was she.

For a moment Lin hesitated. Then he grinned. "No, ma'am. You're with me."

"That gag was old when Noah went on his yachting trip. I got just a minute. Matt's watchin' me like a hawk. Will you lend me about six Forty-Five cartridges?"

"Cartridges? Sure thing. Here. When you run short again, let me know."

"Here. Take this bottle. Present from Tommy and me. And mum's the watchword, cowboy."

"You bet," grinned Lin, and looked after Carlotta as she glided back toward camp. He rejoined Ruth, grinning widely. "What do you make of that?"

"I'd say she had a gun and no cartridges," smiled Ruth. "Hints of conspiracy. That poor Thomas has had a bun on for a week. They aren't at all bad, those two. They're human, anyhow, even if Carlotta does hate me for some reason. If I was the sort that loves scandal, I'd say she is afraid I'll hook the Matthew pickpocket."

But Lin did not seem to hear her last words. He was staring off into the distance. Now he pointed. High up on the distant mountain a signal fire burned.

CHAPTER
EIGHT

" 'Kill that Devil' "

Just before dawn Lin heard Kinkaid return to the camp. The gambler was riding a fresh horse, an iron gray. When he had unsaddled and staked out the gray, he came over to where Lin stood beside his bed. Kinkaid's face was bandaged over the furrow made by the bullet that had almost taken his life the previous evening. He looked drawn and tired.

Lin handed him the bottle that Carlotta had given him.

"Thanks, Rawlins, I could use a stiff drink. Had any visitors during the night?"

"Visitors?"

"Strangers in camp? Like the brother of our Matthew."

"Nope. Nobody."

"We may have 'em for breakfast, then. They'll be after me."

"Yeah?"

"Yeah. There may be some trouble. How game are you, amigo?"

"It depends a lot on what the game is and how the play comes up."

"The men who will come here imagine that I know where there is gold. Much gold. They will want to take me alive so that they can torture me until I tell them where to find the gold. They are tough men, desperate. All of them are killers. The man I killed last night was their leader.

"*Señor* Rawlins, I owe to you an apology. I thought, when we left Los Gatos, that you had been here before. I know now that you are not the man who was here one night. The man who was here is the man I killed, the brother of the man they call Matthew. It was he who shot me from the brush and left me for dead after he'd robbed my pockets. It was he who stole a map and this gold egg.

"I have done you a wrong in my mind. It was that traitor, that snake in the grass, that ingrate whose life I once saved, who owed me for everything he had, who betrayed me. Twice he tried to kill me. The second time he himself was killed. And now come the others who want that gold. They will be five against one. I have won against bigger odds, *mi amigo*. Perhaps, this time, I will once more be lucky."

Kinkaid caressed the gold egg in its buckskin sheath. Lin saw him smile a little.

"*Señor* Rawlins, it has been many, many years since I have put my trust in any man. Yet, I am going to trust you, a stranger, a man who has no love for me, with my secret. I am giving to you the map that shows the location of more gold than you have ever seen.

"More than that, I am going to trust to your care the woman I love. She is not, perhaps, the only woman I have ever loved. I would lie if I said that. But she is the only woman I have known in many years who was pure and decent and all that I am not.

"Should I be killed, Rawlins, this gold belongs to you and to her. Should I be fortunate enough to win against the odds I meet, then I will follow you, and we will share equally what we find. Here, *mi amigo*, is the map."

Lin took the folded strip of oiled silk.

Kinkaid lifted the bottle of whiskey. "To you, *amigo*. And to our future partnership. I drink as a pledge of faith between us. *¡Salud, señor!*" And when he had drunk, he carefully wiped the neck of the bottle with a silk handkerchief and passed it to Lin.

"To our partnership, Kinkaid." Lin drank from the bottle and corked it.

"Now for the plan I have figured out, *señor*. I shall give to that red one the direction that will take him to his promised land. Not that I wish him luck, but that I cannot see these poor fools die here in the desert. Beyond the mountains is their land of plenty. There they can be happy . . . perhaps. *¿Quien sabe?*

"You, *señor*, will take a different course, once you reach the pass through the hills. The map shows the trail. It is rough going and at times there is no trail at all. But you are enough experienced to know how to get there. Take with you the girl called Ruth."

"Why do I drag her along?" Lin, while he had no intention of deserting the girl, wanted Kinkaid's reason.

"Because, *señor*, she is the only woman of this lot that would tempt the vile taste of the men who might visit that colony across the mountains. These other women are thin of blood, unattractive. They will be quite safe. But I fear for the girl called Ruth."

"She is the girl of your love, then?" smiled Lin.

"That is not so hard to guess, *señor*."

Lin held out the folded map. "Take it back, mister. Where that girl is concerned, there's no partnership between you and me. Kinkaid, I don't know your back trail very much, but I know enough. You aren't fit to even look at that little lady. Take your damned map and your damned gold. And if you lay a hand on that girl, by God, I'll kill you."

Lin's voice was low pitched, deadly. His hand was on his gun. But Keno Kinkaid merely smiled and nodded.

"That, *señor*, was well spoken. I know for sure that I can put my trust in you. Keep the map, *mi amigo*. Carry on with the plan I have outlined. When we meet once more, then it will be time enough for gun play. You are a brave man, *señor*, to make such talk to Keno Kinkaid. You will fight to the finish for that *señorita*, no?"

"Plumb to the end, Kinkaid."

"There is one other obstacle that may cause you some trouble, my friend."

"Matthew?"

"*Sí, señor*. Matthew. A bad *hombre*, that red one."

"With a streak of yellow down his back a foot wide."

"*Sí*. And because of that streak of yellow, my friend, all the more dangerous. I would rather make enemies of ten brave men than one bad coward. Matthew has killed before, so he will be ready and eager to kill again.

204

He kills in the dark, from behind a bush or a rock. Watch him, *señor*. Never let him get behind you."

They ate breakfast together, finishing just as dawn streaked the sky. Keno Kinkaid, rolling a cigarette, gave a low exclamation of annoyance. He crushed tobacco and paper in his hands and pointed. Coming over the brow of a hill, not three hundred yards away, were five men on horseback. Kinkaid saddled the big, gray gelding and gripped Lin's hand.

"*Adiós, mi amigo.* Good luck."

"Good luck, Kinkaid."

In the uncertain light, the five men had not seen Kinkaid ride away, hidden by the trees and a long draw. They rode toward the wagons.

Lin Rawlins, his Winchester in the crook of his arm, walked over to meet them. They sat their horses, a hard-eyed, grim-lipped lot. Bearded, heavily armed, well mounted. The spokesman had a greasy black patch over one eye. The cheek under the sightless eye wore a livid knife scar, giving the man a piratical appearance.

Matthew, standing by his buckboard, a shotgun in his big hands, faced them with some outward show of courage. Lin was a little amused to see Thomas, somewhat bleary of eye, sitting on the seat of his wagon, a six-shooter in his hand.

At sight of Lin Rawlins, the one-eyed man gave a startled grunt. "Hang me if it ain't the owner of the Circle Dot. H'are yuh, Rawlins?"

"Able to be up and around, Dillard. What do you want here?"

"I might be askin' the same of you, Rawlins. We're trailin' a wolf. His sign come this way. Seen 'im?"

"What kind of a lookin' wolf?"

"We're after Keno Kinkaid. Where is he?"

"Matthew here is the main ramrod," said Lin. "Ask him."

"You men are after Kinkaid?" A cunning look crept into Matthew's eyes.

"Yeah. He's trailin' with this odd-lookin' layout. Where is he? Spit 'er out, red feller."

"Kinkaid saddled up and rode away last night after supper. That's the last we saw of him. This man, Rawlins, might give you further information. He's Kinkaid's side partner."

"That's a big load tuh swaller, red feller. Last time I seen Keno and Rawlins meet up, they each had a gun drawed. If Rawlins is here, he's here on his own hook. He's got no love fer Keno."

"Kinkaid slipped away last night, Dillard," said Lin. "That's the truth. I sighted a signal fire a few hours after he pulled out."

Dillard nodded, his one eye, bloodshot, slitted, blazed with an evil light. "When Kinkaid left this camp last night, he lit a signal fire that was supposed tuh be lit by . . . by another man. Three uh the boys lit the fire you saw to let him know they was comin' down to meet him. Only they figgered it was . . . it was another feller they was ridin' to meet. Kinkaid hollered to 'em in the moonlight. Then they commenced shootin'. Kinkaid killed two of 'em. The other boy run fer it."

"Who wouldn't run," snarled a man with his left arm bandaged. "With Keno a-throwin' lead at me till them bullets was thick as hail stones? You'd uh done the same, Dillard."

"We'll see who does the runnin' when we come up to him," growled the one-eyed outlaw.

"If Kinkaid comes back," said Lin quietly, "he'd be hidin' in one of the wagons, most likely. And you boys would sure make nice targets."

As if a command had been barked at them, the five were on the ground, guns drawn, sheltered behind their horses. Lin grinned widely.

"Search the wagons," snarled Dillon. "Come on, boys."

"Hold on, men," cried Matthew. "He's not in any of the wagons."

"Stand over, red feller, or yuh might git shot in the belly. Search the wagons, boys."

"There are women and children in those wagons!"

"Wimmin?" Dillard's ugly face leered at Matthew. "Any purty gals?"

Matthew looked at Lin, who grinned back mockingly. The first wagon they came to was the one belonging to Rebecca and Ruth. Rebecca was just climbing down from the wagon. Dillard dismissed her with a grimace.

Guns drawn, they shoved Rebecca aside and two of the men climbed into the canvas-topped wagon. Matthew, white, his eyes shifting fearfully, waited. Now the two men clambered down from the wagon.

"Nobody there, Dillard."

Matthew licked his dry lips. "Where is Ruth?" he asked, his eyes searching Lin's face.

Lin smiled grimly. "Shut yore hairy mug, mister. She's safe."

They searched each wagon. At the wagon of Carlotta and Thomas they lingered some minutes. Carlotta had taken the gun and shoved it out of sight. Then she had whispered something in her husband's ear. Thomas smiled in a blurred manner. He looked a bit startled when he saw her face in the dim light of dawn. She looked like an old hag. Her hair, tousled, stringy, seemed to have turned gray. Her face was blotched and haggard looking, her eyes sunken in black sockets. Three of her teeth were gone.

"Don't look so scared, Tommy," she whispered. "You ain't got the jim-jams. Mother's just made up for the part, that's all. I don't want them burglars to fall for my beauty, see? Alley-oop, Tommy! Do your stuff."

So it was that Thomas pulled the cork on a bottle, and the five outlaws were not backward about emptying the bottle before they left the wagon. They passed up Lottie with looks of disgust.

Their search took almost an hour. Then they remained long enough to wolf breakfast before they rode on.

Lin smiled. Kinkaid now had more than an hour's start.

"Kill that Kinkaid devil," said Matthew to Dillard in an undertone that Lin's ears caught, "and I'll see you are rewarded."

When the five men had ridden away, Carlotta removed her make-up and smoked a cigarette.

Matthew was talking to Rebecca. "You must know where Ruth is, Rebecca."

"I do not. After what she said last night, I don't want to see her again, ever. She's possessed of the devil. She's a sinner, just like that father of hers. He thought more of his horses than he did of me. I told her to pack and go."

"What? Told Ruth to go? You fool! You damned, weepy fool! What the hell right have you to . . ."

"Matthew! Matthew! Cursing!"

"Shut up, you withered old hag, or I'll choke you till you can't see. You sent Ruth away. Where did she go?"

But Rebecca crumbled as if struck down, weeping hysterically. Matthew, muttering, his hands rumpling his shaggy red hair, strode away from the hysterical woman. It was Carlotta who helped Rebecca to her feet and into her wagon.

At Lin's little campfire, Ruth was getting breakfast for herself and him. Lin was shortening the stirrups on the saddle that had belonged to the brother of Matthew. They paid little heed to the raging Matthew as he came up, his eyes blazing.

"What's the meaning of this . . . this sinful performance? Ruth, go back to your wagon. Rawlins, saddle your horse and quit this camp."

Lin got to his feet. He unbuckled his wide cartridge belt and handed it and his gun to Ruth. Then he tossed his hat aside.

"You're a big hunk of meat to chaw and swaller, Mister Red Bull, but I just got to try it. Put up your dukes."

CHAPTER
NINE

"Lin Tips the Prophet's Hand"

A cruel smile twisted the red-bearded lips. Time had been when the self-styled prophet had been the bully of some tough camps. A knife or a gun might make him back up, but in any kind of a rough and tumble fight he was in his glory. Huge of build, with a left or right that could smash a man's ribs or jaw, he looked at the smaller man with eyes of contempt.

"Go to your wagon, Ruth. The lesson I'll teach this young rooster won't be fit for a lady to see."

"If Lin doesn't mind, I'll stay."

"Stay, then," snarled Matthew, doubling his huge fists. There was the glint of murder in his eyes now. Lin Rawlins would not be the first man killed by those hairy red hands. With a rumbling snarl, he rushed.

Lin was not so easily trapped. He side-stepped with the quick skill of a boxer. As Matthew went past, he ripped in a vicious hook that brought a grunt from the big man. Matthew whirled, rushed again, grabbing open-handed this time. Lin ducked, slid away, stepped in a pace, and smashed two swift jabs home before he danced out of reach. Blood spurted from the big man's nose.

"Nice work, Lin," called Ruth excitedly. She had put aside the skillet and coffee pot and stood by the fire, her fists clenched, her eyes dancing with excitement.

"Holy mackerel!" gasped a voice. Thomas, a bottle in his hand, gaped at the scene before him. He had come over to give Lin a little morning's cheer. "Smear 'im, cowboy!"

"Not so loud," cautioned Ruth. "Soft pedal, Thomas."

"I get you, girlie! Oh, oh, oh, and how's that one for a jolt, Brother Matthew? Smash him, Rawlins. Oh, my Lord."

Matthew's big arms had grabbed Lin. With an animal-like growl, Matthew was trying to gouge the cowpuncher's eyes out. Stabbing pains shot through Lin's eyes. Then, with a desperate effort, he got his left arm free. His hard fist was traveling hardly twelve inches as it shot, piston-like, into the big man's midsection. Like a trip hammer those short jolts thudded in under Matthew's ribs. The red-bearded fighter gasped, grunted, tried to evade those terrific jabs. Pain shot through his body. Pain that made him faint and sick.

Now Lin was free from those hairy arms, but, as Matthew retreated, he followed. One, two, one, two. The big man groaned and covered. Lin sent a right and a left to the bearded face. Something cracked. Lin danced away. Swift, shooting pains stung the cowpuncher's left arm from knuckle to shoulder. He had broken a knuckle on that big jaw. But he mustn't let Matthew know. Better end it as quickly as he could, now. One handed, against a man who outweighed him fifty pounds.

Lin stepped inside Matthew's wild swings. The big fellow was bewildered and sick. Now Lin's right swung back. Cocked. His whole weight was in the upward blow that sank, wrist deep, in the soft spot under Matthew's breast bone. Every ounce of Lin's strength had gone into that punch. Matthew's jaw sagged, his eyes rolled backward. He sank in a blood-smeared heap.

Thomas could hold back no longer. His jubilant shouts brought the whole camp running. With them came Carlotta, but she hardly noticed the crumpled Matthew or the victorious Lin, whose back was being slapped vigorously by the shouting Thomas. Carlotta took Ruth's arm.

"Hurry, Ruth. It's your mother . . . I think she's dying!"

Rebecca died in the arms of her daughter. When Matthew, his swollen face bathed, sore in every muscle, came to the wagon of Rebecca, Carlotta met him with dark eyes that flashed with scorn and anger.

"Rebecca is dead. But she told me plenty, the poor creature. As sure as if you'd used a gun, you've killed that poor woman. If I was you, I'd dig a deep hole, crawl in it, and pull the dirt in after me. You dirty, lying, cowardly devil. Too bad the cowboy didn't finish the job. Go away, or I'll kill you."

It was then that Matthew saw the six-shooter hidden under her apron. He turned and walked away.

213

Rebecca was buried there that morning. While Matthew stayed in his tent, drunk as a tick according to Carlotta, one of the men read the funeral service. Ruth, dry-eyed, her beautiful face marred with grief that could find no outlet in tears, stood between Carlotta and Lin Rawlins.

When the grave had been filled with dirt and marked with a wooden slab, teams were harnessed and the wagon train prepared to move on. One of the men drove the team that belonged to Ruth. The girl, riding the horse that had belonged to Matthew's brother, rode ahead with Lin Rawlins.

Matthew, driving his mules, glowered after them. Sometimes his hand crept into his pocket and gripped the gun he carried there. His swollen, discolored eyes glittered with murderous hatred.

Lin and the girl rode in silence. Sometimes her eyes sought his, and he would smile at her reassuringly. Once, when their stirrups touched, he reached over and took her hand, and they rode for a long way thus.

"I never really knew my mother," she said after a long while. "She and I never understood one another very well. She was almost like a stranger, especially after Dad was killed. I wish she could have died happily. She was ill, but kept it to herself. I knew that. It's why I had to stay with her, but something Matthew said to her broke her heart. That red-headed beast killed her belief in everything. God will understand, won't he, Lin, that she wasn't quite right in her mind?"

"He'll savvy, Ruth. Sure thing, He'll savvy."

"I'm all alone now. I suppose I might as well turn around in the morning. There is nothing to prevent my going back, now that Mother's gone. I've enough money to keep me until I can get a job."

In her riding breeches and boots and flannel blouse, a high-crowned Stetson shading her troubled eyes, she looked like a handsome boy. Lin could hardly keep his eyes off her.

Now, as they rode along, Lin told her something of Keno Kinkaid's map, though he left out all mention of the gambler's love for her.

"He wants us to find that lost mine, Ruth. I reckon there must be gold there. But it's a risky game. And it don't seem hardly proper for just us two to go gallivantin' off alone."

She smiled at him, the sorrow gone momentarily from her gray eyes. "It might not be exactly conventional, Lin, that's a fact. But that doesn't worry me a speck. And I trust you as if you were my brother. Lin, let's tackle it. Not that either of us need a lot of gold, but it will be an adventure. Would it be all right to take Carlotta and poor Thomas with us? They've been mighty decent to me. She's regular. And he's a well-meaning sort of fellow. God knows they've come to hate Matthew and this paradise-on-earth racket. Could they come along?"

"Why not? If they can set a mule that far. And that Thomas is a comical duck. We'll have to take along an extra mule pack to carry his hooch and that Zingo stuff. If they come along, you'd be kind of . . . kind of chaperoned, you might say."

Ruth's little laugh made him redden. "Lin, you're priceless! And I like you for it."

"You like me?"

"A lot. A whole lot, Lin." She reached over and gripped his hand.

Lin was blushing like a schoolboy now. "Ruth, there's one thing I left out when I told you about Keno Kinkaid. I didn't tell you he was in love with you."

"You didn't need to, Lin. I knew that already."

"He told you?"

"He didn't need to tell me . . . any more than you need to." She dropped his hand and rode on ahead, leaving Lin to puzzle out her last remark.

After a time Ruth let Lin catch up with her. They rode along again, stirrups touching sometimes, talking over the gold venture that lay ahead of them. It helped melt that lump that ached in the girl's heart.

Once their horses shied, as they passed a clump of chaparral at the beginning of the foothills. Lin investigated. He found two fresh mounds of earth. Two graves . . . Then Dillard had not lied. Keno Kinkaid had added two more to his list of dead.

They would have to make a dry camp that night because the funeral of Ruth's mother had delayed them a couple of hours. They would travel as far as they could before sunset. Their water barrels were full. While the others made camp, Lin and Ruth would take the mules and horses, that were unharnessed, and drive the thirsty animals on to the next water. They would have the cavvy back by dark, and the night wranglers would take charge.

"I'll keep your suppers warm," promised Carlotta. "Gee, Ruth, you look swell in them riding clothes, but I'd like to see you in an evenin' dress."

"Perhaps you will some day. Be back later."

"Little snort, Lin?" asked Thomas, who was quite sober.

"When we return, Tom, and much obliged. Don't take no leather money."

"Even if that cowboy is a collector of antique wisecracks, Tommy," said Carlotta, "he's a good boy. And I'm wonderin' where he learned to handle his dukes. It takes a scrappin' fool to trim Matt."

"A good Zingo massage would fix Matthew up, Lottie, but I'd bust every last bottle before I'd let him have the smell of a Zingo cork."

"That's the old fightin' spirit, Tommy. Rustle some wood while you can still navigate. And don't get too close to that big mutt. He might bite, and even Zingo wouldn't cure hydrophobia. Trot along, honey."

Carlotta kept a watchful eye on Matthew, who was superintending the job of putting up his tent. His face was puffed and discolored, and he was in a surly mood.

CHAPTER
TEN

"Kinkaid Comes Back"

The sun had set, and twilight was spreading its blanket. The campfires were like altar lights against the purple and black of the hills. Children laughed and squealed as they romped. A woman sang. Somewhere a man was whistling.

The tinkle of horse bells announced the return of Ruth and Lin with the horse cavvy. Now, against the sky that was sprayed with early moonlight showed the cavvy and its two guardians, Lin on one side, Ruth on the other. Lin took down his rope to snare the horses for the night wranglers.

There came the flat crack of a rifle. Lin swayed in his saddle blindly, then toppled off to the ground. With a startled cry, Ruth, heedless of danger, spurred around the loose horses and flung herself from the saddle. There was a trickle of blood across Lin's forehead.

"Oh, God! Oh, God!" she prayed, wiping away the blood.

Lin lay as if asleep. Her trembling fingers found the wound, a long furrow across Lin's scalp. By a fraction of an inch the cowboy's life had been spared.

He was stirring, his head in Ruth's lap. His eyes blinked open, and he tried to get on his feet.

"Take it easy, Lin. You've been hurt. Not badly."

"Lordy, my head aches. Was I bucked off?"

"No. Somebody took a shot at you. And whoever it was, he almost got you." Her voice trembled a little. "Thank God that bullet didn't do its work. Without you, Lin, I don't think I could go on."

Lin was hardly aware of the pain that racked his head. Against her protesting hands, he sat up. Smiling, his eyes bright with something that made his heart pound in his throat, he took her hands. "Ruth, Ruth, girl, you do . . . care?"

She nodded, her eyes like stars. Then she was in his arms, but only for a moment. Thomas, running, stumbling, came up. He gave a quick cry of joy when he saw Lin get to his feet.

"Saw you tumble off, Lin. Somebody shot you."

"Who was it?" asked Lin, his arm around Ruth's shoulder.

"Dunno. Couldn't see. Everybody down there's running around like rabbits: And those five toughs riding in with Kinkaid. All confused."

"You say those men are back . . . with Kinkaid? They killed him, then?"

"Kinkaid ain't dead. He was sittin' on his horse, cool as ice, puffin' a cigarette."

"Ruth," said Lin grimly, "get on your horse. Ride like the devil was chasin' you till you reach the creek where we watered the horses. Hide there till I come."

"What are we going to do, Lin?"

"I'm goin' to try to set Kinkaid free. Hurry, Ruth."

Her arms were around his neck, her lips against his. "Good luck, Lin. I'll be waiting, dear."

"Don't worry, honey. I'll be along before midnight. So long."

When Ruth had ridden away, Lin turned to Thomas.

"Let 'em think I'm dead, old-timer. Lope on back to camp. Then bring out your whiskey. Dillard and the other four are all rum hounds. Feed 'em all they'll drink. Let on like you found me dead, got scared, and run back. Can you play them cards, Tom?"

"I'll say I can."

"Then rattle your hocks, pardner, before somebody comes this way. Take along my horse and stake him where I left my bedroll."

When Thomas had gone, Lin took his Winchester and hid himself in a patch of dense manzanita brush. In a short while Matthew and Dillard were searching for him. They passed within a few feet of his hiding place. Lin could hear every word as they searched for his body.

"Too dark," said Dillard. "We'll find his carcass in the mornin'. That feller said he was dead. Shot in the head."

"I'd like to make certain," muttered Matthew, "though I drew a steady bead and saw him fall."

"To hell with 'im till mornin'. I'm hungry, and that Thomas sport was puttin' out some good likker. So, yo're pore ol' Sandy's brother, are yuh? The red-headed warthawg he usta tell us about. His brother, Matt. Red

Matt, as killed the Car-ruthers boys at Trinidad. And yuh got religion, Matt."

Matthew chuckled. "Tell me some more about this gold mine, Dillard." His voice was thick and blurred. Lin reckoned that the big, red bull had been hitting the bottle pretty hard.

"There's a map. Kinkaid's old man drawed it. It locates the gold mine them old *padres* was workin' when they got massacred. An earthquake caved in the drift they had timbered. There was some Injuns and a couple uh *padres* buried alive there. And as the whole side uh this hill slipped, it buried all sign.

"Kinkaid's old man located it and drawed the map. Then he covered all sign and lit out. There was some fellers after him. They ketched him, too. I ain't sayin' who them fellers was, savvy, but there was quite a gang, all told. That brother uh yourn could've told yuh somethin' if he'd had a mind tuh.

"Anyhow, them fellers ketched old Kinkaid, but he didn't have the map. And no torture ever got it outta him where he'd hid it. They got careless and went too far with their torture stuff and croaked the old tight-mouthed son.

"It's a year later when a gent named Sanchez joins us down there in the Blanca Mountains. Sanchez is a fast gun-thrower. He killed a few gents down there, and we don't ketch on that he's pickin' fights and killin' off the boys that done in old Kinkaid. Ner we don't tumble till a few days back that this Sanchez is old Kinkaid's son."

"Has Keno Kinkaid got the map, Dillard?" Matthew prompted.

"Dunno. Sandy claims he found out that Keno Kinkaid had a map. Sandy follered Keno to El Paso not so long ago. I trailed Sandy, him not knowin'. Sandy hired a bartender tuh slip some knockout drops in Keno's whiskey, and, when Keno passed out, Sandy rolled 'im. He gits some money and that big gold aig Keno sets so much store by. But he swears there was no map. Now Kinkaid claim that Sandy swiped the map. That Sandy must've double-crossed us other boys. And somehow Keno's talk sounds straight. It couldn't be, could it, that Sandy give that map to his brother, Red Matt? Huh?"

"No! I swear it, Dillard! Don't kill me!"

"Nobody's killin' yuh, deacon. I'm just friskin' yuh. The other boys is friskin' your stuff at camp. Keep them paws up, er I'll feed yuh some lead pills. What's this? Two pop guns? Shame on yuh, parson! Now pull off them boots and let's see what's in 'em besides feet. *Pronto*, yuh red-muzzled rat."

Lin enjoyed the frisking of the cowardly Matthew. Ten minutes later, Dillard cursed disgustedly.

"You've ruined my boots," whined Matthew.

"What's a pair uh clodhopper boots amongst friends? I reckon I savvy why Sandy didn't let yuh know about the map. Yo're yaller, that's why." He prodded Matthew with his six-shooter. "Git to camp. I'm dry."

Lin heaved a sigh of relief when they had gone. Then he made himself comfortable and settled down to wait until Thomas and his precious whiskey did their work.

CHAPTER
ELEVEN

"Escape"

The followers of Matthew, timid of heart, shocked beyond measure at the events of the past few days, huddled in a wide-eyed group in the largest of the wagons. With them was Matthew, almost as badly frightened as were the others. His face bore the scars of his fight with Lin Rawlins. His breath reeked of whiskey that he told them he had taken to ward off chills that had gripped him. Smothering his contempt for them, his chagrin, his bitterness and hatred, he muttered banal bits of stale advice and consolation.

At the wagon of Carlotta and Thomas, though, there was ribald revelry. Carlotta, cleverly made up, looked like an old hag. Thomas was expanding with each drink. He was a genial host, and hail fellow well met. His grub had fed the five outlaws, and his whiskey was being passed around. Keno Kinkaid, seated with his back to a wagon wheel, his hands and feet bound with ropes, looked on. Now and then Dillard would quit the circle around the firelight, walk over, and slap the prisoner's face, or kick him.

Keno Kinkaid swore under his breath. They had spread a trap, and he had walked into it. They had guessed that he would head for the Blanca country. Cutting across, they had waited for him in a narrow cañon. Before he could defend himself, a rope had tightened around his neck and jerked him off his gray horse. The fall had stunned him. He awoke to find himself a prisoner of the men who once had followed him on cattle raids down here.

He heard Dillard and the others discuss the shooting of Lin Rawlins. Kinkaid's heart was heavy. Matthew, so claimed Dillard, had killed Lin Rawlins. But there was no mention of Ruth. Had she escaped? What had become of her? Kinkaid waited some furtive signal from Carlotta or Thomas, but they gave him no indication they knew of Ruth's whereabouts.

Perhaps she was still with the others in that wagon yonder. But when Dillard, weaving an unsteady course, had gone "to look the she-stock over," he came back with the news that every female over there had plenty rings around their horns. They "was a bunch uh crows."

Could it be that, behind this eager hospitality of Carlotta and Thomas, there was a cleverly laid plan? It seemed unlikely to Kinkaid. Carlotta was plainly tipsy, bordering on the maudlin stage. Thomas was tight as a drum head. They were putting out the whiskey, hoping to bribe these outlaws into letting them and their belongings alone. Kinkaid sneered openly at the fawning Thomas and the slovenly looking Carlotta as they brought out more whiskey. Dillard and his men were getting drunk. They sang and whooped and shot off their guns at the stars. Then two of them got into a quarrel.

Carlotta fed them more whiskey. She sang a song or two and did a jig dance while they clapped their hands to the tune of "Turkey in the Straw." Now each man had a bottle of his own, and they were getting more drunk as time passed.

They got into a discussion about their prisoner. Two of the five were for hanging Kinkaid. Dillard and two others were for torturing him until he gave them some information about the lost map. The fire was dying out, but they did not seem to notice.

Kinkaid heard something move very cautiously under the wagon. Now there was a barely audible whisper in his ear: "It's me, Lin Rawlins, Kinkaid. Sit steady. I'll cut your hands free. Then you take the knife and cut your feet loose. I got our horses ready."

A few moments and Kinkaid was free. Lin slipped a gun into his hand. The men at the fire were arguing hotly. No one of them noticed Kinkaid vanish into the night.

The two men mounted and rode away cautiously. Once beyond earshot, they struck a faster gait. It might be half an hour or more before Dillard and his companions found their prisoner gone. And by then they would be too drunk to follow fast.

"Where's the girl, *Señor* Rawlins?" was the gambler's first question.

"Safe. She's waitin' at the crick ahead of us about five miles."

"You are a brave man, *señor*, and a real friend. I am very much in debt to you, *mi amigo*."

"I couldn't've done much without Thomas and Carlotta."

"Oho! Then the business about the whiskey was part of the plan, no?"

"Shore thing. I hope them sons won't hurt 'em."

"They will be too anxious to follow us, *señor*. They would not suspect anyhow. Dillard is thick through the skull, and the others also are lacking in the brains. Let us look at the map once more, *mi amigo*."

Lin reached into his pocket. He pulled up with a sharp oath.

"It's gone. It must've dropped out of my pocket, back where I tumbled off my horse. If that ain't the dangedest luck!"

"Not so bad as you might suppose, *señor*," smiled the gambler. "Before I gave it to you, I memorized it to the last detail. But if it is found, whoever finds it will follow us. Which, after all, is not so bad. Because, sooner or later, we must meet those five. We must kill them. Only when they are dead, can we ever hope to reach Los Gatos alive with the gold we find. *Dios*, that gold has taken the lives of many men. You are superstitious, *mi amigo?*"

"Not exactly, but this killin' business don't taste so good. It's hell how men will fight for gold."

"For gold . . . or for love."

Lin shot the other man a swift glance. Kinkaid's lips were smiling, but his eyes were hard as slits of steel in the moonlight. The cowpuncher wondered if, in the end, he and this killer would face one another with naked guns. Keno Kinkaid was of that breed who does not give up a thing he desires. And certainly the gambler wanted Ruth as much as he wanted the yellow gold they sought.

CHAPTER
TWELVE

"Bullet-Carved Trail"

At the creek, Lin's shout brought an answering hail from Ruth. In a few moments she joined the two men. She gave a startled gasp when she made out Kinkaid.

"You got away from those men, then?"

"Thanks to *Señor* Rawlins," smiled Kinkaid. "Better that we get going, my friends. We shall need a long start."

Later — some hours later — Lin was to understand what the gambler meant when he had said they would need a long start. Daylight was but a few hours away. Kinkaid rode in the lead. Following him came Ruth, and Lin brought up the rear. The gambler shoved his horse to a long trot. Horse and man seemed to know the trail as well by night as by daylight.

Once or twice Lin rode up alongside Ruth, and their hands gripped in the darkness. Lin was more happy than he had ever hoped to be. Yet, he felt that danger was tagging close at their heels.

Not once did Keno Kinkaid halt until they swung abruptly off the trail and into a narrow cañon. Here he paused. Tall, steep-sided cañon walls hemmed them in. Dawn was breaking across the peaks.

"We start climbing here. The trail passes through a saddle between those two highest points. Keep the feet loose in the stirrups because the trail is fit for goats, better than for the horse. *¡Andar!*"

Black, rocky walls while, above, the dawn lit the sky, and somewhere a waterfall pounded like the surf at high tide. The trail was steep, rocky, twisting like a snake up a cañon wall.

"Do not look down," cautioned Kinkaid. "Look up, always." He was humming as his horse climbed the rocky wall of the cañon, and either he was in a gay mood, or else he sought to cheer up Ruth, for, as they progressed, he chatted gaily, sang little songs, called back bantering talk to Lin, who returned the same sort of talk. Ruth smiled and joined in.

"Poor Carlotta and Thomas," she said once. "I hate to leave them behind."

"We shall meet them again," promised Kinkaid. "*Dios*, they acted brave parts. I do not forget what they did for me."

Lin laughed and held up a bottle. "Tommy's Zingo. And you can believe it or not, but it's taken the pain from that nick in my scalp."

The sun was fully up now. Birds sang. Ruth was getting hungry. It suddenly struck her that they had brought no food.

"When, where, and how do we eat, boys?" she called.

"After we cross through the saddle, then we eat, *señorita*. Wild turkey, quail, rabbit, venison, or plain beef. Always I carry a sack of salt and a sack of coffee beans. A small pot to cook the coffee. And while one never could grow fat on such food, it is better than starving, no?"

They halted at a place where the trail was wide. Kinkaid took a pair of field glasses and swept the desert country below. For some minutes he searched the lower country. His lips tightened. Now he passed the glasses to Lin.

Lin easily picked up the wagon train, Matthew's buckboard in the lead, crawling slowly across the level trail toward the pass that led into the valley beyond which they would find their land of promise.

Then Lin found the five riders. They were almost to the place where the three fugitives had turned from the trail, riding hard, single file. Lin passed the glasses back to the gambler who watched for some minutes. Then he lowered the glasses, and his eyes met Lin's. And Lin knew that the five outlaws had also turned off the trail.

With a smile, Kinkaid handed Ruth the glasses. "Look, señorita, and you will see the prophet leading his children to the land of milk and honey."

But Ruth was not so easily fooled. "What of the five men? I bet they are close behind us."

Lin grinned foolishly. "No use lying. They are. But they'd better turn back if they don't want to get hurt."

"Better that we keep moving," said the gambler crisply. "¡Andar!"

On and on. The way became steeper, more narrow. A switchback trail led up the steep rocky mountainside, and it was less than an hour later when Lin and Ruth knew why the gambler had wanted a good start. For, as they slowly labored up the steep, dangerous trail, a bullet droned past them with an ugly, menacing whine.

The switchback trail had given the men below a chance to shorten the distance between them. Once across the switch-back, they would again gain a long lead, but now they were dangerously close to the five killers behind them. They dismounted and led their horses. Bullets spattered against the rocks. The men below were hidden behind granite boulders. The range was far too long for accurate shooting, but the snarling whine of the bullets was uncomfortable. At any moment a lucky shot might hit one of them or one of their horses. The horses seemed to know the danger and crowded close on the heels of the two men and the girl who labored on foot up the rocky trail. On one side, the granite wall. Below, far below, a sheer drop to death on the jagged rocks.

Again the trail widened, and they were behind the shelter of some huge boulders. Sweat streamed from their faces. They were winded from the exertion, but Kinkaid had pulled the carbine from his saddle scabbard and laid it across a rock. He rolled and lit a thin cigarette. His eyes were steely, cruel.

"*Señor*, you and the *señorita* go on again. Let my horse go ahead. I shall join you at the top of the trail."

Lin shook his head. "Nothing doing, Kinkaid. We'll take equal chances."

Kinkaid shrugged and smiled. "'*Sta bueno, señor*." He took a silver coin from his pocket, flipping it deftly in the air. "Heads or tails?"

"Heads," said Lin grimly.

Kinkaid caught the coin. For an instant it lay in the palm of his hand, then he held it out. "Heads. You win, señor. I stay here. Are you rested, señorita? Bueno. Then go. I join you later."

Lin and Ruth, leading their horses, driving Kinkaid's horse ahead of them, climbed on. A few bullets splashed against the rocks. Now Kinkaid's carbine cracked . . . again and again.

"Don't look back, Ruth. Look up, for God's sake! Up, honey."

Ruth, a little white, obeyed, but she knew what it was that Lin did not want her to see. She knew Kinkaid's deadly aim had found one of the outlaws. Lin had seen the man, down below, pitch sideways from a little brush patch, clutch wildly at the branches that broke, fall headlong into the cañon below. Now the grisly echo of the doomed man's scream floated up to them.

"Steady, Ruth," called Lin, "steady, little pardner."

Kinkaid's gun kept up its rat-tat-tat-tat. Its deadly leaden hail was driving the men below to cover. Ruth and Lin scrambled up the trail, but the guns of the men below were no longer spewing bullets. Kinkaid's uncanny accuracy with a carbine had driven them to cover. Fifteen minutes later Ruth and Lin were at the top of the trail.

Lin pulled his carbine from its saddle boot and squatted behind some boulders. Sweat ran down his tanned face in rivulets, and he was panting so that it was several moments before he could line his sights with any degree of accuracy. From where he squatted, he had a glimpse of two of the men below. Now he began throwing lead at them. He smiled grimly as they ducked out of sight.

Kinkaid began climbing the trail. Lin kept up a steady fire that was returned half-heartedly. The death of their companion seemed to have taken the starch out of them for a time. Kinkaid kept coming. It seemed to Lin that the gambler was moving very slowly. Once he stopped and lay down, then got onto his feet once more and came on. Lin wondered if the gambler was hit. Then, a few minutes later, Kinkaid was beside him.

"Hurt?" asked Lin anxiously.

"Nothing serious. Just a spent bullet in my thigh. Hardly under the hide. If the *señorita* will amuse herself watching the wagon train with the glasses, you and I will get the bit of lead out, *señor*."

"Can't I help?" asked Ruth, making a heroic attempt to smile.

"Nope," said Lin. "Do as he says, honey."

Lin had been calling her "honey" quite without thinking. But he saw the gambler start a little and felt the quick scrutiny of the man's steely eyes.

Now Lin had slit open the gambler's trouser leg and deftly bared the wound. Kinkaid lay back against the rocks, half reclining. Lin had in his saddle pocket the bottle of Thomas's Zingo. He used the pungent liniment to bathe the wound that bled sluggishly. Kinkaid did not flinch when Lin took the lead slug from the shallow wound. It popped out like a pea from its pod. Lin washed the wound with Zingo and bandaged it tightly. Kinkaid took a long pull at the bottle of whiskey that had been a gift from Thomas. Lin also took a drink.

The men on the trail below had quit shooting. Nor did they make any attempt to come up the trail. Lin watched, his carbine ready. He knew that Kinkaid was feeling a little sick and a half hour's rest would do them all good.

A quick cry came from Ruth as she lowered the glasses. "There is a bunch of riders catching up to the wagon train!"

Kinkaid got to his feet, a little unsteady, and took the glasses. For almost five minutes the gambler kept the glasses focused. Then he handed them to Lin without a word.

Lin picked out the horsemen. He judged there must be more than a dozen riders, and they were traveling at a good clip. He lowered the glasses and faced Kinkaid.

"What do you make of 'em, Kinkaid?"

"Who would be following, señor, except men from the Blanca country? Dillard, or maybe the dead Sandy, with too many drinks inside, told of the map. They see the sign on the trail and follow. So now, instead of five, we must fight perhaps twenty men who want the gold we are after."

He smiled thinly. Lin did not like the look in the cold, gray eyes of the man. He read, instead of fear, a sort of triumph there in their glitter.

"They'll be friends of yours, Kinkaid?"

"Does one find friends among wolves, señor?" He walked stiffly to his horse and mounted. "Better if we push along, no? The señorita must be very hungry."

234

Again he led the way. Ruth dropped back and looked at Lin with troubled eyes.

"Lin, don't leave me. I . . . I don't trust Kinkaid. He's up to something."

CHAPTER
THIRTEEN

"Crossed Muzzles"

Keno Kinkaid shot the head off a young turkey. It was a neat bit of marksmanship that hinted broadly of showing off. He smiled thinly at Lin as the dead bird fluttered on the ground. Then he ejected the empty shell from his six-shooter and shoved in a cartridge.

Lin thought the man was slightly drunk. There was an ugly glint in his eyes and a nasty twist to his smile. Lin did not like the way the gambler looked at Ruth. He was sure, now, that he would have to kill Kinkaid or be killed by that quick-triggered gunman.

While Lin built a fire, Kinkaid picked and cleaned the wild turkey. Then he fashioned three green sticks with sharp points. There was a spring of clear water that was pleasantly cool.

Twice, before they ate, Kinkaid took a pull at the bottle of whiskey. Lin did not want any, but he drew his own conclusions when Kinkaid did not offer him a drink. The cowpuncher reckoned that it was just another sign that Kinkaid was planning to kill him.

They roasted the turkey meat on the sticks and ate in silence. The gambler's thin-lipped mouth tightened when Ruth sat close to Lin.

"Did Lin tell you that, if ever we get out of this mess, he and I are going to be married?" Ruth asked bluntly.

"So? I am to congratulate you, then?"

Kinkaid's eyes narrowed to slits, and his smile was a lifting of his upper lip so that his teeth showed whitely. Like the noiseless snarl of a vicious dog. Then he leaned back against the boulder at his back and laughed a little.

"We are not out of this tight spot yet," he said, and let the cigarette smoke drift lazily from his nostrils.

He got to his feet abruptly.

"Come. We lose time worth gold. *¡Andar!*"

Again Kinkaid took the lead over a dim trail that sometimes vanished completely. On and on. Until the trail dropped into a cool, shaded box cañon.

Kinkaid, plainly drunk now, seemed to forget the girl and the cowpuncher. He motioned them to halt there by a tumbling, gurgling creek, and rode on alone. Lin stepped into the shelter of some big boulders and motioned Ruth to join him.

"What is it, Lin?" she whispered.

"Dunno yet, pardner. But it looks like I'll have to swap some bullets with him 'most any time. I was a plumb fool to let you into this mess. I was silly to trust him. He acts loco. Drunk, too. Sit down low, dear. This show might pop open any minute."

For half an hour Lin waited, his six-shooter ready, his Winchester leaning against the rock. His broken knuckle ached horribly. He wondered what was keeping Kinkaid. Was this the place where the lost mine was supposed to be? Was the gambler hunting for its exact location?

Lin's musing was rudely cut short by a rifle bullet that ripped through the high crown of his Stetson. Lin ducked low among the boulders just as a hail of hot lead spattered around him, a split second too late to riddle him.

Then, from up the cañon, a single rifle began cracking. That would be Kinkaid. The outlaws had caught up. This was the end of the trail.

"Lay flat, Ruth." Lin was trying to get a snap shot at one of the outlaws. "Stay down, pardner. We'll show 'em some shootin'."

A man's head and shoulders shoved into sight. Before Lin could draw a bead, the man crumpled. Kinkaid's gun had tallied another dead man.

Bullets snarled and whined. Lin squatted among the boulders, waiting for a mark to shoot at. No use in wasting ammunition. Now he saw a man's leg. His gun cracked. There came a yelp of pain, and the leg jerked out of sight.

"If he lives, he'll limp some," muttered Lin, "and he isn't feeling so happy right now, either. How you making it, pardner?"

"Not so bad, Lin."

"Game youngster. We'll win out, yet."

"Of course we will, cowboy."

The shooting slacked. Dillard's men were growing cautious and were saving ammunition. It was late afternoon. Lin knew that Ruth must be horribly thirsty and badly frightened, but not once had she complained

238

of the heat, of the thirst that choked her, the cramped position she must keep there in the rocks. And never once, even when the bullets sprayed a few inches above her head, did she show any outward sign of fright.

Behind the boulders someone was crawling. Lin cocked his six-shooter and flattened himself in a crevice between two rocks. A croaking whisper hailed him.

"*Amigo*. Rawlins."

"That you, Kinkaid?"

"*Sí*. Do not shoot."

"The same to you, Kinkaid," said Lin grimly, fearing some trick on the part of the gambler. He thought he heard the man chuckle.

The next moment Keno Kinkaid leaped over the granite barricade and dropped inside within arm's reach of Lin. The shower of lead that pitted the rocks had not been futile. Kinkaid was badly wounded, but he smiled gamely, his eyes glittering into the muzzle of Lin's gun.

"The *Señor* Dillard shoots well, *mi amigo*. My luck has soured. Otherwise, perhaps, you would need to pull that trigger, no? Because I came here to kill you, *Señor* Rawlins. Risking their bullets, I crawled along. And not until I jumped over the rocks did they see me."

"You wanted to kill me. Why, Kinkaid?"

The gambler's eyes shifted from Lin to Ruth, then back at the cowpuncher.

"Do not be so stupid, *mi amigo*. Always, when I wanted a thing very much, I went after it. Who stood in my way I pushed aside, understand? You stood between me and what I desired. So I came, *mi amigo*, to push you aside with a bullet. And that cursed Dillard must make the lucky shot for him, eh? But that is life, no? I do not complain. Tomorrow I will be very dead. My death will make many men and a few women quite happy. I do not know anyone who will regret my going. Why should they? Always I have lived for myself alone. Was I not ready to kill you, who had saved my life?"

Kinkaid shoved his hand into the front of his blood-soaked shirt and brought forth his bottle. He sat back against a rock and took a stiff drink. No need of words to tell Lin and Ruth that the gambler was dying.

"Our gold" — Kinkaid smiled crookedly — "I found it. *Sí*. But, *mi amigo*, it is buried beneath many, many tons of rock. There has been another earthquake or a huge landslide. It would take years to move the rock, the dirt that covers that pocket of free gold that has cost the lives of many men, both bad and good men.

"Perhaps the *indios* are right. Perhaps the spot is cursed. Or perhaps the spirits of the murdered *padres* guard it too well, no? *¿Quien sabe?*" He drank from the blood-stained bottle.

"You must believe me, *Señor* Rawlins, when I say I like you. You are a real man. I am in your debt. My final moments on this earth will be spent in doing something to repay that debt. The landslide buried the mine, that is true. But it likewise notched a passage through the cañon wall. What was once a box cañon is now opened. Dillard does not know that. He thinks we are hopelessly trapped. And those other wolves from the Blanca

Mountains, those men we saw catch up to and pass the wagon train, they will think as Dillard thinks.

"When dusk comes, *mi amigo*, you must take the *señorita* and escape through that pass in the cañon wall. I shall remain here and cover your flight. I will pay off what I owe you, *señor*. And I shall, to some small extent, cancel my debt to you, *señorita*."

Neither Ruth nor Lin spoke for some minutes. Kinkaid drank again, then made a cigarette, and lit it. His face was gray with pain, but no whisper escaped his tight lips.

Lin bandaged the wound in Kinkade's groin as best he could. The gambler could not live for many hours. A man with less grit and stamina and will power would not be living now. But in Kinkaid's eyes there burned sparks of fire. It was as if he were already dead, yet still conscious.

"We won't leave you like this, Kinkaid," said Lin.

The smile vanished from the gambler's tight lips. His eyes were slits now. His voice brittle and harsh. "The hell you will not! I am the dictator here. You will do what I command, or as *Dios* is my judge, I will kill you both. In my hand is a gun, *señor*, that can empty itself before you can move a finger. Without boasting, I can say that there is no man alive that can shoot as fast or with the accuracy of Keno Kinkaid. *¡Válgame Dios!* It is not so much, what I am going to do. It is for the *Señorita* Ruth Webster that I make the sacrifice, such as it is."

Ruth's eyes widened. "How did you know my name was Webster?"

"I have seen you sometimes with your father. I knew Bill Webster." His thin lips twisted. "I would much rather kill you, *señorita*, than to have Dillard and those white wolves from the Blanca Mountains get their filthy hands on you. And so, if *Señor* Rawlins does not promise to take you away from here, then I will surely kill you both.

"*Dios*, man, you love this woman! Would you hesitate at anything to save her from such men as those who are coming as fast as their horses can travel? If Dillard's bullet had not hit me, you would be dead now, and I would be riding at nightfall with the *señorita* through the pass. Would you risk the life and more than the life of this girl to stay beside a man who will be dead in a few hours? Are you so stupid? Promise to do what I command. Promise me now or I kill you both. Promise."

"I'll promise, Kinkaid. Not because I'm afraid of your gun, but because I can see it's the thing to do."

"A pencil," gritted the gambler. "Give me pencil and paper. There is something I must write. Something for you both to read after you have ridden through the pass."

Lin handed the gambler a stubby pencil and his tally book. Kinkaid took another drink to ease the pain that was gnawing at him like sharp teeth biting into his entrails. For some minutes he wrote. Then he closed the little tally book and returned it to the cowpuncher.

"Open it when you have gone through the pass. Then you will understand better why I must stay and why you two must go on, because it is the will of the *Señor Dios*. The law of equality. The balance of the scales of justice."

CHAPTER
FOURTEEN

"Dead Man's Legacy"

Dusk. Lin and Ruth stood beside Kinkaid, who sat propped among the boulders. The gambler took the gold egg in its pouch of buckskin from around his neck and looped the thong about the neck of the cowboy. Their hands gripped in a farewell clasp. Ruth bent and kissed the dying man's damp forehead. Kinkaid smiled his thanks, his eyes, for a short moment, softened.

"Go, now," he whispered. "May the *Señor Dios* be kind to you both. *Adiós.*"

So they left him. And even as they slipped away into the shadows to get their horses, they heard Kinkaid's Winchester cracking. They heard Dillard's hoarse voice, pain racked, cursing, even as a group of riders came up the steep trail.

"Quick, Ruth!"

In the saddle now, they raced up the cañon. The twilight threw black shadows across the high granite walls. Then, ahead, the narrow pass. Behind them rifles crashed, the high walls throwing back the grisly echoes.

Then the firing slacked. Ruth and Lin paused there at the narrow pass. Tears still misted the girl's eyes.

244

Then, as they were about to ride on, Lin held up his hand for her to wait.

"Listen! Listen, Ruth!"

"Hallooooo! Hallooo, Lin Rawlins!" came the echoing shout.

"Thank God!" cried Lin. "Honey, that's the sheriff from Los Gatos. It was the sheriff and his posse we watched coming up with the wagon train. Ruth, honey, we're safe." Lin raised his voice in a wild cowboy yell as they rode back the way they had come.

The sheriff met them. He and Lin shook hands without a word.

"Yuh damned young fool!" the sheriff finally said.

"Yuh damned ol' warthog!" Lin grinned.

Two riders came up. One of them was a woman. It was Carlotta. And with her, astride a raw-boned mule, rode Thomas. Thomas was a little tipsy, shouting his joy to all compass points. Carlotta and Ruth, dismounted now, were in each other's arms, laughing and crying.

"I've got to see Kinkaid, Sheriff," said Lin in a low tone.

"Kinkaid is dead, son. But he's taken the Dillard feller with him. Likewise another that's dyin' . . . dead by now, I reckon. Yeah, Keno Kinkaid is dead, Lin. Looks plumb peaceful, like as if he'd bin glad tuh go. His guns was empty. His bottle was empty beside him. The cigarette in his mouth was still lit when I found him. A bad *hombre*, Kinkaid, but game. And when he got Dillard, he got the last uh them he hated."

"How's Matthew and his pilgrims?"

"They're across the hills and into the valley by now. And I gave it to him plain that he'd better stay there and play his hand out. Them fools believe in him. If I told 'em what he is, it'd kinda bust 'em all up. So I told him tuh keep on apreachin'. And if ever he left the valley, I'd see that he went tuh prison fer keeps. Kinkaid gimme his record, and it's a bad 'un. But he almost believes his own preachin' by now, and that valley is shore enough paradise, so the Mexicans claim. Them locoweeds will take root there. Matthew will ride herd on 'em. I reckon they'll be a heap happier than most folks."

That night after supper Ruth and Lin took a walk. When they had reached a lonely spot, they sat down, and Lin read what Kinkaid had written in the tally book.

"To whom it may concern," read Lin in a low voice. "I do hereby bequeath all that I have on earth to Ruth Webster and Lin Rawlins. To be given them the day they are married. John Towne, attorney in El Paso, has a listing of all property that will run in value many thousand dollars. To Ruth Webster and Lin Rawlins I wish all happiness. May God bless their union, always. So I, Keno Kinkaid, pay my debt to Lin Rawlins, who saved my life. And so, I hope, in some small measure, to atone for the wrong I have done Ruth Webster. It was I, Keno Kinkaid, who killed her father, Bill Webster, at Tia Juana, Mexico. For that killing I cannot ask her forgiveness. The duel was a fair one. *Adiós*."

Coffin Ranch

Walt Coburn was contributing a short novel each month in the 1930s to *Dime Western* and *Star Western*, both published by Popular Publications. These short novels averaged about 25,000 words in length, and his word rate at Popular Publications was the same as it had once been at Fiction House. *10 Story Western*, edited at the time for Popular Publications by David Manners, bought short stories of 3,000 to 5,000 words, novelettes of 9,000 words, and short novels of 15,000 words. Walt Coburn was more comfortable with the length of the short novel than with the short story because his fiction was character-driven and shorter fiction tended to rely too much on plot really to accommodate the stories he had to tell. In PIONEER CATTLEMAN OF MONTANA Coburn included reminiscences of Butch Cassidy, the Sundance Kid, and Kid Curry — at one time Kid Curry worked for the Circle C Ranch and saved Bob Coburn's life — and so it is not surprising that occasionally, as here, one or more of them can be found as characters in one of his Western stories. When "Coffin Ranch" was published in the issue for August,

1937 of *10 Story Western*, the editor re-titled it "Fighting Wages at Coffin Ranch" to give the impression of action and gun play, but "Coffin Ranch" remains the more fitting title for a story in which the shadow of death has such a pervasive rôle.

CHAPTER ONE

"'Won't You Come Home, Bill Bailey?'"

With a sheriff's posse crowding him, Bill Bailey headed into the rough country to the south. He was hoping the stolen horse packing him wouldn't give plumb out till he crossed the Mexican line. He headed straight into a wide-mouthed cañon that would either offer him a trail through the mountains or else trap him in a high-walled box.

Bill Bailey was a stranger in a strange land, and had no way of knowing where the cattle trail into the cañon led. He'd lost his bearings a day or so ago, trying to shake off that damned posse. He'd slipped all of them but three or four. And they were crowding so close now that it was making even the calm-tempered, cold-nerved, red-headed Bill Bailey uncomfortable. As his stolen horse followed the trail that twisted through brush and huge boulders, he could hear the men behind him shouting to one another to close in.

"We got 'im!" the outlaw heard the rasping voice of the deputy. "He's rode into Rough Cañon. Close in, boys, and we'll knock his damn' horns off. We got the center-fire son!"

"My saddle's a three-quarter rig," muttered Bill Bailey, sliding his carbine from its saddle scabbard, "not a center-fire. Close in on me, you loose-mouthed badge-shiner, and I'll bite me off a hunk or two of law meat while you bounty hunters are gittin' an outlaw meal."

Bill Bailey's green eyes scanned the rough, brushy sides of the cañon, looking for a trail that would rim out. But he couldn't see one. His one bet now was to take to the brush and put up a fight till they killed him. Through clenched teeth, he hummed a song he'd heard around the honkatonks. It was called "Bill Bailey." Because that was his name, the song had tickled his fancy, and he'd adopted one half-remembered verse as his own. To him it had a twisted, comical, and sardonic significance.

> **Won't you come home, Bill Bailey?**
> **Won't you come home?**
> **They sang the whole night lo-o-ng.**
> **Won't you come home, Bill Bailey?**
> **Won't you come home?**
> **We know we done you wro-o-ng!**

From under a low-pulled hat brim, he twisted his eyes to either side of the cañon. The deputy and his men were getting closer, shooting to drive him on. Then the ping of a rifle echoed in the cañon, the sound flung back by the two walls like a rubber ball. Before the echoes had died, the sharp crack of the gun was rattling as fast as its owner could shoot. Bill Bailey

250

made out a puff of white powder smoke high up on the side of the cañon, where the lone marksman was concealed by rocks and brush.

At first Bill had thought the man up there was shooting at him. But the hoarse, profane shouting of the deputy back down the cañon told him otherwise.

"Turn back, men!" roared the deputy. "The dirty, sneakin' coyote has led us into a trap. He's got friends a-waitin'. They'll shoot tuh kill. Ride back outta here afore we all git bush-whacked. The damned, sneakin' coyote! Ride fer your lives, boys, they're a-shootin' close to us."

Bill Bailey grinned and let his leg-weary horse slow down to a less heart-breaking gait. And he followed the twisting trail.

The lone man on the side of the cañon kept up a continual gunfire that was sending the big-mouthed deputy and his pool-room posse of town glory-hunters back at a run.

Because Bill didn't know how to get up there where the lone marksman was hidden, he let his horse pick its own way, following the cattle trail up the cañon. They began climbing at an easy angle up toward a sort of saddle between two timbered buttes. And when his blowing horse had reached the top of the climb and halted to get its wind, Bill Bailey was not surprised to see a man ride out of the brush, and come toward him at a running walk.

He had expected the man who had driven back the deputy and his two-bit posse to be a friend. This man was a stranger. And in spite of his cowpuncher clothes,

251

Bill spotted him for a dude. A number of items about his garb, also the way he sat his horse, betrayed the rider as a pilgrim. The rider was tall, lean, clean shaven. He was tanned, but there was a pinched look to his face and a grayish pallor to his hollow cheeks that branded him as belonging to that small army of the damned who had been sent to Arizona in a last, desperate fight against that dread, insidious enemy, tuberculosis. Bill figured the dude for a lunger.

There was a handsome, sporting rifle across the man's saddle, and he was holding a quart bottle of whiskey in his hand. Fever-bright eyes, light blue in color, looked at Bill Bailey from under a high-crowned, wide-brimmed black Stetson that was larger than cowboys favored. Those big hats were ordered from the hat makers by show cowboys and dudes. The man's tight-lipped mouth twisted in a faint, mocking grin.

"You're on the Coffin range, stranger. I bid you welcome." His voice had an Eastern accent, and he was plainly drunk. "I have no brass band to play you stirring march music, no key to the city to offer you as a token of hospitality . . . only the right hand and the bottle it holds. Your visit is as a sign from the gods. A few moments ago and all was quiet, and I sat alone on yonder rimrock with the poor companionship of unwelcome specters that marched forth from the wreckage of shattered dreams. I chose the spot on this, the twenty-fifth anniversary of the date of my birth, quite without a friend in this cactus-and-rock-strewn land of yours. E'en as it should be on this last birthday

. . . memories . . . a bottle . . . sitting alone at the feet of the gods.

"And then the quietude is shattered by sounds below in the cañon, and with my field glasses I view a bit of drama in the real. I see a man, the odds stacked against him as fate stacks the cards at times against the luckless, for fate is a fickle wench and enjoys her grisly smiling as she turns thumbs down. Eh? Have a drink. My companionship is not the most cheerful, but the whiskey is twenty-year-old stock."

He uncorked the bottle and handed it to Bill Bailey. "Wipe the neck of the bottle on your shirt before drinking, stranger. Germs." He took a silver cigarette case from the pocket of a shabby hunting jacket, selected a monogrammed cigarette, and lit it. His hands were steady, his voice thin as a razor blade, his sunken blue eyes not blurred. But the man was drunk.

Bill Bailey took the bottle, and his wide mouth spread in a grin. "Here's howdy, mister. And here's thankin' you. My horse was about played out. The men you scared back was a deputy sheriff named Al Donley and some tinhorns he hired at Old Pueblo town."

"I recognized the strident voice of the swaggering Beau Brummel of Old Pueblo."

Then the tobacco smoke started the man coughing. His thin frame bent across his saddle horn, shaking, shuddering in the throes of the racking cough. Bill Bailey swung to the ground and lifted the man from his saddle. He laid the tall, thin form on the ground and stood by, helplessly watching. Blood spilled from the thin-lipped mouth. When the coughing had ceased, Bill found a clean white handkerchief in the pocket of the shabby corduroy shooting jacket and wiped the bloody froth from the gray lips. After a bit, he held the neck of the bottle against the sick man's mouth. The bloodshot, blue eyes thanked him.

They sat for perhaps half an hour in silence. The blood drove the gray pallor from the sick man's cheeks, and the tanned skin and telltale spots across the cheekbones resumed their color. The lunger's eyes, too bright, shadowed beneath, stared off into the distance.

Bill Bailey was a man who understood the golden value of silence. He let the other man speak first.

"They sent me West to die, gave me six months. Four of 'em are gone now." His eyes swung around to look at the cowpuncher. He smiled thinly. "I'm afraid I was near to showing the white feather when you and your friends appeared on the scene."

He took a small, silver stamp box from his jacket pocket and sprung open the lid with his lean fingers. A single white pill was in the box. He looked at it.

"Cyanide of potassium," he said flatly. "Kills a man in a few seconds. Less messy than a bullet." He flipped it into the brush with his thumb. "Damned cowardly, carryin' it about. Eh?"

"No." Bill Bailey shook his head. "No, I wouldn't call it cowardly, mister. You ain't a coward."

"Thank you, friend. But you're quite wrong. However, we won't waste breath arguing such an unimportant matter. Let's have a drink. Then we'll ride on to the ranch. Al Donley won't follow you there. He's not welcome at Coffin Ranch. I've told him so. And my foreman, Jack Crippen, has given Donley orders not to come on our range. I bought the outfit when I landed at Old Pueblo four months ago. The name of the brand struck my fancy. Seemed appropriate at the time . . . eh? Morbid, my friend, but nevertheless quite, quite appropriate. Have another drink. It's twenty-year-old bourbon . . . the cup that cheers . . . past regrets and future fears."

"Got any cows at the home ranch, mister? Milkin' cows?"

"Two or three Jerseys shipped from the East by my doctor, C. O. D. But none of the cowboys know how to milk. And I've never had the patience or skill to make the beasts give down so much as a whiskey glass full of milk."

"Hell! How you fixed for chickens?"

"A brace of the best gamecocks north of the Mexican line," smiled the lunger, taking another drink.

"Fightin' roosters don't lay eggs. Mix that twenty-year-old liquor with enough cream and milk and eggs and you'll make a plumb liar out of that fool doctor back East that give you a six-months' life sentence. Hell, I've seen men fetched to Arizona on a stretcher. One, two, five years, and you couldn't kill 'em with an axe. You got guts, mister, but you ain't usin' 'em. You're layin' down and lettin' that li'l ol' cough lick yuh. I'm no doctor, but I'll gamble I'll have you ridin' bronc's in a year if you'll let me train you and foller my orders. Let's git on to your Coffin Ranch. You just saved my scalp from bein' hung on Al Donley's coup stick. I never was no dairy hand, but I'll juice your

Jerseys and feed you eggs . . . buzzard eggs, if I can't locate nothin' better. The man that give you the six-months' verdict is a damn' fool and a liar."

"Hollingsworth," smiled the lunger, "would get the shock of his frock-coated life if he could hear that. He's the highest paid specialist in New York."

"Git on your horse, mister. We got to git to the Coffin Ranch by milkin' time. Your milkman's name is Bill Bailey.

He's travelin' light from the Montana country."

"You've hired out to Stewart Mollison the Third . . . Stew, to my friends back home, the drinking friends. On other anniversaries of the nativity of Stewart Mollison the Third, those friends toasted his health, prosperity, and happiness in the bubbly stuff from cobwebbed bottles, amid the gay laughter of beautiful women and the . . ."

"This is Arizona, and I don't give a damn if you're Prince Henry the Seventeenth of Russia. You ain't a damned bit better than any common hand to me. We don't want to wear our grandfather's breeches out here. A man's just as good as the guts he's got. And sittin' on a rock with a cyanide pill don't show guts, nor feelin' sorry for yourself because you taken the word of a high-toned society doctor. You got more blue blood than red, because you lack the guts and brains to do your own thinkin' or fightin'. That's the size of it. I'm Bill Bailey the First. And I pay my way where I go. You done me a favor. I'm payin' you back. And if you wasn't sick, I'd slap hell outta you."

"If I wasn't sick, Bill Bailey, you wouldn't be man enough to do the job." The lunger grinned. "Come on, Bill. Sundown is milking hour."

CHAPTER
TWO

"Brand of the Coffin"

At the barn, Jack Crippen, foreman of the Coffin outfit, scowled at the red-haired, freckled, blunt-featured Bill Bailey. They were alone together. Crippen, who stood six feet three in his socks, had the straight, coarse, black hair, large nose, and high cheek-bones that belonged to the Indian side of his mixed ancestry, but his eyes were light gray, like blued steel in the sunlight. They said of Jack Crippen that he was as dangerous as a corral full of mountain lions. But if Bill Bailey was scared, the fear didn't show in his eyes or in the wide grin he gave the Coffin ramrod.

"Long time no see you, Bailey. And if I never sighted you, it would be plenty soon. What's your game here?"

"I hired out to your boss to herd two Jersey cows and some egg-layin' hens he's shippin' in. That's as much as you need to know, Injun. Don't ease that purty white-handled gun of yourn from its nest unless you got the bulge. Because if you do, I'll beat you to it. And I won't shoot to miss. I'm not tellin' this dude, Mollison, your past history, if that what's eatin' on yuh. I'm not even tellin' him you lied like hell when you let on you hated Al Donley. I reckon I know your game

258

here. And I got this much to say ... that stealin' pennies out of a blind man's cup is plumb sportin' compared to your tinhorn cheatin'.

"I hired out to Mollison to pail two Jersey cows and gather the eggs. Crowd me and I'll give you an imitation of a red-headed, short-complected, five-foot-eight Irishman makin' a bunch quitter out of a quarter-breed renegade cross between a rattlesnake and a hydrophoby skunk. You kin send word to your pardner, Al Donley, that he kin locate me here at the Coffin Ranch when he feels lucky. But when he shows up, he better have a gun in his hand. Is there anything else I kin do for you, Crippen? Now's a good time to settle things between me and you. Feel lucky?"

Jack Crippen's slitted, bloodshot, black eyes glared long and hard at Bill Bailey. Then he turned and walked away, his spurs jangling. Bill Bailey grinned at the foreman's back, then went on to the bunkhouse.

He found the dude owner of the outfit talking to a group of cowpunchers inside the old Mexican adobe bunkhouse, passing a fresh bottle of whiskey around. After the manner of cowpunchers, they sized up the red-headed stranger. Bill Bailey returned their stare, nodded to one man he knew. His hand came slowly away from the butt of his six-shooter. He shook his head at the proffered bottle.

"Where do you keep your milk pails, mister?" he asked mildly. And he returned the puzzled stares of the men with a faint grin.

"The cook might know, Bill," said the pilgrim ranch owner, amusement in his blue eyes. "Boys, this is Bill

Bailey. Just hired . . . I'm sorry if I let your name slip, Bill. I'm a clumsy idiot."

"That's all right, boss. Crippen would tell 'em, anyhow. And I was no stranger to Al Donley, who'll know where to find me. I'll see the cook about diggin' up a bucket. You might have one of the boys put them two Jerseys into the corral if they have time."

Bill went out. As he walked away, he heard one of the men express a loud "*Whew!*"

"Is that actually Bill Bailey from Montana?" asked a tipsy voice.

"It shore is, fellers. The original Bill Bailey."

"And just who," Bill heard Mollison asking, "might Bill Bailey be? You chaps fondle the name as though it was a hot potato in your mouth."

"Ask Jack Crippen who Bill Bailey is, boss."

That brought a ripple of laughter. Bill grinned and headed for the cook cabin.

When Bill entered the back door of the kitchen, the cook, a short, round-paunched, bald-headed, walrus-mustached man in a rather soiled floursack apron turned from the stove, a skillet in his hand. He was cussing as he swung around at the sound of jingling spurs.

"How many times have I told you drunken, pie-stealin' sons to keep outta my kitchen? I'll wrap this fryin' pan around your . . . Bill Bailey, or I'm gone loco!"

"H'are yuh, Baldy? Long time no see you. Not since we got you outta that Wind River jail and taken you to the Hole to cook Christmas dinner two years ago."

"Yeah, and when I sobered up afterwards, I woke up in the same damn' jail where you jobbin's sons had put me. I hadn't orter forgive you for that, Bill. And one of them fifty-dollar bills you boys gimme was from that Great Northern hold-up. Was that a proper way to treat the best damn' roundup cook that ever drove four bronc's to a mess wagon and rassled a sourdough keg? I orter bend this skillet . . ."

"Take 'er easy, Buddy. Shove your temper in your flank pocket and tell me just what kind of a spread is this Coffin layout?"

"Mollison is drinkin' hisself to death, while Jack Crippen and the sorriest bunch of would-be cowboys ever assembled is stealin' him blind. Crippen shanghaied me outta the Old Pueblo jail, where none other than that double-dealin', sheep-thievin' Al Donley wears the law badge. I been here a month, but even in that short time a blind man could see what went on. This Mollison dude has more money than brains, which ain't sayin' much. He's got a pair of bum lungs, and he ain't been sober since I landed here. I'm the only human on this place that don't drink with him. Crippen has me on the Injun list. I get double wages if I stay sober . . . not a damn' cent if I take so much as a lemon extract toddy. There's booze enough on the Coffin Ranch to stock two saloons. It's like tryin' to stay sober in town. It's plumb inhuman and torturin' to a man like me, Bill. But what fetches you here? I heard you went to the Argentine. Then somebody said you'd been killed. And not more'n a week ago a feller said you was in the pen under another name. I heard some kind of a story about Crippen and Al Donley turnin' in some boys in New Mexico about a year ago. Is it that you come to this part of the country to pay off Donley and Crippen?"

"Where do you hide the milk pails, Baldy?" grinned Bill Bailey.

"You always was hell for answerin' questions. Excuse me for hornin' into what ain't my business, Bill. But you kin bank on me in a tight. I'm no hand with a gun unless mebby it's a shotgun and ten-foot range. But gimme a meat cleaver or a butcher knife or a skillet, and I'll hold up my end of a ruckus. I don't like Crippen. Donley agrees with me like pizen straight. And you boys treated me plumb handsome up on Wind River. Not all of that foldin' money you fellers gimme was dangerous. I got enough outta what Butch and the Kid and the rest of the Wild Bunch and Hole-in-the-Wall gang put in the hat you passed to send Jan off to trainin' school at Tucson. She finished this year."

"Little Jan's a real schoolmarm now, Baldy?"

"Schoolmarm, hell!" snorted Baldy. "She's a nurse and a top-hand at the trade. She's workin' right now with Doc Kelly at Old Pueblo. He says she's the best nurse he ever had. You mind little Doc Kelly from Montana? He had to git out on account of his lungs. And this dude, Mollison, thinks he's in bad shape. Hell! Little Doc was fetched in on a stretcher. But he wasn't layin' 'em down. He's got guts . . . and brains. And he's got a heart bigger than a washtub. You should remember little Doc Kelly?"

262

"I should, Baldy. He went with me through a Montana blizzard on a fifty-mile ride to patch up a couple of boys hid out in the badlands. And he made the snow red when he coughed, Baldy. I remember Doc Kelly. So little Jan is with Doc! I ain't seen Jan since she had pigtails and her mother was alive and you had that place on the Missouri River at the mouth of Cow Crick. She was a little tike, all eyes, and leggy like a young colt. I fetched her a spotted Injun pony for her to learn to ride. She learned right quick. That was ten years ago."

"You wasn't much more'n a button yourself, Bill, jinglin' horses for the Circle C and aimin' to ride the rough string for 'em some day. And the next we heard, you'd shot a feller and taken to the outlaw trail. That was how long back, Bill?"

The easy grin left Bill Bailey's freckled, tanned face. His green-gray eyes under sun-bleached brows hardened.

"Five years, Baldy. Where's the milk pail?"

"Sorry, Bill. I'm a gabby ol' fool. Had supper?"

"I'll eat when I'm done milkin' Stew Mollison's two Jerseys."

"What! You milk a cow? You ain't drunk, Bill?"

"Not drunk on a couple of nips of Mollison's twenty-year-old hooch. I hired out as milkman for the Coffin spread. The Mollison dude done me a favor. I'm goin' to pay him back. He needs more milk and some hen fruit and not so much booze. Ain't that a milk bucket yonder?"

263

CHAPTER
THREE

"First Blood For The Milkman"

Bill Bailey managed to get a pail of milk from the two Jersey cows. And not until he'd finished milking did he pay any attention to the cowpunchers who sat perched around on the top log of the corral. He'd ignored their grins and snickers and joshing remarks. He handed the filled pail to Baldy and looked up at them, his thumbs hooked in his sagging cartridge belt. His gaze fastened on Jack Crippen, who perched alongside Mollison.

"You and the boys have seemed to enjoy the milkin' show, Crippen. I'm turnin' over the cow juicin' to you in the mornin'. You'd orter make a good dairy hand. From the amount of unbranded calves I seen on the Coffin range as I crossed it, I'd say you shore ain't been workin' hard at cowboyin'. I just taken the milkin' chores this evenin' to show you how it's done. The boss kin expect a full pail of cow juice tomorrow mornin' when you squat on the Injun side of them Jerseys and coax the critters to give down."

Bill Bailey was standing in the middle of the round horse corral. And every man watching and listening, even the pilgrim owner of Coffin Ranch, knew that the red-haired cowpuncher was throwing up a challenge at

264

the big, black-haired foreman of the spread. They looked at Crippen for the next move, expecting a gun play.

"If you was half my size, Bailey, I'd rub your face in the mess your damn' cows have made of this horse corral."

"I am half your size, Injun. Step down." Bill Bailey grinned.

Unbuckling his cartridge belt, he handed it and his six-shooter to the cook. "Hold this, Baldy. Crippen's comin' down to spank me across his lap."

Baldy chuckled. "Whup that big son, Billy, and I'll buy you the best hat Stetson ever made outta beaver feathers."

Jack Crippen unbuckled his gun belt and handed it with the fancy holstered pearl-handled six-shooter to Mollison.

"I hate to tie into a little feller, Stew, but that banty rooster is crowin' too loud fer my ears."

"Fight fair, boys," called Stew Mollison. "Marquis of Queensberry rules. I'll time the rounds."

"Boss," said Baldy, "cowhands never heard of this Queensberry that makes rules. I once knowed a Ike Kingsbury in Montana, but he didn't have no Queenberries. No holds barred. Here's your milk, boss. I'm backin' my old friend, Bill Bailey. And I'm makin' 'er tough on ary you roosters up there that tries to pull Billy off his Injun meat. Have at the big son, Bill Bailey."

No man there, Crippen included, had ever seen the red-headed outlaw in a rough and tumble fight. But

Baldy Clark, roundup cook, who had cooked a Christmas dinner for outlaws up in the Hole-in-the-Wall country, had seen Bill Bailey fight for the sport of it with buckskin riding gloves instead of boxing gloves. "I'll bet the wages I got comin' that Bill Bailey whups Crippen," he called. "Who wants ary part of the bet?"

There was a chorus of takers. Bill looked small and helpless as he faced the big ramrod of the Coffin outfit.

Stew Mollison grinned faintly. "I'll call any wagers Baldy's money won't cover. I'll back Bill Bailey. Who bets on Jack Crippen?"

"I'll give you ten to one." Crippen looked up with a faint, unpleasant grin. "I'll bet all I have and what I got comin' that I'll wipe the cow dirt outta this horse corral and use Bailey's red head for a mop."

"The bet," said Mollison, "will be even money. Call you, Jack. No hard feelings . . . just sportin'. The underdog and that sort of sentiment."

Bill Bailey grinned up at him. "Don't spill any of that cow juice. You got to drink 'er all if I win. If I lose, you kin pour it on me and go back to the whiskey. But if I clean this big Injun's plow, you swap your twenty-year-old bourbon for fresh milk. You claim to have sportin' blood. Money bettin' don't hurt you if you do lose. But I'm wonderin', mister, if you'll call my milk bet?"

"Consider the bet covered, Bill Bailey. And may the best man win!"

As the tipsy crowd yelled, Jack Crippen came at Bill with a jump, his fists swinging. There was a thin, twisted grin on his face. Bill's hooked left, as he ducked Crippen's swing, covered the big man's grin with a smear of blood. First blood for Bill Bailey. He'd split Crippen's lips wide open. He'd cut him down.

Before the big man was back on balance, Bill ripped in a terrific jolt to Crippen's belly. With a grunting gasp, Crippen's long frame bent. He dropped his guard to cover his stomach, and Bill Bailey clipped the big man's jaw with a short hook that rocked Crippen's head.

That was the start of the fight that became Coffin history. Stewart Mollison III and the cowpunchers on the top rail of the corral looked on in gaping, wide-eyed silence. And they saw the unbelievable happen under their staring eyes. They saw Bill Bailey, five feet eight and weighing one hundred sixty-five at the most, moving like a streak, never wasting a blow, hammer and rip Jack Crippen, who had the build of a giant.

The red-headed, outlaw cowpuncher took his time as he punished the bigger man. Deliberately, with a cold-eyed, grinning sort of hatred and fury, he smashed Crippen's face to a bloody, swollen, shapeless pulp. He battered the big man to the ground, taunted him with rasping, slashing insults until he got dizzily to his feet. Then Bill ripped Crippen's blood-smeared face and battered his aching ribs once more.

It kept up until Crippen, slobbering, blubbering, was on his knees, begging for mercy, begging Bill Bailey not to hit him again. In the end Bill Bailey, whose own face was badly battered, one eye swollen shut and one ear ragged from Crippen's teeth, took Crippen's shock of coarse black hair in his two hands. He shoved the slobbering, whimpering, pleading man's face in the cow dirt of the corral. Then he walked away from the quivering hulk.

"I'll take my gun now, Baldy," Bill Bailey said quietly.

"Come around with me to the kitchen, Billy," whispered the beaming cook, "and I'll clean yuh up. I got a bottle hid. And I'm takin' a drink, even if I git fired tomorrow for it."

"You won't git fired, Baldy. I don't reckon Jack Crippen will be workin' here tomorrow."

Bill Bailey had voiced what Mollison and every cowhand that lined the top rail of the corral knew. If Bill Bailey stayed on, Crippen would have to go. The Coffin range wasn't big enough now to hold both men. And it's the law of the range that says the victor stays. The beaten man saddles his private horse and pulls out, like a bull whipped out of a herd by a stronger fighter.

There were no cheers for Bill Bailey. Those were all Crippen men on the corral fence. Crippen had hired them. They'd go with him when he left, as a matter of course. Stewart Mollison III was too much of a pilgrim to understand that. But he was to learn a lot before he was many hours older.

He had sense enough, though, tipsy as he was, not to cheer Bill Bailey. He saw his cowhands looking down at the whipped, sobbing form of Jack Crippen. He handed Crippen's belt and gun to the nearest cowpuncher and climbed down off the corral. He followed Baldy and Bill Bailey to the kitchen. In one hand he carried the pail of milk.

In the little shed off the kitchen that was the cook's wash room, Stewart Mollison III set down the bucket of milk. From the side pocket of his shabby, corduroy shooting jacket he took a silver flask and set it on the wash bench in front of Bill Bailey. There was a curious smile on his face.

"Only a blackguard and coward shirks a gambling debt, Bill. There's the firewater. Would it be welching if I had Baldy strain that milk before I started in on it?"

Bill Bailey grinned through battered, swollen lips. His one visible eye twinkled.

"You'll do, Stew. And I ain't askin' you to quit cold on the hooch. That'd be brutal as hell. It might kill you. Say we make 'er like this . . . you won't take a drink except with me."

"My hand on that, Bill."

"Unless you fire me. It's like this, Stew . . . either me or Crippen has to pull out."

"To the victor belong the spoils, Bill. Crippen came with the Coffin outfit when I bought it. His going won't cause me to shed tears. The job's yours if you want it. Ever run an outfit?"

There was a snort from Baldy, who was coming with a beefsteak for Bill's closed eye. "Bill Bailey's as good a cowhand as ever jiggered a roundup spread, mister. Bill won't steal you blind, neither. Bill never robbed nobody but the railroads in his life. And robbin' a railroad is no crime. Ask any cowhand. Keep the law from closin' in on Bill Bailey, and you got a ramrod that'll put this hen-yard outfit in shape in no time. Boss, I'm takin' a drink with Bill. I've knowed this boy since he was knee-high to a horned toad. And if you can me for drinkin' with this fightin', sorrel-maned, young rannyhan, you ain't the gentleman the blue book claims you to be."

"Bill's the boss, Baldy. You heard him put me on what you call the Injun list. Bill, how about it?"

"This drink comes under the head of medicine, Stew. Drink hearty and pass 'er to Baldy. And when I git washed up, the three of us will have a little medicine talk, as the Injun says. Baldy tells me that Doc Kelly is located at Old Pueblo. He's forgot more about the doctorin' trade than your fancy-priced Eastern specialists ever will know. He's cured hisself of his own lung ailment, and Baldy says he come here on a stretcher. I seen him patch up two of the worst shot-up men you could find in a week's long journey, with only his little black bag of tools to work with and no chloroform to put 'em under. Them boys lived. One was hung. The other is down in the Argentine right now. Doc Kelly's worth more than a corral full of dude doctors. I'm takin' you to see him. He don't wear specs on a black ribbon or frock coats and hard-boiled shirts and a silk hat. But he kin put life back into a week-dead corpse. I'm turnin' you over to little Doc Kelly. Now drink hearty, Stew. And pass 'er along to Baldy and me. This 'un is on the house."

"Look yonder," hissed Baldy, the silver flask halfway to his mouth. "Crippen's makin' a war talk to his coyote pack there near the corral. Bill, trouble's a-comin', shore as hell."

270

CHAPTER
FOUR

"Gunfighters' Payoff"

Jack Crippen, staggering like a drunken man, was weaving his way toward the bunkhouse. His face and clothes were covered with dirt and blood. He had his six-shooter in his hand. He was spitting blood and cursing in a hoarse, sobbing voice. His men trailed him, talking together and looking toward the open shed where Bill Bailey, Mollison, and Baldy Clark were standing. One of Crippen's men took hold of his arm and said something to the big, blood-smeared ramrod. Crippen halted and stood on spread legs, swaying a little.

His voice came in a croaking, sobbing challenge: "No man kin do what you done and live to brag about it, Bailey. I'm damn' near blind and half beat to death, and I can't see good to gunfight nobody. But I'm goin' to make you sorry you didn't finish me. I'm goin' to sell your damned hide to the law for five thousand dollars."

"Take it back to Montana, Crippen, where it'll fetch eight thousand," called Bill Bailey. "I just whupped you out of your job. Take your coyote pack and drift, or I'll double a wet rope and run you off. You ain't workin' here no longer. And you gambled your wages all away.

Saddle your privates and roll your beds. You got about half an hour till dark. And that's your limit."

Crippen snarled and spat out a mouthful of blood. He lurched on to the bunkhouse.

"Where do they keep their private horses?" asked Bill Bailey.

"Down in the lower pasture."

"One of you men wrangle the lower pasture," Bill Bailey called out. "Corral your horses and saddle up. You'll ride your privates when you leave here or else travel afoot like sheep-herders. The Coffin outfit ain't mountin' no more petty larceny things like you."

Two of the men headed for the barn. The others followed Crippen into the bunkhouse.

Bill Bailey washed up, then together with Baldy and Mollison he went into the mess hall, holding the chunk of raw beef against his black eye. Baldy plied them with strong coffee and food, and set a pitcher of milk at Stew Mollison's place. As they ate, they heard the two men corral the little bunch of horses that belonged to Crippen and his crew. The cowpunchers did a lot of loud, drunken talking as they saddled. It was getting dark outside now. Stew Mollison told Baldy to light the lamp.

"I wouldn't make a light," said Bill Bailey. "That flea-bit crew is drunk and ornery. They ain't leavin' without makin' some sort of a play. And I don't like to make a target out of my eight-thousand-dollar hide." He got up from the long bench at the table. "Looky yonder. They done set fire to the bunk-house. And here they come. Lay low! Don't go near the door or windows."

Yelling, shooting, spurring their horses to a run, Crippen's crew rode past the mess hall. Their bullets shattered the windows, thudded against the adobe walls, and closed door. Flames roared inside the bunkhouse.

In the dark shadows of the mess hall, Bill Bailey and Stew Mollison crouched, their six-shooters in their hands. And Baldy, armed with a cleaver, swore into his walrus mustache, because there'd be nobody to eat the big supper he'd prepared.

Then Stew Mollison gave a dry-throated cry of anger. Through the broken windows he'd seen flames shoot up from the main house, a long, low-roofed, rambling old adobe. Before Bill Bailey was aware of the dude ranchman's intentions, Mollison had jerked open the door and was running toward the burning house, shouting at the top of his voice.

A dozen shadowy riders charged past the man on foot, their guns spewing fire. Stew Mollison stumbled, reeled, pitched forward on his face.

Bill Bailey quit the mess hall on a dead run, shooting as fast as he could thumb back the hammer of his gun. One of the riders pitched sideways from his saddle. Another gave a wild yell of pain and reeled drunkenly as his running horse carried him out of sight.

Bill reached the almost motionless form of Stew Mollison. Gathering the limp form in his arms, he raced for the mess hall. Bullets were whining like hornets around his head. He staggered inside with his burden, and Bailey, swearing like a bullwhacker, kicked the door shut after him.

"Looks like the murderin' snakes got 'im, Baldy. Look him over. I'll show them gents the difference between fightin' and foolin'."

As they charged the mess hall and kitchen, Bill Bailey crouched beside one of the low windows and drove them to cover with a one-man volley of lead slugs. He had his own six-shooter and a long-barreled .45 that Baldy had shoved into his hand with brief explanation.

"I'd only be wastin' the lead, Billy. Never could shoot a gun. Scared of the damn' things. Shut my eyes when I pull the trigger. Shot a man's prize milk cow once when I aimed at a flyin' hawk. Take 'er. Mollison's either dead or sleepin'."

For perhaps an hour Bill Bailey held off Crippen and his drunken pack as they bombarded the place. Twice they tried to set the mess hall afire. Each time Bill Bailey drove the firebugs back with a few well-placed shots that crippled the men with the firebrands. Then Crippen and his men headed for town, snarling and shouting and quarreling among themselves, Crippen cursing them. Fire had gutted the bunkhouse and Mollison's ranch house, leaving only the thick adobe walls standing amid the smoking, flaming embers.

Baldy lit the lamp, and they examined Stew Mollison. He had been shot twice, in the thigh and one shoulder. He opened his eyes, blinking. He grinned faintly at Bill Bailey.

"The will of the gods, Bill. Do I rate a drink before I cash in my white chips?"

"Here's a drink, Stew. And you ain't nowhere near dead. I'm goin' to town after my old friend, Doc Kelly. Doc will have you dancin' the Red River jig in no time. Quit actin' like a yeller-bellied quitter, mister. Fight! I've seen men, a heap worse shot to pieces than you are, go on about their work like they wasn't no worse than mosquito-bit. Baldy's goin' to ride herd on you till I git back. Here. This dropped outta your coat. Man, if I had a girl like that to live for, I shore wouldn't talk about layin' 'em down. Play your hand out, Stew. So long."

Bill Bailey grinned and went outside. He headed for the barn. Five minutes later he rode away at a long trot.

"Yonder," said Baldy gruffly, "rides as game a cowboy as ever went to hell and back for a friend. There's a price on that boy's head, and he's got to ride into a town where he'll be shot on sight by the first hidehunter that spots him. They call him an outlaw. Mister, if this old world was as full of such outlaws as young Bill Bailey, it'd be a damn' fine place to live in.

"I'd give a purty to know what fetches Bill Bailey to this part of the country. There's twenty, thirty thousand dollars cached somewheres, and only a couple of men left alive to claim any part of it. That money is supposed to be cached somewheres in Arizona, near the Mexican line. I done heard Crippen and Al Donley talkin' about it in town when they was drunk. When I was in jail and they thought I was dead drunk, they talked in the sheriffs office near my cell. Take another drink, boss. Billy would give it to you if he was here."

275

"Milk will do it, Baldy. Not even Bill Bailey is going to call me a quitter. I'm going to thrash him for that crack when I get well. A few years ago, believe it or call me a liar, I was amateur middleweight champ back in the East. I was captain of the varsity crew and football team. Not even Bill Bailey can call me a yellow-bellied quitter. Trot out your milk."

Baldy chuckled and went into the kitchen. He saw Mollison take the photograph in its handsome leather case and throw it across the mess hall. It landed in a dark corner. Baldy had seen the photograph. It was the picture of a very beautiful girl with a lot of light-colored hair and large, dark eyes and the sort of smile that quickens a man's pulse. And across it was written in a neat, slanting hand: "With all my love, Eleanor."

Baldy poured a big slug of whiskey into a tin cup and filled the rest of the cup with milk. Then he took a quick pull at the bottle, corked it reluctantly, and put it away. He took Mollison's drink into the mess hall, where they had put the wounded man on Baldy's bedroll.

"The drop of liquor in this cow juice is strictly doctor's orders. And nobody's callin' you a quitter."

Stew Mollison's blue eyes, staring into the dark-shadowed corner where he had thrown the picture, were as cold as shining steel in the lamplight. They were bitter, brooding, hard.

"Doc Kelly," Baldy continued, "is the best doctor that ever fished a lead slug out of a cowboy's innards and sewed him up so's he could ride bronc's again. He's done operations with carpenter and blacksmith

276

tools that your high-toned sawbones wouldn't tackle with a million-dollar outfit of hospital tools. He got into trouble because he patched up a couple of outlaws that belonged to the Wild Bunch. They give Doc Kelly enough green foldin' money to choke a mule. Doc never kept a dollar of it. He give it to a hospital that took in charity patients. Doc used to drink a lot. He had to, to keep awake night and day, throwin' hemorrhages faster than a horse kin pitch. He was shipped on a stretcher to Old Pueblo to die. Six months, and he was payin' sick calls. He's too tough to kill. He'll have you in shape to trim Bill Bailey's sails in no time."

Stew Mollison's eyes slid away from the dark corner and looked at the grizzled roundup cook. He grinned and reached for the cup of milk and whiskey.

"Lemme tell you about the time Bill Bailey and Butch Cassidy rode into a town in the Wind River country and stole me outta jail. They taken me plumb up into the Hole-in-the-Wall country. There was a dozen big fat turkeys and all that went to trim a Christmas dinner. I done the cookin'."

Baldy rambled on, a little tipsy. The wounded man half listened. Baldy put more and more whiskey into the milk he fed his patient. When Mollison, exhausted by pain and weakness and drugged by whiskey, dropped into a fitful sleep, Baldy rescued the picture in its beautiful leather case and hid it behind the flour bin. Then he came back to keep watch over the wounded man.

Now and then Stew Mollison muttered in his half delirium. The whispered name on his moving lips was always the same: Eleanor. Sometimes he spoke the name with lingering softness. But more often it was with a bitter twist on his mouth.

CHAPTER
FIVE

"Bill Bailey Confesses"

Bill Bailey reached Old Pueblo around midnight. From the sleepy barnman, he found out where Doc Kelly lived at the edge of town. He found the house easily enough, because lights showed inside, and there were four saddled horses standing out in front of the picket gate. From inside the house came groans and sharp outcries of pain.

Bill dismounted with his gun in his hand and went around to the back door. It was unlocked. He let himself into the lighted kitchen, just as a black-haired, red-cheeked girl in a nurse's uniform entered through the door from the dining room. She halted with a frightened jerk, her round eyes staring at him.

Bill Bailey never knew until later, when he got a look at his unshaved, battered face in a mirror, just what a tough-looking picture he made as he stood there with a gun in his hand. One of his eyes was discolored, swollen shut. His face was bruised from Crippen's fists. His jaw was marred by a red stubble of whiskers. His grin but added to his disreputable appearance.

"Lady," he said in a husky whisper, "will you tell Doc Kelly to slip into the kitchen a minute?"

"The doctor is busy. And you don't need him nearly as badly as three of the four that are ahead of you. You gents certainly celebrate the Fourth early this year. Take a chair. And don't dirty up the floor. I just finished scrubbing it this evening. Why didn't you come in the front way? Or is it that you're hungry as well as beat up?"

"I ain't hungry. But you see, I was playin' on the opposite side of the fellers Doc's got in yonder, and, if they was to sight me, this clean floor of yourn would get mussed a heap more than it is already. Crippen and his boys play rough. Is there another doctor in town?"

"Three others. But . . ."

"But Doc Kelly is the top hand. I know. That's why nobody but him will do. That's why he's got to come along with me now. Those skunks shot a man at the Coffin Ranch. He's mebbyso dyin'. Stew Mollison is a dude, but he's worth savin'. That's more than you kin say for Crippen and his drunken gun-toters in yonder. Your dad tells me you still got that li'l, ol', no-account, two-bit spotted cayuse called Many Spots. Mind the first day you rode him and he shied at a rattler, and you slid off and like to got snake bit? And you quit bawlin' when you was plumb certain the snake hadn't bit your pony? Gosh, you've growed up some since then, Jan."

"Oh, Billy. You're Billy Bailey." Her voice was a husky whisper.

The girl's face had gone a little white. She put the tray of blood-soiled bandages and instruments on the table. She came slowly towards him, her dark, gray

280

eyes searching his face. Bill Bailey grinned and took her two hands awkwardly.

"Those men in there were talking about Bill Bailey. They're . . ."

"Yeah. There's not much time to waste, Jan. No time to talk. They shot Mollison. He's in bad shape. Your dad's lookin' after him. Tell Doc to git his tools and meet me behind that old adobe barn yonder. I fetched a horse for him. Tell Doc to say nothin' to anybody."

"I'll tell him. There's a dun pony in the first stall of the adobe barn. You'll find my saddle with Doc's in the saddle room. Here's the key. Put my saddle on the dun and Doc's saddle on the big bay in the next stall. And shake hands with Many Spots in the box stall at the back. Doc don't know it, but he's taking his nurse along this trip. His housekeeper can shoo Crippen and his yapping warriors out. She can handle 'em. How's Dad? Is he hurt?"

Bill Bailey did not answer. In the doorway behind her he had caught sight of a tall man with his face swathed in bandages. Bill threw the girl aside with a jerk that sent her sprawling. The gun in his hand was cocked when Crippen's scared, hoarse voice came from behind the bandages. His arms shot ceilingward.

"Don't shoot, Bailey! Don't kill me! I ain't got a gun!"

"You're lyin', Crippen. You got a gun, but not the nerve to go for it. Back up. Make a move with your hands, and I'll kill you."

He shoved Crippen against the wall, took a gun from the man's chaps pocket, and flung it behind him. Then he pushed Crippen into the operating room where Doc Kelly was wrapping a bandage around the shoulder of a man who lay on the table, stripped to the waist. Two other men, one with a crudely bandaged leg, the other with his hand swathed in a clumsy, blood-stained bandage, sat on chairs. Bill Bailey's gun swung to cover them. Their hands rose slowly, and fright showed in their eyes. Doc finished tying the bandage and wiped his blood-spattered hands on a red-stained towel.

Doc Kelly was small, leathery, wiry, with a shock of tousled white hair and keen red-brown eyes. He grinned, showing large, even, white teeth.

"Been hearing some reports about you, Billy. You look somewhat the worse for wear, but still in robust health. Emergency visit?"

"These murderin' skunks shot hell out of the dude, Mollison, that bought the Coffin outfit. I'm takin' you to the ranch, Doc. I'll finish tendin' to these fellers for you."

"Hold on, Bill. Don't kill 'em in here. Missus Huggins wouldn't like her house cluttered up, and Jan would back her play. Do your killing out behind somewhere, Billy."

Doc Kelly's bright brown eyes twinkled. He looked at Jan, who stood now in the doorway, rubbing a bruised cheek that had struck the wall when Bill Bailey had pushed her. Her cheeks were bright with color. Then the gray-haired Mrs. Huggins, Doc Kelly's housekeeper, came in, carrying a lamp. She was a large, buxom woman who dwarfed little Doc Kelly and Jan.

"Whatever on earth is happenin' to my house?" Anger blazed in her eyes as she stood at the door, arms akimbo, neat in her spotless gingham. She had brought Doc Kelly to Arizona from Montana. She idolized him, bullied him, fought for him against the world.

"You'll remember Bill Bailey," chuckled Doc Kelly as Jan held his coat after he'd scrubbed up. "Billy's the one that got off with only a black eye and a chewed ear . . . the one with the red hair?"

"Land above, if it ain't the Bailey boy. Whatever on earth you doin' with a gun in your hand in the houses of respectable people? Put it away now, and I'll see if I can find a piece of Jan's cake or perhaps a pie, unless the doctor's stole it."

"Some other time, Miz Huggins. Excuse the gun, but it helps these four mail-order cowhands savvy what I'm talkin' about. All right, Crippen. You and your three brave warriors step outside. You're mussin' up the house. Doc, I'll start 'em walkin' out along the road. They'll be afoot, but I'll be ridin'. Saddle up and ketch up with me, and we'll go on to the Coffin Ranch. If you hear shootin', don't git excited. It'll be me savin' Arizona the expense of hangin' these specimens. Good night, Miz Huggins."

He grinned at Jan. "Sorry I pushed you so hard, Jan. I thought this big 'breed was goin' to shoot. Git along, Crippen."

Bill Bailey herded Crippen and the three wounded men outside. He got his horse and made them walk ahead of him along the dusty road that led out of town, marching them lock-step, prison style.

"If Mollison dies, Crippen," he said flatly, "I'll hang you plenty high. If the law don't do the job, I got friends that will shore be glad to work at it. Keep step there ... hay-foot, straw-foot. Don't bust that lock-step. I'm just trainin' you for the pen at Yuma."

Doc Kelly and Jan, who had changed her white uniform for service-marked cowpuncher clothes, rode up. Bill Bailey grinned and halted the four sullen, sulking marchers.

"Tell this to Al Donley, Crippen," said Bill Bailey. "Tell him he's done played his string out. About face! One, two. Break that lock-step and I'll commence shootin' off your boot heels. March!"

Then, when the four men had scuffed along out of sight in the direction of the lights of the town, Bill Bailey rode between Doc Kelly and Jan.

"You gave your promise to stay in South America, Bill," said Doc Kelly when they'd ridden a way in silence.

"Yeah. I had to break it, Doc. Somethin' happened, and I had to come back. I wish I could tell you about it now, but I can't. I'd heard you was at Old Pueblo and was headed to see you. Somebody sighted me along the trail and got word to this Al Donley. Him and his paid killers set a trap for me and almost got me. They chased me into the mountains. They'd just about had me in a tight when the dude feller, Mollison, saved my bacon. This Mollison is worth takin' along, Doc."

"From all I've heard of him, Bill, I doubt it. I don't care much for his breed. Too much blue blood and not enough of the red. Silk-stockinged aristocracy. *Pah!*

Had more than enough of Mollison's sort when I was at medical school at Harvard. They broad-arrowed me because I waited on tables to pay my tuition. Damn' near broke my spirit. But it's hard to break the spirit of the shanty Irish. Mollison hung around Old Pueblo for a month or so, always pickled in booze. Came West to die. Sorry for himself. *Pah!* Jan, here, has ten times the nerve of your Steward Mollison the Third. Ride on ahead, you two young 'uns. This pacin' walk is just about as fast as Molasses, here, travels. I want to be alone for a while."

Bill Bailey and Jan rode on at a long trot. After a mile or more, Bill Bailey was the first to speak.

"Doc's disappointed with me. You see, I promised him and the governor of Montana that I'd quit the country, that I'd go to the Argentine, and never come back. I had to break that promise. Kelly is as fine a man as ever lived, Jan. I shore hate to hurt him, hate to break his confidence in me."

"Why can't you explain why you had to break faith with him?"

"Because the sign ain't right. And I don't know all the right answers to my own questions yet. When I git all the proofs I'm after, then I'll put 'em in front of Doc Kelly and the governor of Montana, and they'll savvy. But right now I can't talk . . . not even to Doc Kelly."

"Not even to Jan, the roundup cook's kid?"

Bill Bailey didn't answer. For a minute they rode in silence.

"You know, Billy, you were the greatest hero in the world to me when I was a youngster. And nobody, nothing has ever been able to break that hero-worship in my heart. I still don't believe that you ever did a really criminal thing in your life."

"There's a price on my head, Jan. I've trailed with outlaws for five years or more."

"Have you ever killed a man, Billy?"

"I don't know. I've been in some gunfights, like this one we had at the Coffin Ranch. There was a lot of shootin'."

"I don't mean that," said the girl impatiently. "You're hedging. You know what I'm driving it. They claim you killed a man named Shuster, who ramrodded the Rail outfit for a big Eastern syndicate. That was the thing that sent you along the outlaw trail."

"I didn't kill Shuster. I shot him, and for mighty good reasons, or so it seemed at the time. But my bullet didn't kill him. He was plenty alive when I left him at the Rail home ranch. I shot him once. There were half a dozen bullets in his body when they found him dead in his office at the ranch. All exceptin' one bullet hole were in his back. He'd been shot from the outside. Somebody shot him in the back, through the window at night. No, I didn't kill Shuster, though he needed it plenty. But a forty-a-month cowhand didn't stand a ghost's chance of comin' clear at the trial. I broke jail when I learned the cards was stacked against me. Hid out in the badlands with outlaws."

"Were you mixed up in the train robberies and bank holdups you're accused of taking part in? Remember, Billy, it's Baldy's kid that's askin' you . . . the skinny little kid that was all eyes and pigtail braids and pipestem legs and worshipped the red-haired young cowboy who gave her Many Spots. I want you to tell me the truth. How many of those hold-ups were you actually in?"

"You always was the darnedest kid for fool questions." Bill Bailey grinned uncomfortably. "I wasn't in ary one of 'em."

"I knew it! I knew it!" Jan crowded her horse alongside his and threw her arms around his neck. And she kissed him on his battered, bruised, swollen mouth. She burst into tears for what seemed no reason at all, then laughed and sobbed at the same time. "Oh, Billy. Billy Boy." She rocked back and forth in her saddle, her sobs broken with laughter.

"Will you quit callin' a man Billy Boy?" Bill's face was flushed a dull red. "Sounds like you was callin' a sheep dog. Quit it."

Then Doc Kelly rode up, his fat pacer's ears back as Doc kicked him out of his lazy, running walk. "What's all this yelling about? Sounds like a pack of coyotes."

"It's Billy," smiled Jan. "I've gotten a confession out of the hard-riding, toughest, young outlaw that ever followed the crooked trails. He's a fake."

"Stick to your nursing, young lady, and you might amount to something. If Bill Bailey's a fake, I'm the biggest quack that ever packed a pill bag. I thought you were inoculated and vaccinated against moon fever. Fake, eh? Did you by any chance notice the mess he made of Jack Crippen's profile? And those three others certainly weren't hurt by blank cartridges. Fake, eh? *Pah!* You're moonstruck."

But as they rode along together, three abreast, Doc Kelly's bright, brown eyes slid covert glances at the young, red-headed outlaw. Jan, to Bill Bailey's embarrassment, had reached for his hand and rode along now, clinging to it tightly.

"Bill," said Doc, "Jan is eighteen and full of romantic slush. Since she was in pigtails and I nursed her through mumps and measles and whooping cough and chicken pox, you've been a hero to her. You do anything to hurt this child, and I'll have you hung."

"Yes, sir," mumbled Bill Bailey. "I'd deserve hangin'."

"But," began Jan, flushing, "you . . ."

"You heard what Doc said, Jan," Bill Bailey interrupted. "He's plumb right."

CHAPTER
SIX

"Hire for Badlands Outlaws"

Stew Mollison was in no shape to be moved. It would require careful and skilled nursing to save him. Doc Kelly stayed two days, then went back to town, leaving Jan in charge.

"She'll pull you through, if you have the grit and sand to help her, Mollison . . . which I doubt. I'll send you a bill that will put a hole in the bank account you're supposed to have. She's more deserving of the money than the gamblers and saloon keepers. You're under Miss Clark's orders. I've done all I can. You'll get rest and proper nourishment and damn' little whiskey. No reason why those lungs of yours won't heal *pronto*. The man who gave you six months to live out here didn't know the curative powers of sunshine and fresh air. And I'll venture to say he's one of those lap-dog society M. D.s who cater to the whims of fool women and spineless men. But his biggest fee is going to look like chicken feed if Jan Clark pulls you through. We need a hospital at Old Pueblo. I'm going to nick you plenty for its donation."

Instead of getting angry, Stew Mollison grinned faintly and reached out his hand. "Shake on that, Doc. And even if I croak, you get the hospital."

Outside the old adobe house that the Mexican ranch helper had cleaned out and fixed up as a makeshift hospital, Doc Kelly grinned at Bill Bailey and Jan.

"The dude has more fight in him than I gave him credit for, Bill. He'll pull through, with Jan's nursing him. What do you aim to do, Bill?"

"Run his Coffin outfit."

"You forget that Al Donley is the law, even if he has left a few queer-looking signs along his back trail. There's a bounty on that red scalp of yours. Donley and other hidehunters will be after you."

"I'm expectin' some fast cowhands to drift along in a day or so, Doc. I don't think Donley's coyote pack will bother us much. I never lied to you yet. I'm not lyin' now when I tell you that I wasn't mixed up in that big Missouri train hold-up last year, when the conductor and engineer were both killed and two, three passengers shot down. None of the old gang was in on that train robbery when them people got killed and that big bunch of money was taken from the express car. I was in South America then. So was the other boys that got accused of bein' in on it."

"There was a red-headed man in the gang that fit your description, Bill."

"And there's more than one sorrel horse in almost any remuda, Doc," grinned Bill Bailey.

"So I've figured all along, Bill. I've seen red wigs on the vaudeville stage, too."

"Thanks, Doc. I never thought of that."

Doc Kelly held out his hand. "So long, Billy Boy. Jan isn't the only person who won't let 'em put clay feet on an idol. Take care of yourself. And ride herd on Jan."

Doc got on his fat pacer and rode away.

Bill grinned at Jan. "What did Doc mean by clay on the feet of the idle?"

"He called you Billy Boy," said Jan, looking after Doc with eyes that were a little misted. "Wise little old Doc. It's men like him, Bill, that are sure of a place in heaven." And she went into the sick room, closing the door after her.

Bill Bailey saddled a horse and rode alone into the hills. It was still early morning, the sun only a couple of hours high in the cloudless sky. He took a steep trail that brought him to a high pinnacle.

Dismounting, he gathered some dry twigs and got a fire going. Then he threw some green branches on the fire. A high column of smoke rose in the still air. Then Bill took an old slicker he had tied on his saddle and blanketed the smoke. Three times he cut off that smoke column. Three times the smoke rose into the sky. Then he threw dirt on the fire until it was dead. And, squatting on his heels, he rolled and lit a cigarette.

From another high point he sighted an answering smoke signal. A wide grin spread across his tanned, freckled face.

He rode back down the trail toward the ranch. At a fork in the trail, three miles or so down, three armed

291

men were waiting for him. He nodded an almost casual greeting.

"For a man playin' a hide-out game," growled one of the three, a big man with cold, gray eyes and a ragged mustache, "you've shore managed to make a lot of fool racket. Got your name in the papers, and the bounty hunters is buzzin' around like bees around the hive. One of the boys slipped into Old Pueblo last night. The papers was full of yarns about Bill Bailey and the Badlands Gang from Montana. Reward dodgers was posted all over town. What's the idee?"

"I'm roddin' the Coffin spread," grinned Bill Bailey, "and I need half a dozen fast cowhands. I'll mount you on top horses. Stew Mollison pays banker's wages to his brush-poppers. And it's the only cow outfit in the country that furnishes twenty-year-old liquor along with the beans and jerky."

"Sounds like you was full of the twenty-year-old," chuckled a tow-headed, square-jawed, blue-eyed man with heavy shoulders and bull neck.

"Baldy is cookin' for the outfit, Butch. And there's not a better place in the world for us to hole up for a few months. It's one long jump and crow hop from the home ranch to Mexico. Al Donley is the law at Old Pueblo. Crippen is the gent I fired when I took his job. The Mollison dude is the easiest feller in the world to work for.

"Fetch in a wild turkey or two when you come down this evenin', and Baldy will roast us a holiday supper that'll put taller on your ribs. Get your mouths all sot for that twenty-year-old private stock. Somewhere

292

within an hour's ride of the Coffin home ranch is cached that money from the big Missouri hold-up, unless that jasper lied to me in Buenos Aires. And dyin' men don't often lie. Are you Badlands riders hirin' out to the Coffin outfit?"

"Even if you made 'er all up outta that sorrel head of yourn," grinned the tow-headed man they called Butch, "it's still a good bet. Tell Baldy to rassle together the biggest son-of-a-gun-in-the-sack he ever made. We been livin' off the country, and there's wrinkles in our bellies deeper than the Grand Cañon."

Bill Bailey rode on back to the ranch late that evening. Butch and the two men with him had hoorawed Bill about his black eye. They'd called him a clumsy-footed bonehead for getting into the newspapers. But they'd show up with three or four men before dark. Bill's heart was light. He sang softly as he rode back to the ranch.

Won't you come home, Bill Bailey?
Won't you come home?
We know we done you wro-o-o-ong!

At the mess hall he was surprised to see Doc Kelly and Mrs. Huggins eating supper, with Baldy waiting on them right and left.

"The law," said the leathery little cowtown doctor, "as represented by a crooked son of a chicken-stealing weasel named Al Donley ran me out of Old Pueblo. I'm getting a vacation, whether I need it or not. Brought along a shotgun, and I'll keep you in quail . . . a quail a

293

day for Stewart Mollison the Third. We've moved out here, bag and baggage."

"Being run out of town was a blessing in disguise," said Mrs. Huggins. "The doctor was workin' himself to a frazzle. Mister Mollison swears he's going to build him a big hospital for them poor people with ailin' lungs that can't afford to pay for proper treatment. Mister Mollison is a fine gentleman."

"He has you and Jan eatin' out of his hand," chuckled Doc Kelly. "And damned if he hasn't got me wonderin' if I didn't size him up wrong. He turned down two drinks of whiskey. And he told me to write my own ticket on the sanitorium."

"Al Donley outlawed you, Doc?"

"Aiding and abetting a criminal . . . meaning you. Don't look so solemn, Bill. I'm getting a hospital, realizing my life's dream. My mother died of tuberculosis, because we didn't have money to give her the proper care. If I can devote the rest of my days to healing those who can't afford hospitalization and proper treatment, they can list me with Jesse James and hang me in the end. More pie, Baldy, and another cup of Java. I'm as excited as a kid going to his first circus."

So Doc Kelly came to the Coffin Ranch. Within a week a crew of Mexican laborers was at work making adobe bricks. Doc worked far into the night on plans for his hospital, which was to be built at Sycamore Cañon near the home ranch. With Doc worked Jan and Mrs. Huggins. Stew Mollison, out of danger and with the hopeless, bitter look gone out of his blue eyes, getting stronger each day, offered non-sensical suggestions and completely won the friendship of Doc Kelly.

And Bill Bailey and a hard-riding crew of outlaw cowhands worked the Coffin range on the roundup.

CHAPTER
SEVEN

"A Brave Man Flees"

Bill Bailey looked up from some figures he'd been adding in his calf tally book. He grinned at the half dozen cowpunchers sitting around the campfire.

"Mebbyso there's outfits that have better crews, but I'll bet a new hat that no spread in the country has a higher-priced bunch of brush-popper cowhands. This crew, in actual cash money and accordin' to law as printed in black and white dodger notices, is worth just twenty-seven thousand dollars. We may not be top hands, but the law shore values us higher than forty-a-month cowhands."

They had been branding cattle in the rough hills for nearly a month. They were working the Coffin range thoroughly. Fast cowboys on good horses, they were skyrocketing the tally of calves branded in the Coffin iron. And those hard-riding outlaws known as the Badlands Bunch were getting a lot of fun out of it.

The few times that Al Donley and Jack Crippen had tried to surround them and make a wholesale capture, the outlaws had driven them almost to the edge of town. And after ten days without sighting a single posse, one or two of the outlaws began to think that the law had lost interest in them. But Butch and the quiet-mannered killer they called the Kid and Bill Bailey knew better.

"They're plannin' a big hunt," said Butch. "Mebbyso they'll call out a troop of cavalry if they kin git the governor to swing it."

"Mexico is only a few hours away," said Bill Bailey.

The Kid's hard eyes glittered in the firelight. "General Sherman claimed that the only good Injuns was dead 'uns. Me, I feel just thataway about hired posse hands. Let 'em come within gun range, and I'll commence cuttin' notches on my Winchester wood. And if Donley and Crippen don't come back into the hills soon, I'm ridin' to town after 'em. They got somewheres near eighty thousand dollars cached on the Coffin Ranch . . . money from that Missouri train job. They throwed the blame of that hold-up on us boys. I'm after the pay dirt they struck in that express car. I'm for takin' a hot runnin' iron and burnin' them two jaspers till they tell where that money's hid."

"I doubt if they know where it's cached, Kid," said Bill Bailey. "The stuff was in two gunny sacks, accordin' to the feller that died down in the Argentine. It was his job to stuff the money in the sacks and ride like hell while the others took care of the train crew and passengers. Which he done. He rode so fast they never caught up with him. He drifted into this part of the country with all that dough. They was crowdin' him close when he got this far. He couldn't go around the country with two gunnysacks full of money, so he taken ten thousand of it and cached the rest. He said he hid it near the Coffin Ranch. And that's as much as he'd tell.

"We know almost for certain that Donley and Crippen was two of that train-robbin' crew of clumsy, blunderin', would-be outlaws. We locate 'em here near the Coffin Ranch. I make a guess that Crippen spent more time diggin' for that lost cache than he did brandin' Coffin calves. These holes in the ground that we been findin' ain't prospect holes dug by miners. Every odd-shaped rock has holes dug around it. Same with every lone tree that might be a landmark. Them holes was dug by Crippen or Al Donley. They don't know where that money is cached."

"Just the same," smiled the Kid, "I'd like to rub a red-hot runnin' iron along their bellies."

"The Kid," grinned Butch, "is gentle-natured like an Apache."

Then Doc sent a Mexican out to the roundup with a note for Bill Bailey. The note said that the little cowtown of Old Pueblo was filling with strangers. Those strangers might be government manhunters, gathering quietly for one big, swift, deadly attack. Doc thought it was time for Bill Bailey and the Badlands Bunch to quit the country. After all, Doc wrote, Bill had more than paid off his debt of gratitude to Stew Mollison. And if quick-triggered, crafty manhunters like Joe La Fors and Charlie Siringo were on his trail, it was time Bill Bailey got back to South America.

There was a note from Stew Mollison that thanked Bill profusely for running the Coffin outfit for him. In a separate package Bill Bailey found a thick wad of banknotes. They counted out exactly one thousand dollars — Bill Bailey's payroll for his men. And there was a bank draft for another thousand for himself.

I'll drop down to the Argentine some day and see you, Bill, Mollison's note ended. **I'll have a set of fighting gloves in my bag. And I'll give you the licking of your young life, just for the hell of it . . . and for calling me a quitter once. I'll polish you off like a mahogany bar. Good luck, Bill. And God bless your red head**.

Another note, in Jan's neat, schoolgirl handwriting in ink, was strangely blurred in places. He read it twice before he put it away in his shirt pocket:

Please, Billy Boy, go away. Don't take any more risks.

I know you're decent and honest and fine. But proving it to the law is impossible, Doc says. Please, Billy, do as Doc says. Quit the country. Stew has promised to take me with him when he goes to see you in South America. I'm praying for you every night.

With love,

Jan

P.S. The smudges, Bill, are tears.

Bill Bailey gave Butch the money and showed them Doc Kelly's note. Butch read it aloud by the light of the campfire. He looked at them, grinning faintly.

"Well, boys?"

"I'll git Donley and Crippen," said the Kid flatly, "if I have to go to town alone after 'em. It's my guess they located that cache. But they're scared to lift it, scared they'll be nabbed with it. I'll burn the truth outta them two jaspers."

"We come a long ways for that money," admitted Butch. "If they come crowdin' us, we kin slip over into Mexico and thumb our noses at 'em. No use runnin' till we have to. I figger like the Kid does. Donley or Crippen or both of 'em know where that stuff is cached, but they're scared to dig 'er up. We won't run till we're crowded close. Tell that to Doc Kelly in your note, Bill."

And they all added bits of joshing advice as Bill, his face hot and red with confusion, got to his feet and grinned sheepishly.

Bill took a bath in the creek, shaved, and put on his best shirt. He rode off into the moonlight, singing his Bill Bailey song to the stars, headed for the Coffin Ranch. The only light showing was behind the drawn shades of the low-roofed adobe that had been fixed up as convalescent quarters for Stewart Mollison. Bill Bailey reckoned it was about midnight. Perhaps Stew would be reading. He'd stop there for a few minutes before he sought out Jan's quarters. Jan and Mrs. Huggins had a cabin of their own beyond the mess hall.

Bill rode up to the lighted adobe and was about to swing to the ground when he saw shadows moving across the lighted window shade that served as a screen. He could hear Stew Mollison's voice, no longer bitter and brittle, but laughing shakily. And he heard the low murmur of a girl's voice. Bill stared at the silhouettes on the drawn shade. Plainly he saw the shadows of the man and girl go toward each other, arms outstretched. Then they were in close embrace. The sounds of their voices blended.

"I need you," came Stew Mollison's voice, husky, unsteady. "I'm a broken wreck of a man, but Doc says I'll be well again in a year. I couldn't ask you to share . . ."

"I'm doing the asking, Stew darling," Bill heard the girl's voice, sobbing brokenly. "Marry me, dear. We need each other. I'll never desert you, never leave you. I'll nurse you back to health. We'll be together always. Hold me close, dear. Close . . ."

Bill Bailey winced as if he'd been struck across the face. He felt suddenly sick inside. And with that horrible, sickening feeling shutting around his heart was the maddening desire to jerk his gun and start shooting through that damned window shade. The palm of his hand was wet with perspiration as it gripped his gun. He felt as if he were choking. It was a horrible, damnable sensation, with his brain in the throes of conflicting emotions — hatred and something more powerful than hatred and the lust to kill. Still staring at the shadow picture of the embracing figures, he suddenly reined his horse around and rode away at a run. He never looked back, never turned his head, as he spurred for the hills.

So he did not see the door of Stew Mollison's cabin flung open. He didn't see Mollison, wrapped in a dressing gown, a gun in his hand, staring after him, a dazed look in his eyes, nor the girl behind him asking Stew what was the matter. Nor did Bill Bailey see Jan, a woolen robe over her nightgown, in the dark doorway of her own cabin. Jan gripped a sawed-off shotgun tightly, and her eyes went wide with fear that changed to bewilderment as she recognized Bill in the moonlight. She called after him, but he did not hear.

Then Doc Kelly appeared, with his nightshirt tucked into the waistband of his pants, his suspenders drooping, a gun in his bony hand. He was cussing softly.

"Who was that sneaking around in the middle of the night?" he called out. "Look around. See if he's set fire to something."

"It was Bill," called Jan. "He rode away like a wild man, without a word. I can't understand. He rode right past my cabin on a dead run."

Then Mrs. Huggins was waking up in Jan's cabin, asking questions in rapid-fire order.

"Why didn't he stop at my cabin, I wonder?" said Mollison. "Eleanor and I were still up, talking. There was so much to talk about we forgot about time and hospital rules. She was getting ready to go to Jan's cabin, was just saying good night, when we heard the racket of a horse running. And when I grabbed a gun and got the door open, there was a man riding like the devil was after him. You certain it was Bill, Jan?"

"Of course," said Jan so sharply that Doc chuckled.

Then Doc was squinting at the drawn shade behind the window in Stew Mollison's cabin. He was nodding, scratching his unruly shock of white hair.

"Stew, would you mind stepping into your room and walking past the window shade? Or better yet, you and Miss Hollister both go. Shut the door behind you. Stand between the lamp and the window shade and rehearse that good night business. I got a notion . . ."

"And I'm playing the same hunch," said Stew Mollison. "Come on, Eleanor."

He pulled her inside and shut the door. Jan, Mrs. Huggins, Doc, and Baldy, in his drawers and knee-length nightshirt with a cleaver in his hand, looked on. And plainly screened on the window shade they saw Stew Mollison take Eleanor Hollister in his arms and kiss her. Then, dragging the crimson-cheeked Eleanor by the hand, Stew Mollison jerked open the door.

"Did it register, Doc? Eleanor asking me to marry her and behaving like a brazen hussy?"

"It registered," said Doc. "That's what spooked that redheaded, young hellion that would grin in the devil's eye. Nobody got word to Bill Bailey that Baldy, primed with twenty-year-old bourbon, had written Eleanor Hollister that, if she wanted to see the man she loved before he died, she'd better catch the first train West and get out to the Coffin Ranch. How was Bill Bailey to know that Cupid roamed the flats disguised as a roundup cook? So far as Bill knew, there was only one girl on the ranch, and that was Jan. Bill was answering our notes in person. He rode up and saw something of

303

the same touching scene we just witnessed. He won't quit runnin' till he hits the Argentine. Which, all things considered, is the wisest course he could pursue. Fate turned the trick. Baldy, supposing you and I retire to the kitchen. A cup of black coffee, spiked with that Cupid liquor, will not be amiss."

Eleanor Hollister, tall, ash blonde, left Stew and ran to Jan, taking her in her arms. They clung tightly to one another, sobbing a little. Stew Mollison joined Doc and Baldy in the kitchen. Doc handed him a pitcher of milk and a glass.

"It was hell on Bill," said Doc. "It's hell on Jan. But damn it, it's fate's way of doing things. Bill's an outlaw, with a price on his head. The best they could hope for would be a ranch in the interior of South America. An' that's one hell of a place for a girl like Jan. Baldy, dig up that bottle, damn it."

The three sat at the kitchen table, Stew with his milk, Baldy and Doc Kelly with the bottle. A heavy, uncomfortable silence fell over them.

They did not hear Jan slip past in the night. They did not see her, dressed in shabby cowpuncher clothes, ride away from the ranch. While in Jan's cabin Eleanor Hollister, from the East, born and reared in the lap of luxury, held the gray-haired, grief-stricken Mrs. Huggins, humble of birth and housekeeper for a cow-country doctor, who was already mourning Jan, whom she had helped raise, as dead.

"Everything will come out all right," Eleanor kept saying. "Stew and I have half the money in the world and a mortgage on the rest of it. Money can do almost anything. We'll buy and bribe 'em till they declare Bill Bailey a free man."

"Bill Bailey," said Mrs. Huggins heavily, "is an outlaw. The law's hot on his trail right now. God have mercy on that poor child."

CHAPTER
EIGHT

"Midnight Gun Trap"

From a distance so great that Bill Bailey would not
have heard it if he hadn't stopped to wind his horse
after climbing a ridge came the faint rattle of gunfire. It
came from the direction of the roundup camp were Bill
had left Butch and the Kid and the other hard-riding,
cowpunching outlaws known as the Badlands Bunch.

Bill strained his ears to catch the indistinct sound of
the guns. He knew that the law was closing in on the
gang of wanted men, closing a ragged circle around
them. Bill grinned mirthlessly as he rolled a cigarette
while his blowing horse rested. He grinned because the
wily, cool-headed Butch, combining his cold reasoning
with the deadly cunning of the Kid, had anticipated just
such an attack at night, and had selected a camp
ground that had a perfect getaway pass through a rough
cañon that they kept under guard. With Mexico only a
few hours' hard ride from camp, the outlaws could
make a run for it if the fighting got too hot. Odds
against them didn't count to experienced gunfighters
like Butch and the Kid. They discounted big odds with
a splendid contempt that made brave fighters of the
men who rode with them.

306

Bill Bailey knew the folly and uselessness of trying to slip through the circle of posse men. Even if, by some miracle, he did manage to slip through the line of law officers, the chances were good that he'd be shot by the Kid or one of the other boys who would be taking reckless, deadly snap shots at any man who moved toward them. Or Bill might run the law gauntlet only to find the Badlands Bunch gone, riding hard for the Mexican line. It was the unwritten rule that a man, cut off from the rest as Bill Bailey found himself, should shift for himself, play a lone hand.

Bill cussed his luck. That first hot wave of killing hatred for Stew Mollison and his bitterness toward Jan had died a slow, writhing death in his cowboy heart. Stew Mollison had asked Jan to marry him. Bill knew the owner of the Coffin outfit well enough to know that the man, whatever his other faults might be, had a wholesome and decent respect for womanhood. The shadow pictures on the window shade had told him a brief, swift-moving story of love.

And now Bill Bailey was riding away from Jan forever. He was joining the Badlands Bunch for keeps. From now on, he'd take an actual part in their hold-up jobs. In the past Bill Bailey had been an outlaw in name only. Jan had branded him in the right iron when she had called him a fake. Bill had turned to the outlaw hide-outs for refuge. He had been accused of a crime he hadn't committed. He'd shot a man named Shuster, who ran the Rail outfit, because Shuster had spurred and clubbed and ridden to death a green broncho out of Bill's rough string. Bill had thrashed Shuster, much as he'd whipped

Crippen, who was also working for the Rail outfit at the time. And when Shuster had dragged out his six-shooter and opened up on young Bill, Bill had shot him. The bullet had broken Shuster's gun arm at the shoulder. They had been alone in the Rail ranch house. Bill had left the wounded man in the ranch office with a quart of whiskey, after having bandaged the broken shoulder, and had saddled his private horse and ridden away.

A week later he'd been arrested for murder. Al Donley, a deputy in Montana then, had made the arrest. Crippen and Donley had given damaging testimony at the preliminary hearing and coroner's inquest. Bill Bailey, framed for hanging or a life stretch in Montana's pen at Deer Lodge, had broken jail. Safety lay in the rough heart of the badlands.

Outlaws along the dim trails had offered him their friendship. He had done men like Butch and the Kid favors and good turns when he could. They liked him, trusted him as one of their kind, and let him trail with them. But Bill Bailey had never taken part in any of their hold-up jobs. He'd been given the outlaw name, but had shared no part of their game. And to a man, they respected him and liked him for what Butch called "Bill Bailey's damned horse sense and mule-headed stubbornness." Some of them probably secretly believed he had killed Shuster, who had been despised when alive and gained no false glory in death save in the near-sighted eyes of the Eastern dudes who owned the Rail outfit and never came West to learn the real facts.

The Rail owners had posted a big reward for the murderer of their foreman and let it go at that, giving the ramrod job to Jack Crippen, who ran the outfit into debt through his crooked work and sold them out for a price that was a steal to the buyer. That Shuster killing had outlawed young Bill Bailey. And the law had pinned more crimes against Bill's record until he gained an undeserved reputation as a badman, outlaw, and gunfighter. They'd put a price on his head, too. With the reward that the Eastern owners of the Rail had neglected to withdraw, the price on Bill Bailey's head amounted to eight thousand dollars.

Bill Bailey had given his promise to Doc Kelly to go to South America and never return. Then news had drifted to the Argentine, where he and Butch and the Kid and the others were raising cattle honestly, that there had been a train hold-up in Missouri and they were being blamed for it. During that train hold-up the conductor, engineer, and two of the passengers had been brutally, wantonly murdered. One of the men whose guns had done that cold-blooded shooting had had red hair, and the others had called him Bill Bailey. They had worn masks made of black silk handkerchiefs. Long slickers had completed their disguise. And it was from their talk, overheard and remembered by the passengers and train crew and express clerk, that the robbers had been identified as the Badlands Bunch.

Then Bill Bailey had met an American cowpuncher in Bueno Aires who had been wounded in a shooting scrape. Before the cowpuncher had died, he had confessed that he was one of the train robbers who had held up the express train in Missouri and gotten away with a rich haul. His story had implicated

Crippen and Donley. He'd told of hiding the money near or at the Coffin Ranch in Arizona. But he had died before he'd finished his story.

When Bill Bailey and the others had come back to the States to clear their record of rank, cowardly murder and to get the stolen loot from the Missouri train robbery, Bill had hoped desperately to clear his own record of Shuster's murder. Now he was almost certain that Crippen or Al Donley or both of them had killed Shuster. He'd hoped to get proof of that to show to Doc Kelly — and Jan.

Bill Bailey had dreamed a lot of fool nonsense about clearing his record and marrying Jan and settling down on a little ranch somewhere. He'd ridden in from the roundup camp to tell her that he hoped to whitewash his name of all black marks. Butch and the Kid had made out lengthy and somewhat illiterate and profanely strong statements clearing Bill Bailey of all and any part in their outlaw activities. Bill now had those laboriously handwritten statements in the inside pocket of his coat. He'd intended giving them to Doc Kelly. Then he'd seen those shadow pictures on the lamplit window shade — and had ridden away.

Now Bill was alone. He sat his winded horse, trying to think clearly with a brain that whirled. Mollison, Bill told himself, could give Jan everything a woman dreams of having — fine clothes, a beautiful city home, jewels, trips to Europe. He'd give her the Mollison name. Little Jan, daughter of the whiskey-loving roundup cook, Baldy Clark, would be Mrs. Stewart Mollison III.

"Them damn' dudes back East," muttered Bill, "better treat Jan like she was somebody. Or I'll . . ."

Riders were coming, heading toward the Coffin Ranch, along the dim trail that twisted through the rough hills. Bill heard the sound of voices. His heart pounded like a hammer against his ribs as he recognized Crippen's voice. By the loud sound of it, Jack Crippen was drunk and on the prod.

"Don't call me a liar again, Al. I won't stand for it, even from you. I didn't git time to lift the cache. Them damn' fools set fire to the bunkhouse before I had a chance. It's in the steel boxes where we put it, buried deep enough. They ain't rebuilt the bunkhouse. There's only Mollison and Doc Kelly and Baldy and the women at the ranch. If they show fight, we'll wipe 'em out and blame it on the Badlands Bunch. We got our faces blacked, we're wearin' slickers, and we're ridin' Coffin horses. With that red wig on, you'll shore pass for Bill Bailey to them as lives to tell the tale. It worked in Montana to hang Shuster's killin' on Bailey, with half a dozen men ready to testify it was red-headed Bill Bailey they seen ridin' away after they found Shuster dead. That red wig worked on the Missouri job. The three men won't be alive to tell about it. And the women will be scared enough to swear it was Bill Bailey. We'll dig up the money and each take our cut. And no more damned quarrelin' over it. Them gover'ment detectives and the posse will wipe out Bill Bailey and the Badlands Bunch before sunup, or drive 'em to hell and gone into Mexico. You and me split our dough and each goes his way. And don't ever try to double-cross me, Al, or I'll hang you higher than hell for the murder of Shuster."

"Shut up, you drunken fool. Quit shoutin'. Hell, somebody's comin'. Listen. Pull up, Crippen."

Bill Bailey had heard another rider coming from the opposite direction, from the Coffin Ranch, at a long trot. Whoever it was, he was riding hard, shod hoofs crunching and clicking on the loose rock along the trail.

Not a hundred yards from Bill Bailey, Crippen and Al Donley had pulled up. They had probably ridden off the trail into the brush to waylay the rider from the ranch. There was only one way to warn the lone rider of danger. Bill thumbed back the hammer of his six-shooter and pulled the trigger. The roar of his gun sent echoes crashing into the hills. He ejected the empty shell swiftly and reloaded. As the echoes died away, Bill heard Crippen cursing. But the rider had halted and was looking wildly about.

Then Bill's heart seemed to choke his throat. He heard Jan's voice: "Bill? Billy? What's wrong? Answer, Bill! Who shot?"

"Get back, Jan!" he yelled. "Ride like hell! Tell Doc and Mollison and Baldy I got Crippen and Al Donley stopped. If they git past me, they're comin' to the ranch to do some killin'. Ride like hell. Git away from here. You're just in my road around here. Git!"

"I'm going, Bill. I'll go back for help. Bill, that was Eleanor you saw Stew kissing through the window. I love you, Bill. I followed you to tell you."

"I love you, Jan. Now get to hell gone!"

CHAPTER
NINE

"A Law Debt to Square"

Crippen, too drunk to think or act cunningly, let his red hate get the better of his cold, fighting judgment. The whipping Bill had given him had humiliated him, lowered his tough reputation among his men. Here was his one chance to wipe out the disgrace of that beating.

"I'm comin' for you, Bailey. And I'll ride over your dead carcass to take your gal. Here I come!"

Crippen threw caution away with a drunken fling and a snarling curse. He came at Bill Bailey, spurring and shooting. And Bill rode to meet him.

Bill's gun spat flame — once . . . twice. Crippen pitched from his saddle, with a hoarse, screaming yell that broke into a rattle, then faded into silence as his heavy body hit the ground. Bill swerved his horse into the brush to dodge the leaden hail of Al Donley's bullets. Donley had quit his horse and was crouched in the brush.

Bill slid from the saddle with a twisting leap. There was a stabbing, burning pain in his left shoulder, where one of Crippen's bullets had torn through flesh and bone. And one of Al Donley's slugs had raked Bill's ribs.

On foot, he shoved a couple of cartridges into his gun. Then began the dangerous, tricky game of stalking the bushwhacker, Al Donley. Donley was a killer of the worst kind, treacherous, cunning, dangerous. He was as lethal now as a coiled rattler tensed and ready to strike. Al Donley was handicapped by no bullet wounds. And he was crouched, waiting, not moving.

Bill had no time to tie the bullet holes in his flesh, that were bleeding and throbbing with pain. Minutes, seconds counted. He had to kill Al Donley before he bled to death.

"Bill!" he heard Jan call out unsteadily from down the trail a hundred yards or so away. "Are you hurt, Bill?"

"Hell, no!" he lied. "Git goin', you little fool! You're underfoot around here. I got Crippen. I'm gittin' Al Donley next. Damn it, git goin'."

"Don't rush off, sweetheart," called Al Donley. "I always was stuck on you. Bailey's hit in a couple of places. And I got six bullets in my gun, all with his name on them. Hang around, honey. I'll finish off this would-be outlaw directly. He's nothin' but a damn' counterfeit. Never stuck up a train in his life. Never even had the guts to finish shootin' Shuster up north. That was Al Donley and his little red actor's wig. I got 'er glued on my head now. I'm the red wolf that give Bill Bailey the rep he's traveled on. He's as harmless as a sheepherder. Any fool could have killed Crippen. Crippen was drunker than a fiddler's dog and loomed up big as a boxcar fer a target. Hang around, little gal, and wait for a real he-wolf if you like outlaw men.

Come and git it, Bailey. You're fightin' a real man now. Come an' git your bellyful of hot lead, you counterfeit four-flusher."

While Al Donley was mouthing his challenge, lifting his voice to make himself heard by Jan down the trail, Bill Bailey had been crawling through the brush and rocks. Now he was within easy range of the waiting Donley.

"I got you covered, Donley," he rasped. "Stick 'em up."

Al Donley, startled by the proximity of Bill's voice, jumped. Then their two guns were spewing flame. Bill Bailey, on his feet, crouching, swaying dizzily, kept shooting until his gun went empty — and the dark blot on the ground was still.

Then the dread wave of blackness he'd been fighting off swept over his senses, and he reeled drunkenly and fell in a motionless heap. As consciousness left him, he thought he heard the pounding of shod hoofs and the sound of men's voices. Jan seemed to be shouting something.

When Bill woke up, he blinked at the hot, flickering firelight. His vision was blurred, but he made out Jan's face. He heard her voice as she bent over him. And there were men around. He caught the glint of a law badge and the lean, hard-eyed face of its owner. He'd seen that man years before, at the jail where they'd put him for the murder of Shuster, the Rail foreman. The manhunter was none other than the famous Charlie

315

Siringo, rated one of the bravest and cleverest cowboy detectives who ever trailed an outlaw.

"Howdy, Siringo. Before you put handcuffs on me, I'd like to say a word or two . . ."

"Save your breath, Bailey." Siringo's leathery face softened in a bright grin. "The lady's said your piece for you. But she didn't tell me much that I didn't already know or suspect. I trailed Crippen and Al Donley while the other boys were playin' Fourth of July with the Badlands Bunch. I knew you boys were all in South America when the train was stuck up in Missouri. When you drifted back into the country, I guessed why you came back. So I cold trailed you here. And I smelled out Donley and Crippen before I'd been in Old Pueblo two hours. Foggin' Butch and the other boys across the line was more or less of a blind. I trailed Crippen and Donley. Your fast shootin' saved them two killers from hangin'. I read the two statements I found in your pocket. They're blood-stained, but there's enough left of the handwritin' to make 'em out. They prove what I've claimed all along . . . that Bill Bailey never was an outlaw.

"The reward money on these two gents, Crippen and Donley, will be enough to start you and this little lady up in the cow business. I'll see you get every dollar of it. God knows you've earned it and more, Bill Bailey. Only one thing more. It will double that home stake if you could lead me to where the loot from the Missouri train robbery is cached."

Bill Bailey opened his lips to speak. Then he closed them in a tight line, his jaws clenched. That loot, according to Bill Bailey's way of thinking, belonged to Butch and the Kid and the other boys who had come all the way from the Argentine. They'd taken big risks. The loot was covered by insurance. The express company could afford to lose that much to the Badlands Bunch. Bill Bailey looked up into the great detective's keen, searching eyes and grinned.

Siringo smiled faintly. "I knowed better than to expect an answer on that 'un, Bailey. One big reason I've been successful in my line of work is that I think along the same lines as the gents who follow the outlaw trail. I'll leave you now in this young lady's care. She's takin' you on to the ranch. Think you kin make the ride with her?"

"It'll be the easiest ride I ever made, sir," grinned Bill Bailey.

"Thought so. Take good care of him, ma'am. He's shore worth savin'." Siringo rode away.

It was weeks before Bill Bailey was well enough to handle a shovel. One night, when Stew Mollison and his bride had gone to Old Pueblo with Jan to help her pick out a fancy wedding trousseau, and Doc had gone along with Mrs. Huggins, Bill saw his chance. He plied Baldy with some of Stew's twenty-year-old bourbon and finally tucked the old roundup cook into his bunk. With a shovel and pick, Bill Bailey then went to work on the site of the burned bunkhouse.

He gave a grunt of satisfaction when the edge of the shovel struck the hard metal of a buried steel box. Feverishly, Bill Bailey unearthed the treasure box. It was unlocked, and the lid swung open on creaking hinges. Bill's cupped match flame showed stacks of banknotes tied with tape, laid neatly, pile upon pile. And on top of the money was a square white envelope of expensive, heavy linen, the Mollison crest in the upper left-hand corner. Across the white envelope in Stew Mollison's sprawling scrawl was written: **Bill Bailey, Personal**.

Bill opened the envelope. By the light of more matches he read the note:

My dear Bill:

I found this cache when I first bought the ranch. Came on it by accident. I know its history. I've counted the money and have taken the liberty of sending that exact amount, by trusted messenger to Butch and the Kid and the boys. They received it. I have Butch's letter, which I'll show you when you follow us to town. When Baldy is sober, fetch him on to Old Pueblo. Get him in shape to give the bride away. Doc and I are taking charge of all arrangements in town. Siringo is guest of honor. You may now feel at liberty to turn over the loot to him and claim a just reward. After all, Bill, I'm afraid I won't be able to give you that trimming before you get married. Doc forbids it. Says I'm not fit yet to lace on the gloves. But I'd give this

treasure chest to see you line up before the preacher with a pair of shiners.

Did I ever tell you, Bill, I own the damned railroad that runs through Missouri? The train that was robbed was one of mine. Makes for the personal touch, eh? Now use another match to burn this.

Your friend,
Stew

In the gray dawn, Bill Bailey, with the help of Baldy, who was a trifle tipsy and in a mellow mood, loaded the treasure chest and its loot on a buckboard. Then Baldy climbed up on the seat and took the reins. Baldy, in his Sunday suit, proud as the President, clucked to his team and started for town.

Bill Bailey stepped up on his horse and followed at a swinging walk. He sang as he rode:

Won't you come home, Bill Bailey?
Won't you come home?
They sang the whole day lo-o-ong.
Won't you come home, Bill Bailey?
Won't you come home?
We know we done you wro-o-o-ong!

About Author

Walt Coburn was born in White Sulphur Springs, Montana Territory. He was once called "King of the Pulps" by Fred Gipson and promoted by Fiction House as "The Cowboy Author". He was the son of cattleman Robert Coburn, then owner of the Circle C ranch on Beaver Creek within sight of the Little Rockies. Coburn's family eventually moved to San Diego while still operating the Circle C. Robert Coburn used to commute between Montana and California by train and he would take his youngest son with him. When Coburn got drunk one night, he had an argument with his father that led to his leaving the family. In the course of his wanderings he entered Mexico and for a brief period actually became an enlisted man in the so-called "Gringo Battalion" of Pancho Villa's army.

Following his enlistment in the U.S. Army during the Great War, Coburn began writing Western short stories. For a year and a half he wrote and wrote before selling his first story to Bob Davis, editor of *Argosy-All Story*. Coburn married and moved to Tucson because his wife suffered from a respiratory condition. In a little adobe hut behind the main house Coburn practiced his art and for almost four decades he wrote approximately 600,000 words a year. Coburn's early fiction from his Golden Age — 1924–1940 — is his best, including his novels, *Mavericks* (1929) and *Barb Wire* (1931), as well as many short novels published only in magazines that now are being collected for the first time. In his Western stories, as Charles M. Russell and Eugene Manlove Rhodes, two men Coburn had known and admired in life, he captured the cow country and recreated it just as it was already passing from sight.